I0606595

Siblings Matthew and Elizabeth Janssen, nineteen and eighteen, live with their parents in Lilac Cottage in Cape Cod where they had been vacationing when they discovered a time-travel grandfather clock hidden in a secret room. When their parents bought the cottage and everything in it, including the clock, Matthew and Elizabeth are elated at still having access to the time travel device. Summer vacation is over, and the two teenagers now have to plan their adventures around school and family life, making it difficult to get back into the past to solve mysteries. And, boy, do they have mysteries to solve! Not only have a number of young girls been kidnapped and murdered between 1914 and 1927—crimes the siblings are sure were committed by the same man—but the jewels from a jewelry heist in 1900 are still missing. When the siblings find a riddle written by the man who allegedly masterminded the jewel heist, they are sure that if they can just figure out the clues, they can recover the missing treasure…that is, if they can survive their dealings with the murderer of the young girls.

KUDOS for *The Murderer and the Lost Treasurer*

In *The Murderer and the Lost Treasure* by Leonardus G. Rougoor, Matthew and Elizabeth Janssen are nineteen- and eighteen-year-old siblings who have a secret. The cottage where they now live has a hidden room with an old grandfather clock that is a time travel device. They first discovered the clock when they spent the summer vacationing at the cottage. Luckily, their parents decided to buy the cottage and everything in it, including the secret room and the clock. Now the two can go back in time whenever they want, or rather whenever they can work it in between school and family time, since their parents know nothing about the clock or their secret adventures. While looking on the internet, they discover that a number of young girls were abducted and murdered in the area in the early nineteenth century, so the two travel back in time, determined to stop whoever is doing it. With the help of their friends, John and Alice, who live in the past and whose lives Matthew and Elizabeth saved while time traveling over the summer, they narrow down the suspects. Also in 1900, there was a jewel robbery, and the robber left clues to where the treasure is hidden in an old dresser. When the two siblings find the dresser in a shed on their property and discover a riddle hidden inside, they have two mysteries to solve—that is, if they survive their confrontation with the murderer. Unlike the first book, *The Clock*, this one is written in past tense, rather than present, and I enjoyed it a lot more, as present tense isn't my favorite. But tense aside, it is equally as thrilling as its processor, and I found I couldn't put it down. ~ *Taylor Jones, The Review Team of Taylor Jones & Regan Murphy*

The Murderer and the Lost Treasure by Leonardus G. Rougoor is the story of Matthew and Elizabeth Janssen, two teenage siblings. Matthew, nineteen, and Elizabeth, eighteen, have just moved with their parents to Lilac Cottage in Cape Cod. They spent the previous summer vacationing at the cottage, and, at the end of the summer, their parents were able to buy it with all its contents. Those contents include a secret room with a time travel device disguised as a grandfather clock. Over the summer, they traveled back to the early 1900s and saved the lives of two cousins, John and Alice. Now, while surfing the internet in their own time, the siblings discover someone abducted and killed a number of young girls in the area between 1914 and 1927, and also that there a jewelry heist in 1900 where the robbers were killed in a shootout with police before they could fence the jewels, and the stash has never been found. Determined to both stop the murderer and find the stolen jewels, the teens have their work cut out for them, along with their friends John and Alice, who are only too happy to help the time travelers. The story is well-written, fast-paced, tense, and intriguing. Easily fitting into the late YA/New Adult genres, *The Murderer and the Lost Treasure* is one that both young adults and adults will have a hard time putting down. ~ *Regan Murphy, The Review Team of Taylor Jones & Regan Murphy*

The Murderer

and

the Lost Treasure

The Clock ~ 2

Leonardus G. Rougoor

A Black Opal Books Publication

DEDICATION

To my family, Kathleen, Matthew, Elizabeth, and Eva
Also my grandchildren, Cassie and Jamie, who loved,
The Clock, Book 1.

Prelude

On the ferry, he took great care to remain hidden from the young man and teenage girl. Once the ride was finished, the two young people pedaled down one of the long open roads. He would wait for the right moment and then make his move.

"Okay, kid, time for you to be taken care of, then blondie and I can talk. She looks like she'll be quite entertaining," the man said to himself.

He sped up, driving right on the edge of the road. He planned on knocking the nosey boy into the ditch, hard enough to eliminate him, so he could have a chat with the girl, whose long blonde hair was blowing behind her in the breeze.

"We'll find out why you two are spying on me and just who you are. The girl is a little older than I like, but that doesn't mean I can't have some fun with her. I'll kill the boy and then do away with the girl when I'm finished with her," he said, smiling to himself.

Checking all around and seeing no one anywhere, he picked up speed, closing the gap quickly.

Chapter 1

A summer-long vacation at Lilac cottage on Chappaquiddick Island in Nantucket Sound turned out to be the adventure of a lifetime. Murder, theft, and harrowing experiences made using a clock to travel into the past almost fatal.

The home was built in the early nineteen hundreds within one hundred feet of the beautiful shoreline. Although there were some dunes between the cottage and the water, someone long ago had cleared an area between them. Looking through the kitchen and living room windows afforded the occupants a truly beautiful view of the waves breaking on the beach.

The quaint, handsome home was a two-story dwelling with what had been called a good morning staircase. A large landing was built near the top, leading to three short stairways. One led to the master suite and another to a renovated bathroom. The third stairway went to the two front bedrooms overlooking the driveway.

When Leonard and Kate Janssen, Matthew and Elizabeth's parents, tried to buy the wonderful cottage during their vacation, they found it had already been sold. This would have been the perfect place for the family, but it had been too late. Their chance was gone. Attempting to create a lifestyle change for the family, their plans were thwarted at every turn. Each attempt to find another suitable residence on the island ended in disappointment. Although discouraged and feeling defeated, the family refused to give up.

The mystery started with Matthew seeing an unnerving sight at three in the morning as he glanced out the bathroom window facing the beach. Shortly after this event, Matthew and Elizabeth discovered a secret room containing the grandfather clock with its unique abilities. Finding a journal in the clock showed them how to use the timepiece, and the rollercoaster ride began.

This clock, they soon discovered, could transport them to any date in the past. Of course, even this timepiece had its limitations. One could only go as far back as the year nineteen hundred and no farther. The clock could also be used to go into the future, something they had yet to try.

Using the clock in an attempt to alter the past became, at times, a burden of almost unbearable proportions. Whatever could go wrong did, and the two teenagers were at the point of giving up the challenge. The two, trying to fix an event that had happened more than a hundred years in the past, came close to not returning to their own time.

What an amazing summer holiday it had been. The feeling they had when finally they had been able to correct a terrible wrong in the past was almost indescribable. After so many failed attempts, Matthew and Elizabeth managed to come up with a plan that worked. In order to save their friends, Alice and John, in the year nineteen hundred and seven, the pair had to do things that neither of them would ever have thought possible before this.

Of course, Leonard and Kate, all this time, had no idea

what their offspring were up to, with regards to the fantastic clock. In the end, after the teenagers managed to correct things that happened so long ago, everything started to fall into place. The deal on the cottage fell through when the previous buyers backed out, and the Janssens had a chance to buy it, after all. This—and the successful adventure that Matthew and Elizabeth had—turned a dismal time into the best vacation ever.

Back in Des Moines, the family had put their house up for sale, and Leonard and Kate were amazed when it sold in a week. Moving to the island, which was part of Massachusetts, had been a dream come true. No more oil field work in Alberta for Leonard, at least not the long times away that, in the past, had been necessary.

Father and son drove the rental cube van to their new home, with Kate and Elizabeth driving the family car. The cottage, having been bought with all its contents included, had allowed the family to sell much of their furniture. Almost everything they needed had come with the cottage.

Tools, of course, were in the truck, and the males now had a large auto-technicians toolbox that was to go in the garage. At least, it would go in once the leaning building had been straightened out and made safe again. This project the two had been looking forward to completing before Matthew started college. The auto-technicians course was just what Matt wanted to take in college, as he had a real aptitude for that kind of work.

Chapter 2

I'm so glad to be back here," Elizabeth said, smiling with glee. "This is the best place ever."

"I know what you mean," Matthew agreed. "I can hear the waves rolling onto the shore from here. What do you think, Buddy? Are you as happy as we are?" he asked their golden retriever, who let out a bark in response.

"All right, guys," Dad hollered, as he backed the truck to the front of the house in a position to make the unloading easier. "We need to unload the truck and drive it to the rental place in Edgartown. Matthew, can you and Elizabeth shift some of the things in the storage shed to make room for the tools?"

Walking towards the shed, Matthew said, "Sure thing, Dad. Okay, Elizabeth, let's get this done."

The two made short work of creating enough space for the tools to be placed inside the shed. Once this was done, their television, dining room table, and a few dressers, plus their own mattresses were moved into the house, and the family settled into their new home.

With a smile on her face, Kate said to her husband, "I

thought this day would never come. Now, look at us. We live in a beautiful cottage, and we can see the ocean out the kitchen and living room windows. Who would have thought this is how we would be living from now on?"

With everything unloaded, Leonard hopped into the truck, and as he drove away, Kate followed in the car. It didn't take too long before they were back and, although the siblings had moved a number of things, there was still plenty to do.

"How about we unpack our suitcases and bring all the boxes that have our clothes in them upstairs, guys," Leonard said. "Your mother and I will take care of the kitchen things."

Elizabeth nodded, "Okay, Dad, we can handle that. Matthew, can you give me a hand with the bigger ones?" she asked as she bent down to get a grip on a rather-heavy-looking cardboard box.

The two moved everything upstairs and, after vacuuming the drawers, all the clothes were put away. Elizabeth stepped just inside the closet door in her room. All the things that had been in it for years had been removed and sorted. Memories of their trips into the past came flooding back. The feelings she and Matthew had felt, when they read online about their failures to change what they so desperately needed to, went through her head. How she cried when she read about John. The thoughts of what he had endured still brought tears to her eyes.

What a shock it had been to discover the things that had really gone on, instead of what they thought had occurred.

Several times they had almost been caught by people who would not have had a second thought about killing the two teenagers. But this was not the time for any more tears, as the past was the past, and all had been worked out.

With those thoughts going through her head, she wondered if they would be making any more trips into the past. It would have been nice to see John and Alice again, but the wisdom of that decision was suspect. Who knew what the future, or was it the past, would bring? There was one interesting thing about traveling into the past. No matter how long they stayed there, only a few minutes passed in the present. Of course, it did make for a terribly long day if it wasn't planned properly.

"Hey, kids, do you want to come down for supper?" their Dad asked. "Matthew, you and I can have a quick look at the garage. Elizabeth, can you help Mom get the dinner ready?"

"Sure thing, Dad," Elizabeth answered.

Chatting excitedly father and son headed for the garage. It was a short walk on a gravel driveway, and the two made an inspection tour around the leaning building to see if there was any rot and what might be done to make it safe.

Leonard had leaned forward to look through the window. "The foundation seems to be solid enough. It looks like a number of braces will be needed on the inside to hold things in place, once we pull it straight."

"How do you plan to pull the building into position, Dad?"

"I have a two-ton come-along, which I bought a couple of years ago. It's a portable manual hoist that we can hook to the bottom of the tree. Cranking the handle allows me to have two tons of pull, which is plenty to straighten the garage. We'll run a steel cable over the top of the nearest wall and through the top horizontal two-by-fours of the far wall. The cable will be fastened to a support piece at the top of the wall on the other side of the garage."

"Oh, I see what you mean. You'll use the tree as an

anchor and the come-along to pull the building straight. Then if it's safe, we'll go inside and bolt the braces into place. Do you think it will work, Dad?"

"Oh, yeah, I've done things like this before on some of the job sites I've been on," Dad said.

"Will we be using the lumber inside the garage for the project?"

"I'll have to take a good look at it, but, from here, it seems all right. Let's see how dinner is coming along," Leonard said as he patted his boy on the back.

"This is going to be great," Matthew said to his father. "We'll have a nice workshop when we're done and a place for my car in the winter too."

"Nice try, pal, but my car is going in the garage, not yours, ha, ha, ha."

From the front porch, Kate yelled out, "Supper's ready."

The two headed toward the back of the cottage and entered the kitchen.

Leonard stopped by the door. Looking around, he inspected the area just outside the door. With a look of concentration, he turned to Kate. "Hey, dear, what do you think of Matthew and me building a small mudroom or a wash-up area back here? We could pour a small concrete pad and run the drain into the existing septic system. It could be enclosed or just have an awning type of cover over it. We should be able to build it so it doesn't obstruct any of the views."

With a real smile on her face, Kate nodded. "I think that's a great idea. It will save me having to clean up the bathrooms so much."

After supper, the family sat in the living room, enjoying the fire that was burning nicely. The light flickered and cast shadows around the room. After an hour of relaxing, everyone headed upstairs to bed. There was a soft knock on Elizabeth's door, and Matthew entered when she told him it was okay.

"I just want to ask you not to go into the clock room without me, all right," he said.

"You don't have to worry. I won't be going anywhere by myself. I would be way too scared to do something wrong and end up stuck someplace and not being able to get back," she informed him.

"Do you think we might want to see John and Alice again or maybe try some new spots? It would be really interesting to see some of the things that have happened in this area," Matthew said with a faraway look.

"Maybe I'll look online when I get the chance and find out what might be interesting to see," she said.

"There is one thing I think we should check out. We need to find out how long John owned the cottage and who has lived here since then. I don't want to appear in the clock room and run into someone unexpectedly when we come out of the closet."

She giggled. "Oh, you're coming out of the closet, are you?"

"Very funny. You know what I mean."

"I'll check into that later, remind me," she said.

And so ended the first day of living in their new home.

Chapter 3

Just before going to bed, Elizabeth logged onto the computer. Online sites had provided a never-ending supply of information. Everything from archived newspapers, to old police records, could be found on search engines like Google.

Going online, she went to a site that explored the history of this area. There were several stories of interest that sidetracked her attention before she could look for previous owners of their cottage. One was a tragedy of the abduction of a young girl eight years old. The story said that the child, named Cassandra Boothe, had been taken from her home. A massive search had taken place, including a house to house, but no trace of the girl had been found.

Years later, the decomposed body of a young girl had been found buried in a cave on the mainland not far from Chappaquiddick Island. The perpetrator of the crime was never apprehended. According to the article, the family of the deceased never got over it after the body was recovered.

Another story exposed a long-time resident of the area

as being a spy for the Germans during the Second World War. He had been caught, but not until many secrets had been passed along. He had told the authorities that he had been forced into revealing secrets by two men who befriended him in a bar, but no one had believed him because there was never any trace of them found.

There was a third story that told of a shootout between the police and a small group of criminals thought to have been the thieves that stole a valuable jewelry collection on loan to a local museum at the turn of the century. Unfortunately, the criminals had all been killed in the exchange of gunfire. It had also been reported that a book containing clues to the hiding spot of the jewelry had never been found. It had been estimated that the treasure was, in modern times, worth many millions of dollars.

There were a number of other stories, but Elizabeth was too tired and made the decision to look further into this tomorrow. Lying on her bed, she drifted off into a deep sleep.

The following morning at the breakfast table, plans were discussed. Looking out the window, the family saw before them the sand dunes rising slightly towards the ocean. There were grasses swaying in the breeze on some of them, and it was obvious that previous owners had cleared some of the sand away. This provided a beautiful view of the beach and the rolling waves crashing onto the shoreline. The road leading to the cottage was on the other side of the building. This way, the scene wasn't spoiled by the garage and driveway.

Off in a daydream, Matthew remembered that there once had been a resort called Mariner's Lodge in the area long ago. This and many homes of the early nineteen hundreds had long since burned down or been removed. This created a quiet little haven with no close neighbors for the family. Matthew and Elizabeth, having been in the past many times, had firsthand knowledge of how gorgeous the area had been in its heyday.

As Matthew was asked a question, his attention was drawn back to the present.

"We'll need to find you a car to go back and forth to school, Matthew," his dad said.

"Thanks, Dad, you're right, but I think a small pickup truck might be better. That way we can use it to haul stuff too."

"Good thinking. We'll check online to see what there is for sale around here or on the mainland," Dad agreed.

"Will it be possible to drop off your sister on your way to college each day?" Kate asked. "That will save us having to get another vehicle or having her try to catch a bus."

"I don't see why not. I can always teach her how to drive, too. How would you like to learn to drive a stick shift, sis?" he asked her.

"I don't know. Is it very hard to learn?"

"Actually, it's pretty easy once you get the hang of it," he said. "I'll go online later and look for one too."

"What are you and Mom going to do?" Elizabeth asked her father. "I overheard you saying that you're going to town this morning,"

"We need to get groceries, first of all. We were thinking of opening a Bed and Breakfast, at one point, but realize that the house is too small, and then we thought of converting the storage shed over because it is large enough. So we're going to see the people at city hall about it today."

"Do you think it would bring in enough money during the summer months here?" Elizabeth asked.

"I'm not sure this is the best idea myself, but you might as well check and see if it's feasible or not," Matthew piped in. "Would it be all right if we move a few of the things in the shed into our rooms. There are a couple of dressers and a nice freestanding mirror in there. If you want the mirror, Mom, we can always move it into your room."

"What do you think dear, is that all right?" Leonard asked his smiling wife.

"I don't have a problem with it, although I would like to look at the pieces to see if we need them in the master bedroom," she said.

The decision made, Leonard and Kate prepared to go into town, saying they would be back in three or four hours.

Chapter 4

Matthew and Elizabeth headed to the shed and opened the door. All was as they remembered it. There were tarps of various types and ages covering things. The building, being of good quality, had kept everything inside dry and well preserved. When the two first explored the contents of the structure in the past, they were surprised at the things they had discovered. Taking off the covering, Elizabeth examined the free-standing mirror. The frame was made from an ornate dark hardwood that must have taken a skilled craftsman many hours to make.

"I hope Mom doesn't want this mirror. It will look gorgeous in my room," she said, admiring the piece.

"It sure would. I'd love to have the large dresser with the hidden compartment we found last time to put in my room. Where do you think the cedar chest would work the best? Would it go at the end of the bed, or can you use it elsewhere?" he asked.

"That depends on what you want to use it for, I guess."

"What do you think is under that tarp in the back corner? We never did look at it. Let's have a peek," Matthew said, walking toward it.

As they made their way to the corner, they had to push a few things out of the way first and carefully removed the dusty old canvas tarp. Elizabeth sneezed as the dust entered her nose. When the tarp was off, standing before them was an ancient small dresser with a peculiarly shaped mirror held in the upper frame of the unit. There was a place for a person's legs so they could sit on a low chair or stool.

The top of the dresser had enough room for a writing pad. It measured about twenty-four inches wide and just over a foot deep. The two sides rose above the writing area about eight inches leaving just enough room for a person's arms to rest while writing.

There appeared to be no entry into or reason for one of the higher sections. On the right-hand side there was a drawer in the raised section, about twelve inches wide, but on the left side of the dresser, the front of the raised section was solid wood. There was a drawer about six inches below the top just like on the other side of the piece, making it seem a little lopsided. It reminded Matthew of the dresser with the false top they had found containing a journal during the vacation.

"Hey, sis, does this remind you of the dresser we found Alice's journal in?"

"Are you talking about this front spot here that looks like a drawer should be there, the same as the other side?" she asked, pointing to the indicated spot.

"Yeah, the dresser looks odd, doesn't it?"

"It does," she agreed. "I bet there has to be something hidden in there. Just like the clock and that dresser over there against the wall."

"Why don't we clean up the free standing mirror and carry it to the house. We can bring it into Mom and Dad's room. Then we'll do the same with this small dresser and put it in your room. If we put your laptop and a few other things on it, maybe they won't even think about putting it in theirs," Matthew suggested.

"I like that idea, and then we can figure out how to get into what I'm sure is another hidden compartment. This is getting exciting. It reminds me of our adventures last summer."

The two worked at transferring the pieces into the home, which took the better part of an hour. With a little time left over before their parents said they would be home, they started to bring the larger dresser Matthew wanted into the house and got it to the bottom of the stairs. This was the one with the hidden compartment that they found during their summer vacation.

Elizabeth was too tired to be able to carry it up the stairs. "Hold on, Matthew. I don't think that I can carry it up there. My back and my hands are sore."

"Gee, I would really like to have it in my room before Mom and Dad get home. I'm sure if they see it down here, they'll want it in their room. Then Dad will surely find out about the secret cubby hole."

"Would you be able to use the dolly to get it up the stairs?" she asked.

"Excellent idea. I should have thought of that."

He ran to the shed, grabbed the dolly, and carried it into the house. Elizabeth tipped the piece forward, and he slid the lip under the bottom of the unit. The strap was then tightened around the dresser, and he backed up to the first step.

One by one, the stairs were ascended. When he reached the landing, he had to stop to catch his breath. Just as he took hold of the handles again, the sound of the car pulling into the driveway was heard.

"Darn it," he said. "Help me by lifting on the bottom,

so we can get it into my room before they get into the house."

The two worked quickly, and, as the dresser was brought to the door, they realized that it had to be turned sideways in order to fit. Matthew quickly undid the strap and removed the cart from under it. They brought it to the side of the dresser and pushed it back onto the cart, tightened the strap and he wheeled it into place in his room, quite out of breath.

"Hey, guys, can you help with the groceries?" Mom called from the front door.

"You go down and help, while I clean out the dresser real fast and throw some of my stuff on top of it. I'll be down as quick as I can," he said, breathing heavily.

"On my way, Mom," Elizabeth shouted.

Matt grabbed a rag and wiped off the top and then opened a drawer and did the same inside. He took a few of his clothes out of the closet and put them in the drawer and closed it. Grabbing a few books and the lamp from the nightstand, he placed them on top of the piece.

That ought to do it, he thought.

Picking up the cart, he headed downstairs to help with the groceries. When all was done, he asked, "Did you find out what you went into town for, Dad?"

"We found out that we won't be able to start a B and B here. The shed can't be converted, due to some by-law, and the house isn't big enough. The ideas were gone over, and the answer is no."

"Are you disappointed?" Elizabeth asked.

"Not really. To tell you the truth, it would tie us up during the nicest part of the year. It's probably a good thing this house doesn't have another bedroom or two," Mom said.

The two kids glanced at each other thinking about the hidden secret room the clock was in. They would have to make sure their parents didn't ever find out about it. That would surely ruin any future adventures they were certain were on the horizon. Matthew made a mental note to always make sure the control panel door on the clock was closed when they left the room. If they made a trip, the door to the room had to be locked, too, so Mom or Dad couldn't walk in, discovering their secret. Unless you knew what to look for, you would never realize there was an extra room hidden there.

Thinking about the secret room reminded Elizabeth about the stories she read online the night before. She was eager to let Matthew know about them. "Any ideas as to what you will do, Dad?" she asked.

"I've worked in the oil fields getting projects up and running. I'm considering starting an online consulting business. I may have to go to the sites periodically, but nothing like I used to do," he replied.

"That sounds great. What about you, Mom?" Matthew asked.

"Funny we should get on this subject. I went to the little bank in town this morning to do a little business. While I was there, I was chatting with one of the customer service representatives. She told me that there's an opening at the branch for a part-time position. While I was there, I put in my resume. They told me I would hear one way or another by the middle of next week," she said with a smile on her face.

"That's great. We hope you get the job. You've worked full time for so long, it will be nice to ease off a bit," Elizabeth said to her.

"Oh, I almost forgot to tell you. The services for television and internet will be upgraded up tomorrow. They need to be changed over into our names and upgraded to meet our needs," Leonard informed the pair.

Matthew and Elizabeth went upstairs to conclude their

earlier endeavors. On the way up the stairs, Elizabeth shouted down to her mother, "Hey, Mom, We put the free-standing mirror in your room. I found a small dresser with a mirror on it that I can do my homework on and put that in my room instead. I hope that's okay with you."

"Thank you, that's very kind of you, dear."

When they were finished cleaning the dressers, every-thing they needed was put in or on them. Elizabeth asked her brother to come to her room. She fired up the computer and showed him the stories she found the night before. The article about the jewelry theft piqued Matt's interest immediately, especially since they had already traveled back to a period close to the time when the rob-bery had taken place.

The article stated that it had always been believed that the perpetrators were residents living on the mainland in the Providence area. The police caught up with the gang in the countryside outside Edgartown. They were fol-lowed after getting off the ferry at Woods Hole. The shootout occurred when one of the police officers prema-turely made contact with one of the robbery suspects.

One of the suspects, named Frank Barnes, had been a long-time resident of Martha's Vineyard. He was a furni-ture maker, known for the intricate furniture he made. As a sideline, he occasionally made granite headstones. Be-cause of the intricacy of his work, he needed to charge too much for the stones and as a result, only did a little work in this area. It had long been thought that a diary of sorts, holding clues as to where the jewelry had been cached, had been hidden somewhere in the area. This, of course, had never been substantiated.

"The shootout happened about four years after the robbery took place. I wonder how the police found out that they were even involved." Elizabeth asked, looking at her brother.

"Wow, just think! That Frank guy lived a short distance away from here in Edgartown," Matthew said.

"Yes, it sure is something. It doesn't say too much about the other men or where the police thought they might have been going."

"Do you think that they might have been going to retrieve the jewelry?" he asked.

"It could be, otherwise why would they be traveling together in a group," she replied.

"What is the other story you were talking about?"

"It's about a child that was abducted in the summer of 1914. They only discovered the body years after she disappeared. It says they found her buried in a cave on Martha's Vineyard three years later. It even shows where the cave is. Aquinnah is at the eastern tip of the island. Maybe we could go there sometime when you get your truck. What do you think, Matt?"

"I like that idea. It will be nice being able to explore the islands. Do you think you'd like to travel back to see John and Alice sometime?" he asked.

"You aren't thinking of getting involved with Alice again, are you?"

"No, I see that it wouldn't be a good idea to try that."

"Then I really would like it. We'll have to wait till Mom and Dad are gone for a bit, though."

"Make sure you keep a record, like you did on our vacation, of where and when we go anywhere, all right? That way we won't overlap any of our away times," he said.

"I still have the journal, so that won't be a problem."

"There is one thing bothering me, sis."

"Oh, what's that?"

"Remember John said that he wanted to come to our time for a visit?"

"Yes, I remember. What about it?" she asked.

"I'm not sure it's a good idea. What happens if he learns something here and uses it in the past. It could really alter things in our time," he said with a concerned expression.

"I see what you mean. It could have disastrous effects if it was something big. Maybe we'll have to explain this to him and guard against it. Either that or we'll have to talk him out of coming here. Let's think about it and come to some decision later."

They end up going for a walk on the beach with Buddy, their Golden Retriever. Things had changed from when they first came here for the summer-long vacation only a short time ago. My, what an exciting time that was. Everything the two did, attempting to change the past ended in dismal failure. Only coming up with a final desperate plan did they manage to succeed in their quest.

Elizabeth and Matthew both remembered how chilling it was to see the figure of Alice running down the beach. Even Buddy had been frightened by that scene.

"Are you and Dad going to fix the garage when you get your truck?" Elizabeth asked.

"Yeah, we were making plans about how to safely pull it back straight and bracing the walls to keep it square. We'll brace the inside properly, and that should do the trick. If all goes well, we should be able to make it safe to work in."

"That sounds like a plan to me," she said. "By the way, when do you start school?"

"In just over a week from now is the first day of school. Dad and I will be looking for a pickup soon. Boy, I can hardly wait," he said excitedly.

"You were serious, when you said you'd teach me to drive, weren't you?"

"Of course, sis. We're pals, and, besides, I might need you to drive me once in a while," he said, smiling at her.

Buddy decided that there had been enough talk and barked at them before running into the water. They both joined him in the water for a swim, throwing their towels on the beach. Half an hour's worth of play and they headed back to the cottage for supper.

The meal finished, Matthew and Elizabeth did the dishes much to their parents' surprise. When this was taken care of, they all spent time in front of the fire. An hour later, the two siblings excused themselves, leaving Leonard and Kate relaxing on the couch.

In her room, they looked over the dresser they brought in from the shed.

"I wonder if there is a cavity in this side here," Elizabeth asked, pointing to what looked like a disproportionate part on the left side.

"If it's like the clock or the dresser in my room that has the secret compartment in it, I'm sure one has to be here too," he said, looking at the spot she indicated.

"The clock and your dresser having European influences, look like they were built by the same person. The style of this is more of an American type," Elizabeth pointed out.

"Clean your things off, and I'll pull out the drawer."

This done, Matthew looked inside the opening where the drawer had been and rapped the wood with his knuckles. There was a hollow sound, bringing a smile to his face. "There's a piece of wood just above the opening that I can move just a little so that probably means there's an empty space inside there," he said.

"Now, all we have to do is figure out if there's a way to open it. There's no point in building it like this if not to hide something. I'm starting to get excited, Matthew."

At this point, there were voices coming up the stairs. Matt quickly replaced the drawer and sat on the bed as Elizabeth sat on the chair in front of the dresser.

After a minute, there was a light knock, then Mom entered the room to say goodnight.

"Thanks for putting the full-length mirror in our room. I just love it. Is that the dresser you were talking about? I can see why you would want it to do your homework on, it's lovely," she said. "Good night, you two."

"Night, Mom," they said in return.

They then began to make plans to locate, the following day, a way into the dresser's secret storage compartment.

They fell asleep rather quickly that night, unaware that many adventures and dangers awaited them in the very near future.

Chapter 5

The next morning arrived with a thunderstorm looming on the horizon. Leonard advised everyone to make preparations for the hard rain that was approaching. Mom and Elizabeth checked all the doors and windows to make sure there were no gaps for the rain to come in. Leonard and Matthew checked the outside of the house to make sure the downspouts were properly attached and the soil sloped away from the house. With shovels in hand, the two corrected any grade problems around the outside of the house and shed. The car window was closed, and the shed and garage doors were also secured.

When all that was done, the family sat in the living room watching the lightning in the sky as the dark clouds got closer and closer. A few drops hit the windows and soon turned into a deluge of water coming from the sky. The thunder vibrated the glass as grains of sand bounced against the windows. The wind blew in gusts that seemed to threaten the very cottage itself.

That storm was even worse than the one they experienced on their vacation. Buddy whined each time a clap of thunder rattled the windows. He stayed close to Elizabeth, trembling constantly. Despite their efforts to keep the rain out, there were still a few places where the water gained entry. Leonard made a mental note to fix these spots. He knew that this type of weather was common for the area, and they needed to be ready for it.

The girls wanted a fire to warm the room up, and Matt tried to start one. He realized quickly that a strong downdraft was blowing the smoke into the house and gave up, coughing. The phone rang, and Kate answered it. The man who was to come and upgrade the services told her he had to wait for the storm to pass before he could do the job. A particularly close lightning strike accompanied by the crash of thunder caused the power to go out. Both the girls let out a shriek but recovered quickly, getting up to light candles. The rain, wind, and lightning went on for an hour and a half. As quickly as the storm came, it left again.

The sun shone again as the clouds blew across the sky. The candles were no longer needed, and the cleanup began. Water was dried, and windows opened as the temperature rose. Matthew and his dad went outside, cleaned the window glass, and picked up any debris the wind had brought to the cottage.

"Wow, that sure was something, Dad," Matthew said.

"You're not kidding. I guess this is something we'll have to get used to. The places where the water got in will have to be fixed. I'm glad the garage is still standing. We'll have to get to the job of straightening it soon."

"Okay, Dad, whenever you're ready I'll help with that," he said as a voice called out to them.

"Hey, boys, it's time for lunch. We're going to have sandwiches because the power is still out," Mom said.

It took two hours before the electricity came back on. A cheer erupted from all the family when the kitchen light started to glow once more. Half an hour later, the serviceman called informing them he would be there shortly. It took the man forty-five minutes, and all the changes required were completed.

"Your dad and I are going to town to pick up the items necessary to fix the leaky places in the cottage. He also needs some nails and bolts to fix the garage. Do you two need anything?" Kate asked.

"Could you pick up a few D-size batteries for my flashlight? I could use a notebook, but that can wait till just before school starts," Matthew said.

Elizabeth told her that she had all she needed for the time being. The parents drove off a few minutes later, leaving the pair to their own devices.

"Let's have a look at that dresser. I'm curious as to how we can access the secret interior," Matthew said.

Off they went to her room, removing everything from the drawers and off the top. The first thing they did was to turn it around so they could see the back. In the upper right corner was a slightly faded ink stamp.

"Can you read what the writing says?" Matthew asked.

"I'll use my magnifying glass to make it bigger."

Doing this, she got close and then tilted her head to get a better view while Matt shone a light on it.

"It says that this piece was built by…Frank Barnes of Edgartown on Martha's Vineyard. Isn't that the man who was named in the article about the jewelry robber's shootout?" she asked.

"Yes, it was. I think it's even more important now that we find a way inside this thing. Wow, it seems incredible that we should stumble upon this piece. What are the chances?"

The two studied the back of the dresser, finding no hints. Laying it on its back they searched every nook and cranny, again finding nothing. Standing the piece upright, they scrutinized the two ends thoroughly.

"So far we've checked everywhere except the front and top. I sure hope we find something here," Matthew said.

The two went over every inch of the front and top and still found nothing.

"The only place left is the inside and the mirror frame, so let's check the inside first, that's where I would make the access point," Matthew said.

They went over every square inch of the interior and still no way in was found. Frustration was building up.

"What the heck? This is really hard to figure out. It's as hard to get into as the clock would have been if we hadn't found the journal. Maybe we're looking for something too obvious," Matthew said.

Stepping back and carefully looking the piece over, he started trying to think more like he would if he was making the dresser himself. He set the piece on its feet once more. The frame of the mirror was pushed and pulled and even twisted.

Finally, at the corner of the frame where it met the main part of the dresser on the left side, a little lever moved a trifle. It was almost directly over the spot where the hidden space was.

Matthew twisted the lever slowly to its maximum and was rewarded by the sound of a panel dropping into the empty space where the drawer had been removed. "Wow, I thought we were stumped for a while there. This is great. Take a look inside and see if you can see anything, Elizabeth," he said, grinning.

Kneeling down, she looked inside then reached in, moving a piece of wood panel and pulling out a thin journal.

"Just to keep the suspense going, let's put everything

back together in case Mom and Dad come back early. We don't want them asking us about this," Elizabeth suggested, even though Matthew would much rather have read what was in the book. "I wonder how many people have had possession of this dresser and how it ended up in the shed," she said.

"Good question."

Once they were done, they sat on the edge of the bed and opened the journal to the first page. In it, they found a brief account of the robbery and the plan to wait a considerable amount of time for the authorities to give up the investigation. Once this part was done, there were several blank pages, then a page with a rhyme. The two read it over quite a few times till it dawned on them that this was a clue as to where something might be hidden. This now took on a new light as they read the words one more time. Matthew closed his eyes as Elizabeth slowly read out loud.

> "'To the cross, you have to go
> Where they stand row on row
> An obscure corner you will find
> Where the sun it always shines
> In the stone, it will show
> Where to next you will go.'

"My goodness, what on earth does that mean?" Elizabeth asked, shaking her head.

"Darned if I know," he said. "I think the only one who would know was the one who wrote it. To tell you the truth, I wonder why he would make this riddle in the first place. He already knows where the jewelry is hidden, doesn't he?"

"Maybe it isn't for him at all. It could be that he wrote it and then hid it in the dresser, just in case something happened to him. His friends, I'm sure, would be able to figure it out. I'm not sure if we'll ever be able to decipher this, so we might as well think about when you want to go back to see our friends."

"How long did Mom say they would be gone?" Matthew asked.

"It's three o'clock, so I doubt that they'll be much more than an hour. Is that enough time to decide when to go back to and make the trip?" she asked apprehensively.

"Get your journal, and we'll see what time we want to go back to."

This she did, and they made the plan to go back to July 10, 1908, for no reason in particular. This was a time approximately one year after the two finally managed to change the past.

Into the clock room, they went, after taking a quick look out the window to make sure their parents weren't home early. Elizabeth stopped and walked back to her room, leaving Matthew with a puzzled look on his face. She picked up her cell phone and called her mother.

"Hey, Mom, I was just wondering if you have time to pick up some apples before you come home. By the way, where are you now?" she asked. She listened for a second and, saying bye, hung up. "They're still in town and won't be back for over an hour," she told Matt.

"That's pretty smart of you. I didn't even think of doing something like that," he said, quite impressed.

The little panel at the front of the timepiece just below the clock face was opened. It was about two inches high and ran the width of the front. Two buttons on opposing sides of the clock were pressed in to allow the panel to swing down on a cleverly hidden hinge system.

With the panel now opened, they saw the familiar series of six dials on the left side and two more plus a switch on the right side. The day, month and year to go back to, were set by the six dials and the duration of the stay back in time by the two on the other side. The maximum time they could go back in time was ninety-nine hours and the least was one hour which was what they set it for.

The weights were set, and the switch then turned on. Finally, the pendulum was made to swing, and the two waited for the clock to do its job at the top of the hour. Both felt a little apprehension as the moment arrived. Even though they had made many trips to the past already, it was still an exciting event. Now, they could use the clock anytime they had the freedom to do so. The room clouded over, and they were gone.

Chapter 6

When the air cleared, they found themselves back in the uncle's home. This came as a surprise to them as they thought that the clock would have been in John's home. Luckily, the room was empty, and the two climbed out the window once again, as they had done many times before.

"I thought John was getting the clock. How come it's still in the uncle's house?" Elizabeth asked.

"I think we should find John and ask him."

Off they went in search of their friend. Everything here was as it had been the first time the pair traveled into the past. There was a feeling of nostalgia as they surveyed the scene before them and breathed in the familiar aroma of the warm flower-scented air.

The first spot they looked for their friend was the dock where all the pristine boats were kept. There was no sign of him there, so they headed to his home. After knocking on the door, a moment later, it opened, and there was John. He had a shocked look on his face, and, when he recovered, he stepped forward to hug his two friends from the future.

"Boy, am I ever glad to see you. Does this mean that you still have access to the clock?" he asked excitedly.

"Our parents ended up being able to buy the cottage where the clock was stored, after all, and so we can use it whenever we want. At least when we're alone," Matthew said.

"I thought your uncle was going to give you the clock," Elizabeth asked.

"Oh, that's going to happen when I buy Lilac cottage in a few months. He's helping me with the finances. He has done a complete turnaround this past year. You would hardly recognize him now," John explained.

"That's wonderful, John, Elizabeth said. "We're so glad to hear that. Is Alice somewhere to be found? We'd love to see her too."

"I'm sorry. She's on vacation at the moment, but she'll be back next week. I'll tell her that you were here. Maybe you can come back then."

"Yes, we'll try to do that. Oh, by the way, we found a riddle in a hidden space in a dresser and wonder if it means anything to you. We think it may have something to do with the Jewelry Collection heist that happened a few years ago," Matthew said.

He showed him a copy of the riddle. John read it over once, then again. A puzzled look crossed his face. "Sorry, but it means nothing to me. Let me keep it, and I'll give it some thought."

Matthew didn't bother to inform John that the man who wrote the note was still alive and would sometime in the not-too-distant future be killed in a gunfight with the police. It didn't seem important at the moment. The three chatted for a while, and the familiar beep came from Matthew's pocket. It was signaling them that the clock would take the two back to their own time period shortly.

Elizabeth told John that they would come back

sometime after he moved the clock to Lilac Cottage. Matthew asked exactly when he would take ownership. Then he asked John to build the secret room as soon as he could after getting possession of the timepiece. Matthew drew up the plans for the hidden entry and explained its workings to him.

John agreed to do this, and Matthew gave him a prospective date when the two time-travelers would try to return.

Matt and Elizabeth found a private location and soon after disappeared.

Chapter 7

The air cleared, and the two were standing in front of the clock in their own time once more.

"Well, that was interesting. It was nice seeing John again," Elizabeth said with a smile.

"Yes, it was, too bad he doesn't have any idea what the puzzle means. It is bothering me, I think we could find the hidden jewelry if we could decipher the message," he said, frowning.

"Don't worry, Matt. I'm sure we'll figure it out eventually. Maybe we're not looking at it the right way. I don't know what the right way is but it obviously isn't the way we are," she said, patting him on the back.

"Yeah, you're probably right. When I relax and let things happen, they sometimes fall into place themselves," he realized.

At that point, Buddy met them as they walked back into Elizabeth's room. A thought struck Matthew just then. "I think that we have to make sure Buddy doesn't go into the clock room at all. He might try to go in there when Mom or Dad is in here, and that might make them suspicious. What do you think?" he asked.

"I think you might be getting a little paranoid, but I can see it happening, so, yes, it's a good idea. Whenever we go back, we'll make sure he is kept downstairs," she agreed.

Not long after, Leonard and Kate arrived back home and, as things were put away, Leonard let Matthew know they may possibly have found a vehicle for him.

"We were driving past a small car lot and found a nice looking Toyota truck. It's the smaller version, not like the F-One-Fifty or the Ram-Fifteen-Hundred. The bigger vehicles burn up too much fuel, so we thought this one might interest you. We can go look at it in the morning if you like."

"That's great, Dad, can you afford it? I don't want to be a burden to you," Matt said, genuinely concerned.

"No, no, the price is actually less than we were planning on spending, and it's in really good shape with low mileage too," Leonard insisted.

"Wow, I can hardly wait. Thanks, Dad," Matt said, smiling from ear to ear. He thought that he was lucky to have parents like this. He also felt a little bad for having to keep the clock a secret, but he knew what would happen if they found out.

After dinner, father and son went to the garage to look things over. The steel cable was ready, and Leonard drilled a hole through the side leaning away from them. The hole was above the top of the wall over the header. On the other side of the building, midway along the wall, a brace was set up. With this done, he drilled another hole. This one went through the header. The smaller entry door was forced open, after being stuck because the wall was slanted by the leaning of the building. The cable was then fed through the first hole far enough to reach through the second hole.

Leonard propped up another timber against the second

wall to prevent the building from leaning any more. Entering the building, he stretched the cable, feeding it through the hole on the far side. Matthew picked up a heavy walled pipe, and the cable was then wrapped around it and fastened.

Leonard tightened the cable while his son held the pipe up till it was tight against the wall horizontally. With the come- along attached to the bottom of the large tree, the cable was tightened more and more.

There was a creaking as the building slowly straightened out. They pulled it just a fraction past straight and placed the braces against the far side wall, preventing it from going back to the leaning position that they had found it in.

"Good work, Matt. We'll leave it this way till we can brace it from the inside tomorrow after we look at the truck. Does that work for you?"

"It sure does, Dad. This went easier than I thought it would."

"Three things make a job like this easy. Experience, the right equipment, and good help and I had all three."

The next morning, the whole family drove to the car lot and took the four-year-old truck for a spin. Matthew loved the truck, which turned out to be a stick shift. This was just what he had wanted because he already had a little experience with standard transmissions. His past friends had vehicles like that. A deal was struck, and preparations were made for payment. They went for lunch while the oil was changed and everything gone over by an independent auto tech. With the tech's approval, insurance was put on the vehicle, and it was driven home with Matthew happily behind the wheel.

Back in the garage the men finished all the bracing and removed the cable. The building was tested and found to be sturdy. The interior was cleaned, and the concrete floor swept. The tool boxes were brought in and the garage was now functional. Even the main door worked as it should.

Life at the new home settled into a routine. Everyone was happy, and Kate received a call informing her that she had been hired. They asked her to come in so she could be shown her duties. She would have to work every second Saturday, but that couldn't be helped. The wage was agreeable, and the staff pleasant to work with.

Leonard took the time to set up his online business, and it wasn't long before he was contacted by former employers with work to be done. There would be monthly trips to tie everything together for him, but those would only last a week. Every second week would see him at corporate offices for meetings, but these were just for a few days at a time.

School started with both teenagers settling in nicely. They made friends easily, and the courses, they found, were not too difficult. Living considerably farther away from school than the other students made visitations unlikely, and this actually worked well for the two. This way, they had more time to themselves for trips into the past. If they didn't have the clock, it would have made life a trifle lonely for the pair.

"We haven't made any headway with the puzzle so what do you say we look at some of the other articles. Maybe we can help someone in the past." Elizabeth suggested to her brother.

"There's one thing I think I might have figured out. The robbers met four years after the theft. They came to Martha's Vineyard on the ferry and got into the shootout there. This means that the treasure has to be in either Martha's Vineyard or on Chappaquiddick Island. If it was somewhere else, they wouldn't all have met in that spot. They would have met on the mainland."

"Yes, I think you're right. That's great thinking, Matt. We'll have to familiarize ourselves with the two islands, and I bet the pieces will fall into place, one at a time. Good going, bro," she said and laughed as she patted him on the back.

They read some of the articles describing a time long gone by. There was the one telling them about the young girl, Cassandra Boothe. She had been abducted from the family home in Edgartown and found dead years later in a cave. There was a black-and-white photo of a young girl along with a description. Cassandra had light reddish brown hair, green eyes, and freckles. She had a slender face and body and was considered a pretty girl.

The person who buried the body had remained unidentified, despite all efforts by the police investigating the crime. Elizabeth pulled up a map on Google and found the spot where the cave was located. That coming weekend, they planned to go and see the site.

After a little more browsing, it was discovered that there were a large number of other murders and disappearances of young girls scattered through a thirty-five year period. The girls were all close to the same age, and the circumstances each time were very similar. It had been suspected many years later that a serial killer may have been responsible, although no real evidence of this was ever found.

Another story involved the murder of a man in Martha's Vineyard in 1927. There was a photo of Albert Morris with his wife and two children. The family fell on hard times and had difficulty surviving after that. The murderer was never apprehended.

"How do you feel about taking a trip back and seeing if we can find out who the murderer was," Matthew asked.

"Oh, I don't know. I think things could go sour very

easily if we make a mistake. I'm a little scared by this," she answered.

"To tell you the truth, I think that the clock came into our lives for a reason. I really think it's our duty to try using the clock to make a difference in the lives of people who have been wronged so badly."

"Where on earth do you get these lines from? Have you been watching some television show where they say things like this?" Elizabeth asked.

"Well, maybe, just once or twice. It does make sense, though, doesn't it?" he said seriously.

"Okay, just what do you think we should do, or haven't you thought that far ahead?"

"Give me some time. I'll come up with something. It doesn't have to be this particular case, you know. We could tackle something a little less challenging at first if you're too afraid," he said to her.

"I am nervous, but yes, I think these people deserve our help. I'll put a little thought into it too and, between us, we may be able to come up with a feasible plan," she replied, wondering if this was a good idea, even though she was the one who brought it up. She doubted that it was, because the feeling of dread she'd had several times during the vacation was back.

Monday morning brought a new day with the sun shining warmly and very few clouds in the sky. Matthew went outside to look over his new truck. It was a nice deep red and shone beautifully. He sat in it and tried out the stereo.

This is great, he thought. Who would have thought his parents would buy a vehicle this nice for him. He remembered his promise to teach Elizabeth how to drive the stick shift as she came out of the house. He drove toward town and got on the ferry to Edgartown, after dropping her off at school, and continued on to the college.

He was happy he chose, with the help of his parents, that trade to get in to. The auto-tech course at the college had a very good reputation. His father had explained to him that cars would always be around, and a good auto-tech would be able to find a good-paying job in any city in the country where he might want to live.

During his lunch break, he had a few minutes by himself and thought about Albert Morris, the man murdered in 1927. Matt wondered where he could get more information about the crime. Maybe a little more information about the man himself would provide some clues as to the identity of the murderer. A plan started to form in his mind about going back to see what could be learned a day or two before the crime.

On the way home, he informed Elizabeth about what he thought they should do.

"I think that's a good idea, Matt. Maybe we'll find enough information about it to do something," she said. She couldn't believe that she was actually getting somewhat excited about it.

After supper, the two got onto the computer to gather what sparse knowledge there was. They found where he lived and what he did for a living. He worked in a plant that turned whale blubber into lamp oil and soap products. The plan was to go on the weekend if they were alone long enough to make the trip.

Trying to locate clothes suitable to wear in 1927 was easier than it was for 1907. The two made their preparations as the week slipped by. They thought it best to go back for one hour to inform John of their plans. Then, when arrangements for travel were made, they'd go back for longer to see if Albert worked during the day or at night. His body had been discovered on a Friday late in the afternoon, August nineteenth. The exact time of death was not given, but the authorities believed he had been killed the night before. They would need to find him early enough on that day to possibly do something about it.

The end of the week came, and Kate informed the family that she would have to work on Saturday. Leonard was going to be home for the weekend and would be online with clients, discussing plans for oil field upgrades and maintenance. This did not work well with what the teenagers had in mind. The two kept a wary eye for an opportunity which failed to materialize.

"Unless we get some alone time during the week, we'll have to wait for next weekend," Elizabeth said.

"I think you're right," he agreed.

As the week progressed, Leonard made good headway on the job. Matthew asked what Elizabeth thought about an idea he had and, when she felt it might work, he made a suggestion to his mother. "Hey, Mom, Dad has been working hard since we've moved here. Why don't the two of you go out for lunch or dinner on Saturday? It might be nice for you both to relax a little while."

"That's a wonderful idea, but it will have to be after I get off work at three o'clock. What will you and Elizabeth do for supper?" she asked.

"We can have macaroni and wieners. Elizabeth loves that, and we haven't had it in quite a while," he said.

"I'll go talk to your dad and see what he thinks."

Kate walked into the living room where Leonard had his desk and computer set up. She made the pitch, and the plans were set.

Matt headed up the stairs and let Elizabeth know that everything was a go. They made the rest of the preparations. Matthew, as usual, was all excited, but Elizabeth knew that it had the potential to be dangerous. It had happened before, and her hands trembled ever so slightly.

"We need to have some protection with us, all right, Matt," she said nervously.

"Okay, but I doubt anything will go wrong. We're only going to gather a little information," he told her. "But I'll bring my slingshot and a wooden walking stick, so you'll feel safer."

"Thanks, Matt."

The weekend arrived, and Saturday afternoon after she got home from work, Leonard and Kate got ready for a few hours of relaxation. They had chosen the seafood restaurant in town and decided to take a stroll around the scenic streets before entering. The sun was shining and the mid-September weather was balmy and pleasant. Buddy was left behind with the kids, who spent the afternoon on the beach. The dog had been happy just to lie down and rest after a vigorous workout chasing a Frisbee and the occasional gull.

"Okay, they're gone. Get the stuff while I set the date on the clock, Elizabeth."

Matt opened the door at the end of Elizabeth's closet. The same door, that had been concealed for so many years, lead to the hidden room that housed the clock and a few other items. Because the window had been darkened the room was very dim. He thought it might be a good· idea to run an extension cord into the room and plug in a lamp. The only concern he had was forgetting to unplug the cord and place it in the room. His parents would then soon discover the room, and then the clock and the trips into the past would come to an abrupt halt. Buddy was asleep on the rug in the kitchen, oblivious to what was about to happen. The door to the secret room was closed, and the two siblings stood in front of the clock.

Using the six dials on the left side, the date set was Thursday, August 18, 1927. The duration would be one hour, using the two dials on the right side. The weights were wound to the top, ensuring that the clock wouldn't stop prematurely, and the arms on the clock were set to two-fifty-five with the switch activated. The clock would send them back in time at the top of the hour.

"So, sis, are you ready to go?"

"Have you got everything we need in the canvas bag?" she asked.

"I do, let's go. Boy, I'm all excited. I can hardly wait for this."

He reached into the clock and started the pendulum swinging, and then he closed the door gently.

The five minutes passed slowly and, when the timepiece reached three o'clock, the room once more clouded over.

Chapter 8

Once again, the air cleared, and the pair had appeared in John's house this time instead of the uncle's. Matthew called out to let John know that they were in the clock room.

"I'm downstairs, Matthew. I thought you would return many years ago," he said when the two came into the kitchen.

"We're going to, but we thought we would solve a murder case first. I know this is confusing, but it will clear up when this case is finished, and we come back to see you in your past. It's even confusing me," Matthew told him.

Elizabeth filled in a few of the blanks. "We need your help to get to Edgartown. We're only here for an hour, right now, to see if you can arrange a ride into town for when we return. We'll be back as soon as we can after you make the arrangements. We need to get to this address," she said, handing him a piece of paper.

"Certainly, I can get things ready while you're here. When you come, everything will be ready. It will take close to an hour to get there. What time do you want to get to this address?" John asked.

"We would like to be there by three o'clock if possible," Matthew said.

"Then I suggest that you get here by one, so we have plenty of time. I'll get my helper to take care of things at the bakery while I'm gone. Let's go to the garage and get the car ready. I bought a used Tin Lizzy a few years ago. The automobile I had before this had been breaking down too often."

The three went to the garage, and Matthew lit up as he feasted his eyes on the Model T. As boys did, the hood was raised, and they studied the engine. Elizabeth chuckled to herself as she watched them.

The three gathered a few items they thought would be necessary and waited for the journey home. John, being much older than the travelers, found that he was most interested in discussing what the future was like. Matthew and Elizabeth tried not to elaborate too much, and John asked why. Elizabeth relayed their fears about things from the future being accidentally used in the past and what the consequences of that would be.

"Hmmm, I see your point. If I do come to see you, I will have to make sure that I don't find out how things work or learn what major things will happen between now and then," he said with a thoughtful look.

The beep in Matthew's pocket indicated that the two would be going home in a few minutes, and they headed to the house. It would not do to have someone witness them vanishing as they went back to their own time.

The trip home was made and, after they checked on Buddy, the clock was reset for one o'clock. They were soon on their way back to see John again and then on the drive to Edgartown.

When they arrived at their destination, they saw that

Albert Morris lived in a poorer area of town. After talking to a few neighbors, the three found out that Albert's employment was rather sporadic. He worked several types of jobs that included fishing boats and a place that turned whale blubber into lamp oil. The lamp oil production was quickly changing and would be a lost art soon, according to the locals.

While they were watching Albert's home, a young boy came out and walked along the side of the gravel road.

"One of us should ask the boy where his father is while John and I stay here," Matthew said, looking at his sister.

"If you want me to go, just say so," she said laughingly.

Elizabeth casually walked down the street and struck up a conversation with the boy. After chatting for a few minutes, she came back to where the boys were standing.

"The dad is in the house, getting ready to go out to meet some men. James doesn't know who they are but says that his mother doesn't like them," she explained.

"We'll have to stay out of sight so we don't raise any suspicions," John suggested.

The three picked a spot and waited for Albert to leave the house. After about half an hour, he came out of the rundown little home and headed toward the town center. Once there he met with two unsavory-looking characters.

John, Matt, and Elizabeth managed to hide close enough to overhear part of the conversation.

"Do you understand what it is you have to do?" the swarthier of the two men asked.

"Why do I have to do this?" Albert asked.

"They will never know that you're involved. All you have to do is drive the stolen automobile. We'll be the only ones with handguns," the other man said.

"I can't do it, I say. Please don't make me do it," he pleaded.

"You will do it, or I'll pay that pretty little wife of yours a visit. Would you rather that happen?" the first man asked threateningly.

"No, no please don't do anything to my wife."

"You just make sure you're there tonight in front of the theater, and you had better not fail us, or else. Make sure you have your mask," the swarthy man told Albert.

With this, the two men left Albert standing there with a fearful look on his face.

"How can we help him deal with these men? I'm sure they're planning a robbery, or they wouldn't need guns," Elizabeth said.

"Gosh, I'm not sure what to do here. Where is the theater, John? Is it far from here?" Matthew asked.

"It's near the shoreline in the town center. Why do you ask?"

"Let's go there and see what we're dealing with. Maybe we can come up with a solution to Albert's problem. He doesn't want to be part of this but is being forced into it," Matthew replied.

"This has to be why Albert is murdered. The men want him to drive the getaway car, and then they'll dispose of him so they won't have to split the loot. I'm sure of it," Elizabeth stated.

When they got to a spot across the street from what looked like a fairly recently built beautiful theater, they surveyed the area. There were many shops along the street on both sides with colorful displays in the windows, depicting the current fashions and the latest products for sale. There was a large sign in front of the doors leading into the theater itself, announcing the long-awaited one-night performance of a popular opera singer.

"I bet this is why they want to rob the place tonight.

They expect to have a large crowd and lots of money in the till," Matthew said.

John looked at the two." Do either of you have any ideas?"

Matthew looked at Elizabeth for a suggestion but received a blank look. He got that faraway look in his eyes as he thought over possible scenarios. After a moment, he turned to the others. "Where can I get a sheet of paper, a pencil and an envelope?"

"I can go to that store on the corner and buy them easily enough," John said and started walking away. He came back five minutes later and handed Matthew the items.

Matthew found a flat surface and began to write. When he was done, he read what he had written and added a few more lines. Folding the paper and inserting it into the envelope, he wrote on the front of it. Handing the envelope to John, he gave him instructions and John left to do what he had been asked.

"Do you think this will work, Matthew?" she asked.

"I sure hope so. This is the safest way I could think of. If it doesn't, I have an alternate plan but that one leaves us more vulnerable, so I hope we won't need it," he said, his brows knit together in concentration.

The three left to go for supper after John finished his task. While the group waited for the time to pass, they talked about things they all planned to do.

"You said that you'll be coming to see Alice and me sometime before now. Do you have any idea when that will be?" John inquired.

Elizabeth was the first to answer. "We're thinking of trying to save the girl who was abducted and found years later in a cave."

"I remember reading about that. It was in all the newspapers for the longest time. Do you think that we can do something to help her?"

"We would like to try, especially because she is not the only one who disappears. We may not succeed, but it might be worth an attempt. Why, would you like to help us? You do know that you won't remember helping us now?" Mathew informed John.

"It's funny when you think about it, but yes, I want to help, even though I won't remember any of what we're doing now. It won't have happened yet," John said, smiling as he thought about it.

The time for the show approached with many people purchasing tickets. The crowd was very large and there was a happy feeling of excitement in the air. The patrons slowly made their way into the theater. The gentlemen there for the performance were in expensive suits and overcoats and the ladies were dressed in their finest gowns. Most of the people entering had a refined air about them.

As the last of the crowd passed the entrance to the interior, a car drove slowly by and parked on the same side of the street as the theater, and about a hundred feet away. One man got out of the front seat on the passenger's side while another exited the rear from the driver's side of the automobile. The man from the rear stepped up to the driver's window, pulling a firearm inconspicuously from his pocket.

The gun was pointed at the driver as the man spoke to him with threatening gestures. The two men left the car and walked toward the theater. As they came closer, it became obvious that they were the men that were seen earlier talking to Albert Morris.

John, Matthew, and Elizabeth walked down the street toward the car on the opposite side of the road. When the two men were out of sight, they crossed the street. There were only a few people on the sidewalk here and there, at this point, because the patrons had all entered the theater already. When no one was near, Matthew and John pulled jackknives out of their pockets, and, as they passed the car on either side, they stuck the knives into the tires. As the tires went flat, Albert jumped out of the car confronting the pair.

John and Matthew turned on him, as John put up his hand to stop the man from continuing, and informed Albert that the robbers were intending to kill him after they got what they wanted. John and Matthey advised him that he should leave while he could. The color drained from his face, and he didn't even think to ask how they knew this.

"They'll come to my house and kill me, anyway, when they find I'm not here," Albert said.

"Maybe not, if all goes well," John told him.

At this time, there was a commotion at the theater's entrance. The two men came running out, and there was gunfire as police officers pursued them. There were shots returned, back and forth, leaving the two men dead outside the theater. There were shrieks from ladies who had just witnessed the event, and everyone in the vicinity had backed against the walls of the closest buildings. Both men lay on the sidewalk face down on the hard surface with blood creeping along the bodies staining the concrete.

Albert stared at Matthew, John, and Elizabeth, stunned, with his mouth hanging open.

"Go home and take care of your family, Albert," Matthew said.

At this point, the man's wits came back to him and he ran away from the scene.

"I guess we didn't have to flatten the tires, after all," Elizabeth said. "But it could have turned out way differently. Let's get out of here before the police see us and ask why we're here."

A short time later, the familiar beep sounded once again and, in a hidden location, the three prepared for the moment the travelers vanished into thin air yet another time.

"What made you think of writing the note to the theater owner, Matthew," John asked.

"I figured that the owner would heed our warning much more readily than the police because it's his money on the line. The police might have thought the note was a prank. I guess the owner called for police protection after receiving the note."

"Good thinking, I hope we will meet again. I will always get older, and you will stay about the same age, but I can live with that. I do enjoy solving these crimes," John told them.

The three said their goodbyes as the air clouded over.

Chapter 8

The two reappeared in the clock room. This had not only been an exciting day but a long one too. The only problem was that it was still mid-afternoon and a long time before sleep.

"Wow, I didn't think we would be able to fix Albert Morris's death that easily. I really think we got lucky this time. I remember all the failures trying to fix things during our vacation," Matthew said.

"Me, too. Good work thinking of sending the note to the owner of the theater. It sure did the trick. I think I'll look online to make sure Albert didn't die some other way," she informed him.

Firing up the computer she checked to see if things had indeed worked out for the Morris family. When she got to where the story was last time she looked, there was no mention of his death. Instead, there was an article of the attempted robbery of the theater and the death of both would-be thieves.

"That's absolutely great. I'm so glad he didn't die needlessly," Matthew said.

"That is wonderful. Mom and Dad are going to be out

for a while yet, so I think I'll have a nap," Elizabeth told Matthew.

"I'll do the same and set the alarm for an hour and a half, and then I'll wake you up."

After their naps, they headed down to see Buddy. The trio went for a walk along the beach, enjoying the sunshine and having a good feeling about their first adventure. When the walk was finished, Matthew headed for the garage and did a bit of tidying up. He swept the floor and moved some lumber, so plans for a workbench could be made. He grabbed a broom and cleaned away the cobwebs that had accumulated over the years.

Elizabeth came into the garage to see how things were coming along. They discussed the plans for the building. The family tools were already there, and the doors hinges had been lubricated to swing open freely.

"Do you and Dad plan to paint the outside? It looks like it could use it," she said.

"Dad hasn't said anything, but that's a good idea. I think he does have plans to paint the cottage, though."

"What will happen if he looks through the window in the extra dormer and does some investigating? He will definitely find the hidden room, and that will put the Kibosh on any more traveling for us," Elizabeth pointed out.

"Oh, boy, you're right. I don't like the possibility of that happening at all. We'll have to come up with a plan to prevent that from happening."

"If he mentions the painting, try to postpone it until next summer. Maybe we'll think of something by then," she suggested.

"I have an idea right now. I want to run an electrical cord into the room for light anyway. We won't need the little bit of light that comes in through the window then. When they are both gone for a few hours, I'll make a cardboard pattern. When I have that made, I can get some old wood and build it in the garage and trace the pattern onto it. If I do it right, it should fit inside the dormer, close to the glass. That way if by chance he is up there and looks through the window, all he'll see is the wood. It will look like a wall is there, and the only reason for the window is decoration," he said, smiling at her.

"That's a great idea, Matthew. How on earth do you come up with these things? I sure am glad we're a team. You make things a lot easier."

"Thanks, sis, but you come up with a lot of good stuff, too."

After getting a bite to eat, Matthew got a piece of cardboard left over from the move and cut out the pattern. After a bit of fiddling around, it fit nice and snug and would do the job if he could make the wooden insert properly. It was getting close to when their parents would be coming home, so things were put away, and the room locked up.

"Hey, guys, we're home," came a shout from the front door a half an hour later.

"Hi, Mom, how was your time at the restaurant?" Elizabeth asked.

"It was really nice, thanks for suggesting it. What did you two do while we were gone?" she asked in return.

"We cleaned out the garage, but other than that not much," Elizabeth answered.

At this point, Matthew and Buddy came into the room. The dog ran to Leonard, looking to be patted, letting out a pleased bark when he was. To conclude the evening, a fire was lit, and the family played a few board games before retiring for the night.

The next morning, with the homework all done, Matthew and Elizabeth went for a ride in the truck. They toured the island and, on a deserted road, he started the first driving lesson. It took a bit of practice, but after about half an hour, Elizabeth got the hang of it. She drove around on the back roads, getting more familiar with the using of the stick shift. Seeing as how she was quite comfortable by then, he taught her how to stop and start on inclines. This is, of course, was much harder, but soon even this became manageable, too.

On a drive along a street near a group of buildings was a small church with a cross on top of a steeple. When Elizabeth saw this, it reminded her of something, but she couldn't quite remember what it was. She was sure it would come to her at some point.

Back at the cottage, there was a family discussion about whether or not any projects needed to be done before winter came. A few items were raised and talked about.

"I think we need to consider painting the cottage at some point," Leonard said.

"I think that we should look after the eave troughs and make sure they're in good shape first. But even before that, I think it would be best to get the garage in shape for the car this winter. We don't know how long the good weather will last here, so painting the cottage should wait for next summer when I'm off school," Matthew suggested.

"All right, yes, that's a good idea, Matthew. Let's get out to the garage today and see what we can do to prepare it for winter. Next weekend, if I don't get called out of town, we'll tackle the eave troughs to make sure they're in shape for the rains and winter weather. Are you saying you want to try painting the house next summer?"

"Yes, it can't be all that hard. I helped Jimmy's dad paint their garage before," Matt informed his father.

"I've got a good idea. Why don't we fix up the garage now and then paint it before the weather turns? That way

I can see how good you are before turning you loose on the house. What do you think, son?"

A deal was struck, and the two headed toward the garage. The roof was in fair shape and should last another year or two. They grabbed shovels and fixed the grade around the perimeter so the rainwater would flow away from the building.

A few minor things were fixed as well as the shutters on the two windows, which luckily were on the sides and didn't crack when the dwelling was straightened out. On the inside, some of the lumber was cut and nailed together and a workbench took shape. It was built with a shelf inside about halfway down.

"That didn't take long did it, Matt?"

"No, it didn't. It looks pretty good, and I'll bet it'll stand up for quite a while. Do you think we should anchor it to the wall?"

"That may well be a good idea because I'm going to attach the vise to it and heave on it now and then," Leonard said.

Another half hour and they were done.

"I'll get some paint this week, and we'll start painting the outside next weekend. What do you think about getting a small wood stove in here so we can work in the bad weather?" Leonard asked.

"I like that idea. It's hard to work when your fingers are numb," Matthew said, laughing at the thought.

With the work done, the two headed to the home, and Kate suggested a barbecue. This was met with a cheer as everyone was quite hungry.

The hamburger patties were brought out as the unit heated up. A salad was put together and fries were cut while the oil was being heated. Drinks were put on the patio table, and Buddy got ready to lay a guilt trip on whoever happened to be available, so he'd be able to join in with the family for some of the eats.

"Matthew, you'll have to feed Buddy first. I don't want him begging for food," Kate instructed her son.

Needless to say, Buddy was disappointed when his food was put in the dish, just when the hamburger patties were starting to sizzle nicely on the fire.

Later when the two youngsters had time, Elizabeth mentioned the incident driving past the old church. The thought had just come back to her.

"The first line in the riddle mentioned a cross. Do you remember, Matthew?"

"Yeah, I remember."

"I think that it's obvious that we need to look at a church for the rest of the clues to make sense," she said.

Pulling the journal with the riddle in it out of the drawer, they studied the first line.

"I think you may be onto something," Matthew agreed.

"What does the next line mean?" she asked.

"'Where they stand row on row.' What do you think that could mean?"

"The first thing that comes to me would be the gravestones or maybe a group of trees planted in rows. Could there be some other hidden meaning in the words?" she asked.

"I think we'll have to drive around a bit and see where all the churches are and check the grounds. We might be able to find some clarification as to what that line means."

"I'll go online to locate the churches. It'll save us a lot of time," she told him.

"'In a corner obscure you will find, where the sun it always shines.' Now, what on earth does that mean?" Matthew asked, puzzled.

"Your guess is as good as mine. How can the sun always shine?" she answered.

"I think I'll go to bed. It's been a long day, and we have to be ready for school in the morning."

The weather was nice and warm all week, so Leonard picked up the paint for the garage. Friday, he was called out of town, and Kate had to work Saturday. This worked out well for the two siblings, and Matthew told his father that he would start painting the garage.

While he had the chance, Matthew got the wood needed to close up the extra window in the house. He took great care to nail it together securely and then laid the template on it and traced the pattern onto the wood. Using his dad's jigsaw, he cut the piece to size, carried it into the house, and tried to place it in the window. The insert ended up being too tight in certain spots, so he put marks where a little sanding was required.

This took a few attempts, but he finally made it fit snugly in place. A few well-placed screws and backing blocks to anchor everything securely, and things were good. Taking the extension ladder he inspected the work from the outside and was pleased to see that everything looked perfect. The planks even went in the right direction.

With Elizabeth's help, they managed to paint the entire outside of the garage by the time their mother got home.

"I'm amazed at the job the two of you have done. Your father will be impressed by this, and you aren't even covered in paint," Kate said, laughing.

"Thanks, Mom. We're glad you like it," Matthew replied with a grin.

Having the inside of the window boarded up had been a relief for them. That way, it was very unlikely that the clock room would be discovered unless, of course, they became careless. Matthew expressed this concern to Elizabeth, who suggested that they make plans to always lock the room, whether they were in it or not, even if they were home alone, because their parents could surprise them by coming back unexpectedly sometimes.

When he had the chance, Matthew took an extension cord and ran it into the clock room. He found a lamp that was unused and brought it into the room. That was okay but not ideal.

"I think that an electrical outlet is needed in this room. I'm going online to see how to tie into an outlet in one of our rooms," he said.

"Is that safe to do?"

"It wouldn't be online if it wasn't. I'll turn off the power first before I start the job," he replied.

After a bit of research, he found what he needed. Going into both bedrooms, he located an outlet that was close to where he wanted power in the hidden room. He got everything he needed from the garage and went to work. An hour later, he had a new power source where he wanted it with an on/off switch too. The new outlet box was fastened to the wall with a cover plate and all was well.

"Wow, I'm impressed with you, Matthew."

"The directions were easy to follow so it wasn't very difficult," he said. "At least, we can see in here without a flashlight now. With the switch being close to the closet door, we can turn on the light as soon as we enter the room."

Buddy, up to now, had been fairly quiet, but enough was enough. He let out a bark, indicating he wanted to do something.

Getting the idea, the three of them went for a walk along the beach and gave the dog a good workout. When they got back to the cottage, Matthew suggested that they make plans to go back to a time before Cassandra Boothe had been abducted.

"I'd like to see if we can do something to prevent her disappearance. Maybe we can find out who the person responsible is," Matthew said.

"Al right, I'll check online for all pertinent information and you take care of Buddy."

With the details written down, the clock was set for May 24, 1914, the Sunday before the abduction. The little girl didn't get taken until late Wednesday afternoon that week, but that gave the pair a chance to assess the situation and maybe make plans for an intervention. The clock was activated, and Matthew, as usual, was excited, but Elizabeth again had feelings of unease. Too many things had gone wrong before and, to her, it was no game. The last thought in her mind as the room clouded over was the question of whether or not there would be complications with this incident.

Chapter 10

One moment they were in an old room and the next they were standing in front of the clock in a nice clean newly built space. They made their presence known, and John called back, asking them to come downstairs. The cottage was the same as it was in their own time, only much newer.

The two found, to their surprise, that Alice was there too and the reunion was a happy one. The reason for their trip was made known and, although John had plans that couldn't be changed, Alice said that she would be happy to take Matthew and Elizabeth where they needed to go.

When Alice found out that this wasn't a one-time incident but the beginning of a long time event with many girls disappearing in the following years, she was appalled. She said that she, although now married and several years older than her friends, would do all she could to help. Her husband was away on a business trip, and she would find someone to look after her three-year-old son.

Matthew who once had a crush on the younger Alice was surprised that she was married and had a baby already. He was surprised, at least until he realized that times were far different then than they are in his own time. People of this era got married much younger, and wives stayed at home with their children. Did women even have the right to vote yet? He couldn't quite remember when things like that had changed. He decided not to ask, not wanting to open a can of worms.

The horse was hooked up to the buggy, and off they went. It was a good thing the clock had been set for six hours because it would take time, to get to their destination and do the surveillance.

Once they reached town, they went to a spot near the address on Morse Street. Most of the homes there had picket fences and wooden exteriors. There were sidewalks along most of the streets, and the properties were well maintained. The trio did a walk by the home and noticed the girl playing on the porch. Cassandra was oblivious to them as she played with her dolls. She talked to them, periodically chastising one.

Matthew kept a wary eye out for anyone in the area who might be watching. The three separated and checked several streets in the vicinity. North Summer and Water Streets were traversed. Cottage Street, Fuller, and Peases Point Way were scouted too. There were many people walking that Sunday afternoon, but no one looked too suspicious. There was one man who looked fairly long at Cassandra and said something to her, but she waved as if recognized him, so he had been dismissed. Matthew took a mental picture of him anyway, just in case he saw the man again.

The clothes they were wearing seemed to fit in with the current trends, so they received no undue attention. The three hung around for a while and went to Main Street to eat the lunch they had brought with them.

"It gives me a funny feeling to see the two of you

again. You haven't changed at all, even though years have passed for me," Alice said.

"It feels the same for us. We saw John thirteen years from now, and the difference gave us an even stranger feeling," Elizabeth said.

"John and I have talked about using the clock, but ever since he was trapped in the past for so many years, he can't bring himself to do it," Alice told her friends.

"I can see where it would be daunting. The feeling of making an error must always be in the back of his mind. It's probably best to leave it alone for now. We'll come to see the two of you now and then if that helps," Matthew said.

Lunch finished, another circuit was made to see if anyone suspicious might be in the area. On Morse Street a little distance from where Cassandra lived, they saw the same man they'd seen earlier. He was acting nonchalantly, as if he was enjoying the weather, but Matthew thought he might be up to no good. Matthew got the two girls and let them know his suspicions.

The man was about five foot nine and weighed in the neighborhood of one hundred and eighty pounds. He had light brown hair, was clean shaven, and wore glasses. To Matthew, he looked a little geeky or maybe just a little bit off.

When the man noticed the three watching him, he quickly walked away. They tried to follow him but, after turning a corner, by the time they got there, he had disappeared.

"Where did he go so quickly? Do you think he lives in this area and ran into his house?" Elizabeth asked.

"He could have run through someone's backyard and gotten away from us like that," Alice suggested.

"If we wanted to find that out, we'd have to stay here, but we don't have the time anymore. In two hours, we'll be back home. Do you think we should warn the parents about what will happen?" Matthew asked.

"I'd like to do that, but what if they ask how we know this, what are we supposed to tell them? Oh, we're from the future, and we read it in the paper. I'm sure they'd listen, right after they called the police on us," Elizabeth joked.

"The only thing we can do is to come back when the abduction takes place and be here waiting for him. Do you think John could come with us so we are able to subdue the man," Matthew asked Alice?

"Oh, yes, certainly, I'm sure he will want to be here. I'm not sure I'll be able to come, though."

"That's all right. You've helped enough already, we really appreciate it," Elizabeth told her.

A little more scouting around and it was time to head back with Alice. When they arrived, Matthew helped un-hitch the horse and put it in the stable. Ten minutes before the clock did its thing, John came back from wher-ever he had had to go.

They filled him in on what had gone on and asked if he could help on Wednesday. He said he needed to do some work for a customer at his job but would arrange to do it earlier. They made plans to meet at John's house in time to get to Edgartown. The best time, they agreed, was two hours before the crime took place at four-thirty. They all agreed that Matthew and Elizabeth needed to be dressed differently so they wouldn't be recognized by the man if he was indeed the perpetrator.

It amazed John each time the two disappeared before his eyes. The look on his face conveyed the fact that he still wanted to use the clock sometime, but had to work up his nerve first. Too bad he had gotten stuck in the past on that first and only trip when he went on to save Alice. He had told Matthew and Elizabeth that he still shuddered over this when he thought too much about it. Maybe he'd talk more to Matthew about it if this case came to a satisfactory conclusion.

Chapter 11

It looks like the man we saw could possibly be the one who takes Cassandra Boothe," Elizabeth said.

"It sure does. Why else would he run when we spotted him? It's a good thing John will be with us. We should have no problem overpowering him and taking him into custody," Matthew answered.

"I don't think we should go back today. I'm tired from having spent six hours there. Mom will be home in an hour and a half, so a nap is out," she said.

"We, actually, could go back again now. If we go back early on Wednesday, we could sleep there for a few hours. What do you think about that?"

"Excellent, that's a great idea. We'll only lose the time it takes to prepare for the trip back. John will go do his job and come back to wake us up. We'll be back here before Mom gets off work," Elizabeth agreed, smiling brightly.

The preparations were made. The clock was set for departure and the length of time to stay in the past.

They both thought that if they stayed for about two hours past the time of the abduction, it would give them plenty of time to do whatever was necessary.

The room clouded over, and they were on their way. The pair arrived at eight in the morning on Wednesday, May the twenty-seventh. John was a little surprised to see them that early in the day so they explained their reasoning to him. He listened to their explanation with a smile on his face.

"The two of you are very clever. I'm quite impressed at how you plan these adventures," John remarked. "I have to go to work and will be back at one o'clock. If you get hungry, there's food in the kitchen, just help yourself."

John left at that point, and the siblings went to sleep quickly, despite the fact that they were a little apprehensive about what was to come.

They were both awake and had had a bite to eat by the time John got back home. The horse was hitched to the carriage and, after a few preparations, they were on their way. It took a little longer this time to get to the address because of a delay at the ferry crossing.

When they slowly made their way to the hiding place they had selected, they were still three-quarters of an hour ahead of time. The wait was done in silence for fear of alerting the murderer.

At just before four-thirty, the three noticed a man who had been watching Cassandra's house from a distance, moving to a better spot.

"Do you see the man hiding over there?" Matthew whispered, pointing in the direction where the man was.

"Yes, I see him," John said.

"Let's see if we can get behind him and prevent the abduction," Matthew said as he started moving.

Remaining hidden, the man stayed in the bushes. He sat there for a moment concentrating so hard that he didn't notice that the three were coming up on him from behind. All of a sudden, they made their move. A bag was dropped over the man's head, and a rope was tied around his shoulders and arms.

The man was then led away from his hiding place along an overgrown path. This took several minutes as the man was struggling and trying to talk to them, but no one was listening. He was tied to a tree with one loop of the rope across the man's mouth, silencing him. John contacted the police by phone explaining what had happened. He told them that the man was tied up and waiting for them.

From a safe distance, the three watched the proceedings as the police took the hood off the man and then untied him. There was a discussion, and they all went running to the house where Cassandra lived. What took place was a shock to the group. What they surely thought was a criminal getting ready to abduct a child had instead turned out to be an undercover policeman. From what they could hear, the man was watching the child on a tip from an unknown source.

The child, who had been playing on the front porch, moved to the backyard after entering the home. It had now become clear that someone had been hiding behind the house and had taken the child. This all happened as the three had captured the plainclothes policeman. It was suspected that, because the child went to the backyard, she might have been taken, despite the fact that she was being watched from the front of the home.

"Oh my, we botched this up terribly. The kidnapper was in the backyard the whole time. We would have missed him, even if we hadn't interfered," John said.

"We wasted a lot of time waiting for the police to come. Why didn't they warn the parents that this might happen?" Matthew said dejectedly.

"I don't know how we could have gotten this situation

so wrong," Elizabeth said as she started crying. "What do we do now?"

Matthew, the first to regain his composure, made an observation. "We haven't actually lost anything at this point, you know. What has happened would have happened, even if we hadn't interfered. The authorities don't know anything about us other than the fact that we tied up the policeman. We will have to come up with some other solution to this incident."

"Well, we can't come back here a second time. We made that decision during the summer. We don't know what will happen if we go twice to the same place. If we have already made the trip to a certain time, will we run into ourselves? Anyway, we'll have to figure out how to fix this after we get back home," Elizabeth told them.

With heavy hearts, the three headed back to John's home. Very little was said on the ride, as each was lost in their thoughts. Matthew seemed the most optimistic of the group. He had always managed to come up with a solution to problems at hand. Once they reached John's home, Alice was told what happened.

"That is a shame. You must be very disappointed. I'm sure you will be able to correct this at a later date," she said.

"Yes, that is what we will have to do. We'll go to the site of the next abduction and see who it is we're dealing with. Once we have his identity, we can make plans to deal with him," Matthew said optimistically.

The familiar beep came from Matthew's pocket, letting them know the visit was almost over. The four went indoors and soon said their goodbyes as the siblings disappeared.

Chapter 12

Somewhat somber, the two went downstairs after locking up the room with the clock in it. Buddy, at least, was happy to see them. Matthew took the dog for a run along the beach to take his mind off things for a short time. They played and enjoyed the warm sunshine and the sound of the surf as it rolled onto the shore.

Maybe it was a mistake to grab the policeman so early. They probably should have waited to see what transpired before acting. Would they have been able to stop the real perpetrator if they had waited? Matthew had his doubts that it would have ended much differently.

So what are Elizabeth and I going to do now? he thought.

A plan slowly unfurled in his mind. First, they would have to look online to see if the next kidnapping still took place. The time and date would be noted. There would have to be an exploratory trip in order to assess the proper method of dealing with the murderer.

Once this was done, they'd have to decide whether to tackle the problem alone or involve John and Alice. Because Alice had a child of her own now, he was reluctant to bring her into the situation again. This much done, he headed back to the cottage.

Mom would be home soon, so Mathew asked Elizabeth if she would like to help him prepare supper. They got out a nice steak and defrosted it in the microwave oven. The potatoes were warmed up, too, and put on the barbecue. A salad was tossed, put in the fridge, and instant pudding had been mixed up, ready for dessert.

Mom came home and was so pleased with her children that she couldn't resist hugging them. "This is wonderful. My feet are a little sore, and I wasn't relishing the thought of making dinner tonight, thank you."

Even Buddy got patted in all the excitement. Matthew threw the steak on as his mother went upstairs to change. This turned out to be a wonderful meal, as the two siblings even did all the dishes.

They all spent the evening in front of the fireplace, relaxing and chatting. At nine o'clock, Leonard phoned, letting everyone know he would have to remain at the site, he was working at for another week. He said that he would be home the following Sunday evening. Everything was going exceptionally well, but he did miss his family. Kate was left alone to read as the youngsters went upstairs.

The computer was fired up as Matthew told his sister his thoughts on how to handle the situation concerning the murderer. Once the story came on screen, the two read about the events as they had now changed somewhat. The police believed that the officer was subdued by accomplices in order to allow the kidnapper to make good his escape.

"What the heck? Why would they think that?" Elizabeth asked.

"Because that's what I would think, too, if I was them," he said, somewhat subdued.

Elizabeth went on to the story of what was suspected to be the next taking of a child two years later. She read aloud to Matthew who was sitting on the floor, leaning against the wall.

"'A child aged seven has disappeared from her home in West Tisbury on the afternoon of Saturday, June the seventeenth, at approximately four-thirty. There are no witnesses to this horrible incident. The parents of Jenny Adams have no idea why their child would be taken. There are no leads as to the identity of the culprit.' There's a follow-up article that states, 'there are no further developments in the case. There are no clues as to what happened to the child, and she still hasn't been found,'" she read.

"I think that we need to make another of our exploratory trips back into the past, this time to the scene of the second abduction, in order to familiarize ourselves with the area. We'll have to enlist some help from John or Alice for acquiring transportation to Dark Woods Road in Edgartown. I sure hope John is able to assist us again." Matt explained his reason for not wanting to involve Alice any more than necessary. "I think we'll have to find a way to repay John for some of the costs we incur when we use the ferry and meals we have there. Do you have any ideas about this?"

"Maybe we could bring some food or a gift," she replied. "Other than that, I don't know."

"We were going to go to the cave where the body of Cassandra was found, but we got sidetracked. Maybe we could go there after school this week, just to have a look around."

"Sounds like a plan to me, Matt. How far is it from Edgartown?"

"It will only take about forty minutes to drive there from home. So if we go from school, we should be able to make it home before Mom finishes work on Wednesday. It's a good thing that students can use the ferry for almost nothing. It sure would add up if we had to pay regular prices," he said.

After school, the two connected at the ferry and drove to Aquinnah. Locating Clarksville Cave was fairly easy, and they scouted the area surrounding the cave entrance. There were plenty of places a person could hide if they didn't want to be seen. The only problem was that they didn't know exactly when Cassandra was brought there. Going into the cave gave them an eerie feeling.

"I feel funny about being in here, Matt."

"I think that's because you know what happened in this cave. Otherwise, I doubt that you'd feel that way. What I wonder about is where Jenny was buried, her remains were never found. There are half a dozen girls that have disappeared that the authorities know about. I wonder if the person responsible took more in other areas of the country?" he asked.

"I doubt we'll ever find out for sure."

They saw a little marker at the extreme end of the cave in the darkness. Other than that, there was nothing there but their imagination. The excursion was concluded and the pair headed for home.

As they pulled into the driveway, Elizabeth asked, "Do you have any ideas on how we can find out who the kidnapper is?"

"All I can come up with is going back to when Jenny was taken and watch to see who does it. If we can find that out, we'll be able to decide what to do to prevent the crime."

"By the way, have you given any thought to the riddle we're trying to solve?" she asked.

"I haven't thought a lot about it, but I think you're right about the first line referring to a church, although it could be at the entrances of a school or just a burial site. The second line talks about something standing row on row. It may be possible that it's referring to a cemetery. Headstones stand row on row or trees, maybe even a number of buildings."

"The first thing that comes to mind for me is headstones. What about 'in a corner obscure you will find, where the sun it always shines'? In a corner obscure could mean in the corner of the cemetery or maybe the corner of a headstone," she replied.

"Yes, it could, but where the sun always shines? What on earth does that mean? It can't shine at night or when it's cloudy, so it must mean something else. Besides, which church or cemetery is it talking about? I know it must be on one of these two islands. This is where Frank Barnes lived. It would make more sense if he was talking about a church not far from where he lived, right?" Matthew questioned.

"Definitely, I'll look into it, and we'll go look at the ones closest to where he lived first. Maybe we can do it this weekend, or are you planning to see about Jenny first?" she asked.

"I'm not sure yet. I'm going to think this over for a few days then we can talk about it."

The week went by uneventfully and, on Friday after school, Elizabeth met Matthew at the ferry. She had checked online to see where the churches and cemeteries were near where Frank Barnes had his little shop on Main Street.

Driving to the address on Main Street, they looked at a small building with living quarters above it. The shop that was there now catered to the sweet tooth in people. The candy shop window was filled with trays of handmade confectioneries that piqued Matthew's interest.

"Ooh, they look really good," he said.

"We have other things to do, Matt, so let's go see the local churches."

They drove past St. Elizabeth's where Matthew made a comment.

"Hey, sis, they named a church after you."

"Ha, ha, very funny."

There were no cemeteries of note at the Federated Church or The Old Whaling Church. The two main spots for burying people back in the nineteen twenties were Westside Cemetery on Cooke Street and Town Hill Burying Ground on Town Hill Road outside of town.

The two took a quick ride to Town Hill and slowly walked through the rows of old headstones. The weather had worn many of those markers, but most of the names were still easily read. They looked at all four corners of the field for something that would make sense of the line in the riddle.

"In a corner, you will find, where the sun it always shines," Matthew said out loud. "I don't see any spots like that here, so it must mean something else."

"I think we'll have to look at every stone in this place. Maybe that will give us a clue."

They each started looking at the headstones, beginning at opposite ends. At the end of half an hour, they met near the middle.

"I don't know about you, but I haven't found anything at all, there's nothing much here."

"This looks like a poor man's burial place. It said in the article that the stones Frank Barnes made were costly so that means the people buried here wouldn't be able to afford one of his," Elizabeth told her brother.

"You're right. The place where we may find what we need is probably in Westside Cemetery. Do we have time to search there today?"

"No, we'll have to save it for another time. Mom will

be getting off work soon, and if we're not home when she gets there, there will be questions," she pointed out.

They managed to beat their mother home by fifteen minutes and worked feverishly to get supper started. This way, it would look like they had been home for a considerable period of time. Buddy was happy to see them and would have liked to go out to play but found that this wasn't going to happen anytime soon.

"I appreciate you two doing this for me," Mom said. "It saves me a lot of time when I get home from work."

"We're glad to help where we can. How do you like your job, Mom?" Elizabeth asked.

"I like it a lot more than I thought I would. The people I work with are really nice, and the hours are short enough that I'm not worn out by it all."

"You're working tomorrow too, aren't you, and Dad will be home Sunday as well, right?" Matthew asked.

"Yes, I am, Saturday is a nice easy day at the bank, and I'm looking forward to your father coming home."

After the dishes were done, Kate sat in the living room, balancing her checkbook, and then proceeded to read a novel. Matthew took Buddy out for some activity. He barked excitedly as they headed for the beach with Matthew carrying a ball for his pet to chase. An hour later, Buddy was worn out as he had done most of the work in this game of fetch. Kate was still reading, while her children headed upstairs to make some plans.

"Have you decided if we're going to use the clock tomorrow or hunt through the cemetery in town? We should look around the churches in town too. There may be a small burial spot in some of them that aren't listed online," Elizabeth said.

"I thought about it and, while we have the time, with mom at work and dad still out of town, we should go back to the time when Jenny was kidnapped. We may well be able to identify the abductor and then come up with a concrete plan to deal with him. We can go to the churches and burial sites pretty much any time we want. What do you think?"

"As usual, you're right. I'll open up the computer, and we can decide on the date we'll go back to," she said as she sat down at the desk.

The screen showed an old photo of a young girl. The story read, *Jenny Adams, age seven, disappeared from her home at approximately four-thirty in the afternoon Saturday, June 17, 1916. No clues as to the identity of the kidnapper have been found. There has been a massive search conducted with no results. The parents are distraught and make a plea for their child's return.* The story continued in articles printed at later dates, but nothing was discovered as to the whereabouts of the missing child.

"So what do you want to do? Are we going to make an exploratory trip or just go back to the date Jenny was taken and see what we can learn then?" Elizabeth asked.

"I think we should go to the day she is taken and see who does the deed. Then we can figure out how to take care of the person. Does that work for you, sis?"

"Okay, I just had a thought, though. I know we decided against it before, but do you think we should take my digital camera with us. That way we can take a long-distance photo of the culprit and use it to possibly identify him when we get back," Elizabeth suggested.

"That's a great idea. We could print the photo off on the printer and have John help us use it to find out who the man is."

Elizabeth located the camera and plugged in the charger, while Matthew went to his room and found a few items he wanted to bring with them.

As the two lay down in their beds, thoughts of what

tomorrow would bring ran through their heads.

Matthew thought that this was going to be a great adventure, and he could hardly wait to go back again. The only thing that concerned him was the fact that John might see the camera and want to see how it worked. This, of course, could not be allowed to happen, because it would spell disaster if the technology were to be discovered years earlier.

Matt wondered if he could give John something that would not cause any disruption in the scheme of things. Thinking of toys brought an idea to mind. He had a yo-yo in the drawer of the night table next to his bed. Before heading out tomorrow, he would see when it was actually invented and see if he could help John and Alice invest a little money into it. He drifted off to sleep with a smile on his face, thinking of how they might be able to help their friends and maybe save the child at the same time.

Elizabeth, the most cautious of the pair, struggled with many different thoughts as she lay in bed. Her mind dwelled on the more sinister side of things. What would happen if they actually ran into the man, and he realized what they were up to? If he was armed, he might well dispose of two nosy teenagers if he felt threatened. What would happen if someone took the camera away from her? That could cause a huge adjustment to history. It might even change things so much that their own future would be in jeopardy. She would have to talk to Matthew in the morning about her fears. Elizabeth finally drifted off into a less-than-restful sleep.

In the morning, everyone met in the kitchen for breakfast. It wasn't long after this that Kate headed off to work. At that point, Elizabeth voiced her concerns about the camera.

"I see where you're coming from, but I've taken a few precautions to prevent this from occurring. I'm also going to take back my wooden yo-yo to give to John. It will become popular in a year or two from the time we give it to him. It was actually invented years before in the Philippines and was made into a commonplace toy by a Pedro Flores in California. If they wait for the right time, they can invest in it and make a little money. This way we can pay them back for all their help. What do you think, is it a good idea or not?" Matthew asked.

"I think we should wait to give it to them. We'll ask if they want anything for their help and if they do, we can give it to them at that time. You never know if a thing like that could make some changes to our time," she replied.

"All right, sis, I'll hold off on it then. Let's get things started, and we can head back to see John. It's Saturday where we're going to, so he should be home."

The dials on the clock were tuned in, and the mechanism wound to the top. The length of their stay had been set at one hour, in case preparations needed to be made by John. A second trip back would give him the time needed to get ready.

The pendulum was set in motion, and the arms of the clock worked their way to the top of the hour where it needed to be to make time travel possible. The room became hazy, and the siblings were once more on their way to the past.

Chapter 13

The air cleared, and once again Matthew and Elizabeth found themselves in the clock room in John's home.

"Hey, John, are you here?" Matthew called out.

There was only silence, and they realized that they would have to go out to find either John or Alice. Hopefully, they wouldn't have to look too long. They headed out the front door and, as they stepped out, they met a man standing thirty feet from the front door.

"Who are you and what are you doing in John's house?" he asked quizzically.

"We're friends of John and Alice," Matthew replied. "My name is Matthew, and this is my sister Elizabeth."

"I'm Alice's husband, Sam. She has told me about you two. She said that you helped her and John out of a real pickle years ago. She has never really explained everything, but she and John owe you a lot for your help. She described you to me, but she said that you were teenagers then. You still seem like you are that age now. This is curious, I will have to ask her about it," Sam said, cocking his head to the side.

He was a man in his middle twenties standing about five feet ten inches tall and weighing around one hundred and ninety-five pounds. His brown hair was tossed by the breeze and he had a pleasant-looking face. He walked over to the pair and shook hands with them. He had a grip like iron, Matthew found out.

"Do you know where John is, Sam?" Elizabeth asked.

"He is in Providence on business and won't be back for a few days. Didn't he tell you this? You were in his house, so I assumed you saw him already."

"Actually, we just got here and walked in. The door was unlocked," Elizabeth said, looking at Sam with a sweet smile on her face, discouraging any more questions.

Matthew caught this and thought that she was learning to use her charms rather well.

"We will need to find a way to Edgartown in a few hours. All we need is a ride there, and the cost of the ferry, but with John not here it complicates things," Elizabeth said with that same disarming smile on her face again.

"I'll see what I can do for you. I think that I'll have the time to take you myself. I'm sure Alice will come along too. She'll want to see you again."

"That would be wonderful, we really appreciate it," she said.

"When do you need to be in Edgartown?"

"We would like to be in the town center by three o'clock," Matthew told him.

"All right, meet me at the stable at one o'clock, and we'll be on our way. Unless you would like to come for a visit to our home while you're here? We could have you for lunch. I think Alice would like that," Sam said to the pair.

"That would really be nice, but unfortunately we have

to be somewhere shortly and we can't change our plans at the moment. Thank you kindly, though. We'll return by one o'clock," Elizabeth stated.

The siblings walked away and, in fifteen minutes, the soft beep sounded. They found a hiding place in order not to be seen when the clock did its job again.

At home, they took care of a few things, had lunch, and brought a few things to eat. Then they were sitting in front of the clock again.

When they exited, John's home this time, they came out the back door, being careful no one was around to see them. They met up with Sam and Alice who now was older than she was last time the three saw each other. Alice had a look on her face that would have betrayed her if Sam had been looking. It must have been a surprise to see people years later and have no visible changes in them. James, Alice and Sam's son, was now five and looked at the pair shyly as they made the trip.

The ride to the ferry was pleasant in that June of 1916. The four chatted along the way and, despite the age difference, found they had things to talk about. Of course, it would have been different if John had been there. He would have been asking about what the future was like.

The two were taken to the ferry landing, and Alice slipped Elizabeth enough coin to pay for the fare.

In a whisper, Elizabeth said to Alice, "We will pay you back when we can."

"No need, it is both John and I that owe you. Anytime you need us for anything, we will be there for you. You are on your way to save someone else, aren't you? We will try to help any way we can. If Sam wasn't here, I'd go along with you now," Alice told Elizabeth as she gave her a hug.

The two got on the ferry after a quick goodbye and were soon in Edgartown. The walk to Dark Woods Road took fifteen minutes, and they found a place to hide so they were able to watch the home where Jenny lived.

"You know that we can't try to interfere with the proceedings. We're here to find out the identity of the person responsible and go from there," Elizabeth told her brother sternly.

"I know, but it won't be easy. I'll take a walk around the street and see if there are any better hiding places or if the girl can be taken some other way that we won't be able to see from here."

"No, I should be the one to do that. I will be much less of a threat to a man than you are, and he will ignore me much more readily than you," she informed him.

"All right, but be careful and don't make it look obvious what you're doing."

Off she went, looking like she was out for a stroll. She walked around the streets while Matthew kept an eye on her and the girl's home. They still had almost an hour before the event was supposed to occur.

When Elizabeth came back, she told her brother that there was a blind spot on the other side of the home that the young girl could be taken from, that wasn't visible from where they were hiding. The two moved away and made their way to a better spot. Unfortunately, that place left the child vulnerable from still another area.

"Maybe we should split up and cover all our bases better," Elizabeth suggested.

"I don't like that at all. I don't want anything happening to you. By the way, have you seen Jenny anywhere while you went for your walk?" he asked.

"No, I haven't. She must be in the house or isn't home yet. The story did say that she was taken from her home."

"Are kids still in school at her age? You would think that a child would not walk home alone, wouldn't you?" he asked.

"I think we have to split up, or we'll lose this one too. I'll stay where you can see me and be able to signal you if something happens. Please, Matthew, I really feel I have to do this."

"All right, go, but you make sure you don't leave my sight, you hear?"

Elizabeth left her hiding spot, moving away from the home and coming out of hiding on the far side across the street. She was hidden from view of the dwelling and anyone on the road. Matthew had the camera ready in case he needed it. It was now half an hour till the reported time of the abduction. There was the occasional person walking in the area but no one suspicious.

Matthew was looking down the road as an automobile drove slowly by the home. He noticed that Jenny had come out the front door and down the steps. She headed to the yard and took a seat on the swing hanging from a large limb of a maple tree near the street. There was no fence and no sidewalk between the home and the road.

The car backed up when the driver saw the child. He looked around, and Matthew took his picture as the man swung his head around. He called out to Jenny, and she waved to the man as he talked. It seemed obvious that she knew him. The man waved back and drove away.

"Crap," Matthew thought. He hadn't needed a false alarm. At that point, he looked at his sister who turned her head toward him, and he just shrugged. Elizabeth came out from her hiding place, walked along the street, and out of sight for a moment and then came up behind her brother.

"I think the man in the car saw me watching him. When he looked around, I wasn't hidden properly, and I think he saw me there. I'm sorry, Matt."

"That's okay. I got his picture, so if it is him, we may be able to track him down. Unfortunately, I didn't get the plate number. I was too busy trying to see his face," he said.

Another vehicle drove past, and then another, but nothing happened. Several people that went past their hiding place seemed to glimpse the two hiding. They were no longer hiding as well as they could because the tension had been building up in them. They didn't want to miss seeing who was responsible for taking the girl and had gotten careless. Things hadn't turned out the way they had hoped for.

Jenny was still playing on the swing as the time of the incident came closer and closer. An older well-dressed lady walked by and chatted briefly with Jenny who smiled at her, and then the lady continued on her way.

They waited and waited, and as the time arrived, nothing happened. In frustration, after another half hour, they got up and walked around the streets staying within sight of the girl. She finally got up and walked toward the front door and into her home. The two would-be detectives stayed in the area for a while longer and realized that something was terribly wrong when a police car went past the end of the road traveling along Main Street.

There was a commotion, as people had heard that there had been an incident on the next road over. People were making their way to the scene. The pair came out from where they had been hiding and blended in with the crowd. The details of what had happened shocked the youngsters as they heard what had just occurred.

A young girl was missing. Someone called Abigail had not been seen for over an hour. A rumor had it that a man driving an automobile had been in the area and might be the one responsible for the girl's disappearance.

Matthew signaled Elizabeth, and they left the scene. The time to go home was approaching, and they needed to be out of sight soon.

"Excuse me, folks," a man said to them.

"Yes?" Elizabeth answered.

"Did you see anything suspicious in the area that may help the police find the missing child?"

"I'm sorry, but we just got here and stopped when we saw the crowd gathered," Elizabeth answered.

"If you think of anything, can you come to the station and let the desk officer know?"

"We certainly will. I hope you find the child," she said to what must be an officer in plain clothes.

Matthew touched her arm, and they left the area as unobtrusively as possible.

"My goodness, we come here to identify a murderer who was supposed to take one child, and we inadvertently cause another girl to be taken instead. This is twice we've managed to get things wrong. How can we fix this? This little girl will be murdered, and we are the cause of it. Saving one to have another abducted is worse than failing the first one," Elizabeth sobbed as tears rolled down her cheeks.

Matthew put his arm around her shoulders and tried to comfort his sister, but to no avail. The sound of the beep in his pocket brought him back to their immediate needs of finding a secluded place.

As the air clouded over around them, a dark mood settled over the teenagers. Both started to wonder if they were actually the ones that should be attempting to change the past. Too often things had gotten worse rather than better.

Chapter 14

Once they were home, the computer was started, and they read the story about Abigail Sanders living on Mariners Way, one street over from Dark Woods Road, having disappeared. The date was Saturday, June 17, 1916, and the time was thought to be shortly before four thirty in the afternoon.

Abigail was described as being nine years old, having a slender build with long flowing red hair. Her eyes were green, and she had a happy disposition.

There was a plea for anyone with information to come forward. A photo of the girl was on the same page, as well as a picture of very-sad-looking parents. The story of Jenny Adams was no longer there.

"We managed to stop Jenny's kidnapping but caused Abigail to be taken instead," Elizabeth said dejectedly.

Another story had been printed three weeks later. It stated that the body of Abigail had been found in a wooded area on the other side of the island.

"The spot where they found her body was not very far from where Cassandra was discovered," Matthew observed. "I think we are probably dealing with the same person in both cases."

"Do you think it was the man you took the photo of, or could it be one of the other drivers that saw us in the bushes when we got a little careless?"

"To tell you the truth, it could be any one of them. I'm leaning a bit toward the man in the picture but can't say so with any conviction," he answered. "Of course, it could be someone else entirely. We might have missed seeing a person who went by when we weren't paying enough attention."

"Oh, Matthew, what do we do now? That poor little girl must have been so frightened. It doesn't say what that horrible man actually did to Abigail, but it must have been awful. I feel so bad that we caused her to be taken. I'm sure that the person who was going to take Jenny saw us and changed his plans."

"I feel bad, too, and I'm going to try to figure out a way to fix this. I'm going for a walk on the beach with Buddy. Maybe I can think of something while I'm gone. It's hard, but can you check and see who the next girl to be abducted is and get as much information as you can about that case?"

"I'm going to lay down for a short time first. I'll take care of that when I get up."

Matthew went downstairs, and his pet met him at the back door, eager to go out and play. The dog seemed almost to sense that something was wrong with his master and rubbed against his leg, trying to help. Out the door, they went with Matthew's thoughts staying in the past where their efforts to make things right had ended in disaster.

"What did we do wrong? How could we have tackled the problem better? What can we do to fix this and apprehend the serial killer, saving all the children that awful man murders?" he said to himself. "Why is he doing this?"

Buddy barked an answer, but his input was ignored, so he ran after a seagull that had landed not far from the two. Matthew watched the dog as he chased the gull without any chance of catching it. He felt that he had as much chance of getting the perpetrator as Buddy did with the bird.

Maybe another line of attack was needed to turn this situation around. Unfortunately, he couldn't think of anything. He had found in other circumstances that turning his attention to another problem helped bring out his creative side. He decided to play with the dog for a while then maybe tackle the problem of the riddle to take his mind in another direction for a while.

The two went for a run down the beach. When they finally came to a stop, Buddy ran into the surf for a time of wet frolicking. Matthew watched the small waves come onto the shore and then recede. The scene was tranquil, and he felt himself slowly relaxing somewhat.

He thought of one of the lines of the riddle they were trying to decipher. *Where the sun it always shines.*

"Now what on earth can that mean," he said. "The sun can't always shine, so it must refer to something else."

He thought about it for a minute and came up with a thought. "Maybe there is a tombstone with something on it that emits light, like a gas flame he had seen on tombs of very important people. This, however, was short-lived as he hadn't heard of anyone really important being buried on the island. Besides, the riddle was written after the jewelry robbery, which occurred in the first few years of the nineteen hundreds. He doubted that natural gas would have been piped into a cemetery at that early a date.

Another thought came to mind. He recalled that Frank Barnes made some high-end headstones and, with a little investigating, it might be possible for Matt and Elizabeth to find out if any were in one of the cemeteries in the area. That idea made sense to him, and he felt that he may just have made some headway in solving part of the riddle. There was another thought somewhere in the back of his mind, but no matter what he did he couldn't bring it to the forefront. Oh, well, he was sure it would make itself known as those thoughts had many times in the past.

Realizing that he had paid little attention to his pet today, he called Buddy and played with the dog for a bit. The two jogged back to the cottage and, after rinsing the salt water from Buddy's fur, Matt took a drink from the hose himself.

Looking at the clock on the kitchen wall, he realized that his mother would be home in just over an hour. He went up the stairs to see how Elizabeth was handling the disappointing situation. When he knocked on her door, a voice groggy from sleep answered.

"Come on in, Matt," she said.

As he entered the room, it became obvious that, as well as sleeping, she had also been crying.

"I'm sorry that we couldn't make things better, but I'm sure we'll be able to fix this one way or another. There's an idea in the back of my mind and, sooner or later, it'll come to me. I know it's about a way of possibly discovering who the abductor is. It may be nothing, but I have hopes it may work out. I'm going to do some online research later to see if that gives me any clues," he said. "Do you want to help me get supper started? It may take your mind off the dilemma."

"Let me wash my face, and I'll be right down."

The two tried their hand at making a meatloaf. They found one of their mother's recipes and got to work. When it was in the oven, Matthew peeled potatoes to go with the meat dish. They were going to mash them after they were cooked. A salad was made and, when all the preparations were completed, Elizabeth found that the distraction had made her feel much better.

She realized that Matthew usually came up with solutions to things.

He was the one who had thought of how to turn the tables on those dreadful people during their summer holiday. She thought he was truly a resourceful person and was glad he was there to help.

"Hey, guys, I'm home," Mom said from the front door. "What smells so good? Did you two cook supper again? You know that you're spoiling me. I could get used to this." She walked in and hugged both her kids. "I'm just going to change. How long before it's ready?"

"You have about fifteen minutes. We'll set the table and have everything ready for you when you come down," Elizabeth said and, turning toward her brother, whispered, "Thanks, Matt, this has helped me a lot."

"No problem, sis, we have to stick together."

With supper done, Elizabeth sat down in the living room with her mother as Matthew built a fire. When things were going nicely, he laid on the couch, intending to chat, but as soon as he did, he started to drift off. The mother and daughter looked at each other and almost laughed as they saw him doze off.

"He must have had a hard day," Mom said.

"He went for a long run with Buddy along the beach. Maybe it wore him out. I see Buddy is having a nap too."

Mom let out a chuckle as she saw that the dog was actually asleep too. "Maybe making supper with you was more of a strain than he's used to. Thank you, dear, it means a lot to me when the two of you pitch in like that."

"That's all right, Mom. We feel you and Dad really went out of your way to move us here, and we just want to show our appreciation."

Matthew woke up with a start a short time later when Buddy decided to lick his face.

"Whoa, what happened?" he said a bit shocked that he may have dozed off.

"You fell asleep as soon as you got on the couch. You must have been pretty tired," Mom told him.

"Too much fresh air I guess. I think I'll go to bed. Boy, am I bushed."

Elizabeth nodded. "I think I'll head up too, Mom. Good night."

"Night, night dear," she returned.

Because she had slept for a while in the afternoon, Elizabeth decided to find the information Matthew had asked for. It didn't take long, and she had what she was after. After writing down what she found relevant, she went to the story of the next victim. It seemed that all the girls she read about so far were under the age of ten. What would possess a man to do the things this one had done, she wondered. How did an aberration like this come about?

When she got the information on the third and fourth victims, she moved on to the fifth. She had a list written on a piece of paper.

First—Cassandra Boothe age 8 disappeared May 27, 1914, found 3 years later

Second—Abigail Sanders age 7 disappeared June 17, 1916

Third—Yvonne Routar age 9 disappeared August 14, 1917

Fourth—Anna Krause age 7 disappeared July 3, 1918

Fifth—Rebecca Jacobs age 6 disappeared March 21, 1920

Sixth—Alison Mason age 8 disappeared April 6, 1920

Seventh—Margaret Thorne 9 disappeared August 29, 1926

Eighth—Johanna Baxter 7 disappeared March 19, 1927

Ninth—Barbara Campbell 8 disappeared October 22, 1927

She looked at the list and noticed the gap between 1920 and 1926.

"I wonder why he stopped for six years. Did he learn to control himself? Maybe he was in jail for some other offense, or it might be possible that he moved away and continued his practice somewhere else," she muttered to herself.

It had been getting late, and her eyes were closing on her, so after brushing her teeth, she went to bed. Normally, she fell asleep easily, but tonight the gravity of the situation weighed heavily on her mind. Would they be able to find out who that person was and if they did, how would they stop him? These thoughts continued in her head for a time and, in the middle of an idea, she drifted off into a restless sleep.

In the morning, it felt like she had hardly rested. Her eyes looked like she had been up most of the night. It was a relief that it was Sunday and there was no school. Heading for the bathroom, she turned on the shower and spent a little more time in it than usual. The hot water had a refreshing effect on her and, when she finally exited, she felt much better.

As she got dressed in her room, thoughts of her research went through her head, and she recalled that some idea had been forming in her mind as she lost consciousness. It was there in the back of her mind, but she was unable to retrieve it. Oh, well, it couldn't have been that important—or could it?

Matthew was already having breakfast with their mother. She put on a happy face which she carried off fairly successfully. After a bit of trivial conversation, Mom asked if they had any plans for the day.

"Nothing much so far. We may go to the beach and do a little exploring. Is there something that you have in mind?" Matthew asked.

"I have to pick up your father after lunch and will do a little shopping at the same time. Is there anything either of you need?" Kate asked her children.

Elizabeth shook her head, and Matthew said, "Not that I can think of. We're running low on luncheon meat if you have time for that. Pastrami would hit the spot for my sandwiches this week at school, though."

"Good idea, we haven't had that in quite a while."

The rest of the morning was spent doing some chores around the house as the kids both pitched in to help. This made things easier for Mother, and she let them know it. Matthew buffed the pine wood floors by tying rags to his feet and doing the *Ali Shuffle*. His feet were moving back and forth so quickly, all that the two saw was a blur. They got a real kick out of watching him glide around the room as he polished it to a high sheen. Only Matthew would think of doing the job this way.

As their mother left, she told them she would be gone for at least three hours. When they were alone, Elizabeth told her brother that she had done a little research and had a list of names in her room. The two went over the names and dates came up with the same question about the gap between some of the crimes.

"I wonder if we can find any information about any-one going to prison from that area. It would explain that part of it. It's either that or he moved away for a time, possibly doing the deeds in another part of the country," Matthew said thoughtfully.

Elizabeth typed her question on the Google browser and, after a bit of surfing came up with nothing. She then looked for anyone of note that left town and later returned but drew another blank.

"I'm not sure of what other questions to ask at this point," she said.

When she had typed in about the discovery of Cassandra's body, hoping to find something they had missed earlier, there was a notice giving the time of her funeral.

A light went on in Matthew's eyes as he remembered what had been going through the back of his mind on the beach with Buddy. "Elizabeth, this article just helped me remember something that's been eluding me. I was wondering if it might be a good idea to go to the funerals of the girls to see who attended them. If a person shows up at all of them, he might just be the culprit. It might be his way of getting a little more satisfaction from the crimes. It's obvious that he does this for a reason, and this may just help us locate him."

"If it turns out that we can find someone suspicious and he matches one of the drivers that drove past Jenny's house when we were hiding, we will have a starting point. The crimes were committed all over both islands, and only someone with an interest in the children would attend more than just one or two in their own area. They wouldn't have any reason to attend any out of their own district," she exclaimed excitedly.

The fear of running afoul of this man had temporarily been pushed aside.

Doing a search of all the funerals, they figured that that day would be the best time to make a few of the trips back in time to start the surveillance. Elizabeth suggested taking her smaller camera instead of Matthews, which had a telephoto lens. It would be far easier to keep concealed. They made the rest of their plans, took care of

Buddy, and set the date of the first burial on the clock. The room clouded over, and they were on their way.

Chapter 15

The two met up with John and filled him in on what was going on. Luckily, John happened to be free and could go with them, using his car that he had recently obtained to get them there in plenty of time. They also asked John if he could think of any methods of transportation that he and Elizabeth could use if John wasn't around when they came back at the dates Elizabeth gave him.

He thought about it and said that he had a bicycle and when he could locate another he would put them in the shed by the house. He'd make sure that they were always in good repair and leave a key where the two could locate it. All they had to do was give themselves the extra time it would take to pedal to their destination.

"How can we pay you for this," Matthew asked.

"To tell you the truth, I am thinking of starting a bakery. I have gotten quite good at making cookies and cakes. If you can get me a recipe for something that becomes popular soon, maybe it will help my business somewhat. Do you think that might be possible, or do you think it could create complications down the road?" he asked.

"I think we can find something that is popular without having it become a huge sensation. Sure, we'll look into it for you, this will be a way for us to pay you back somewhat," Elizabeth told him.

After they returned at the agreed time, John drove them to their destination. The three stayed away from the burial plot far enough to be unnoticed. Matthew and Elizabeth wore hats, so their faces were hidden. They also had different clothes on so, if the driver of one of the cars was there, he wouldn't become suspicious.

The clothes they wore had been purchased at a used goods store in Edgartown in their own time. Having checked online ahead of time, it had been easy to find things that fit into the era they were going to. The only reason they had even noticed the store was because of the clothing rack on the sidewalk. It had been fun going through the things no one wore anymore.

When the procession reached the grave site, the three were in a position that had them facing most of the mourners. The small casket holding little Cassandra was brought to the grave site.

With Elizabeth standing behind the other two, she took photos of everyone there. The camera was placed just above Matthew's shoulder so it remained out of sight from anyone who may have glanced at them. There were only two people that she couldn't get a decent shot of, so they changed positions in order to get the picture.

Matthew tried to memorize the men there and compared them to the drivers of the automobiles that had gone past Jenny's home. Two of them seemed like they were familiar, but that wasn't an indicator of guilt at that point. They could both have been neighbors and there to express their sympathies.

With that done, the three headed back to John's home and were soon back in their own time. Knowing when the next funeral was, plans were made for John to try being available to drive them. Matthew thought of a way for John to get in touch with the siblings without anyone traveling in time.

"John, why don't you leave a note in the clock? You can place it behind the dial mechanisms. We haven't had any reason to look there so far, so we won't find it prematurely. Make the note very small and just write the date we need you to drive us and put a yes or no on it. That will tell us if you are able to drive us to the funeral on that day," he said.

"That's a great idea, Matthew. I would never have thought of it. We can communicate that way for all the funeral dates. Because you say that you haven't looked in that spot yet, there won't be any chance of the note being discovered and removed prematurely."

The beep sounded and shortly the two were gone.

After they got back to their own time, Matthew looked inside the clock. He found a note and read that John was once more able to drive them.

After getting a few items they might require, the dials on the clock were reset, and they were on their way to the past once more.

John had been in his home waiting for their arrival. This time, the funeral was for Abigail Sanders and the burial was in the cemetery outside the town. The parents were unable to afford a plot in the one in town and that, hopefully, could help to catch the perpetrator.

They got there a little early and waited out of sight amongst the trees. When the service was underway, they moved to a spot that allowed Elizabeth to once more photograph everyone there. Matthew studied the faces and came to the conclusion that three of the men were the same as at the last funeral. This again was not conclusive because they could have lived in the same area and were there out of respect for the family.

The funeral after that one was for Yvonne Routar and took place on the far side of Martha's Vineyard. This, the three believed, would be a more promising venture. As they drove back to John's, he said he would put the note in the clock again. This time, they were a little behind schedule, and the time travelers disappeared before their arrival back at John's home.

Checking on Buddy first, they decided to make one last trip that day and go to bed earlier than usual that night. It would, by that time, have been a very long day indeed. They both had school in the morning and needed to be at least somewhat refreshed. Checking to see if John's note was in the clock and seeing that he was once again available, the dials were set, the clock wound up, and, after a bite to eat, they were on their way again.

John was ready, and they were off to attend yet another funeral. This time, they arrived as the service was already in progress. Standing on the sidelines, the pictures were taken and, to Matthew's surprise, two of the men he had seen at the previous funerals were also there. This was too much of a coincidence to be ignored. They decided that if either or both these men were at the next funeral, they or he would have to be checked out. Why would a person be at all these burials and not have a good reason? Could it be that more than one person was responsible for the deaths of all these girls?

As they drove away, Matthew shared his thoughts with the others. They too found it very incriminating that the same men were attending all the services. The three made plans for the next meeting, and the two were on their way home shortly thereafter.

Chapter 16

All the trips had now taken their toll on the would-be detectives, and they were both thinking of taking a nap. The only problem was that their parents were due to come home within the next hour. Elizabeth got the bright idea of calling her mother to check on their arrival time.

The two were in luck, the flight had been delayed, and Kate and Leonard wouldn't be home for at least two hours. Elizabeth expressed her sympathy to her mother and ended the call.

"They won't be here for at least two hours so we can sleep for a bit," she said with a look of relief.

The nap was the very thing they needed, and they were up in plenty of time to have the sleepiness gone from their faces by the time their parents got home.

The homecoming was pleasant, and the family caught up on what had been going on since Leonard had been on the job.

"Things on the site have been progressing very well, and it looks like I will be doing a considerable amount of work from home. There will be times when I need privacy and, with the office being in the living room, it will be important to have a quiet household. I'm sorry if this interferes with life for you, but unfortunately it can't be helped," Leonard said.

"That won't be a problem, Dad. We have lots of things to keep us occupied, so no need to worry about us," Elizabeth told him.

Leonard smiled. He was indeed a lucky man. He had a beautiful wife that he got along so well with, and two great kids who were growing up into very responsible young adults. A slight tear formed in his eyes, something that didn't happen very often and, noticing this, his wife hugged the man she loved so dearly.

After a few days at school, the two siblings met at the ferry terminal on Martha's Vineyard. They wanted to go to the cemetery to look at the headstones. The riddle still needed to be solved and, if they could find a stone that Frank Barnes made, there would be a chance that they could make some headway with the riddle.

They checked all the tombstones near each of the corners in the cemetery. Nothing gave them any clues that were obvious. They started looking at the rest of the stones, checking one row at a time, with each taking a different row in order to speed things up. As they were concentrating on the job at hand, a voice called out to them.

"Is there someone you are looking for? Maybe I can help you locate them."

The two spun around, startled, and looked at a priest who had come upon them unobserved. Neither of them had a quick answer to the question and just stood there, looking a bit confused.

Matthew made an attempt to express himself. "I, ah, we were just, ah, looking."

Elizabeth gathered her wits a little quicker, "We

thought that it would be interesting to see the names and dates on these headstones. There is so much history here, and we thought this would give us an idea about the people that lived here so long ago. I hope that's all right with you, sir, or should I call you Father?"

"Father is what most people call me, and it will be fine, as long as you are careful not to damage anything," the priest said then smiled and walked away toward the exit.

Matthew watched the man leave and then turned to look at his sister. "How on earth do you come up with this stuff so quickly? I'm tripping over my tongue, and you just act like everything is fine."

Elizabeth let out a little giggle and continued studying the headstones. The two made their way through the cemetery as quickly as they could because it would soon be the time that they were expected home. She saw a symbol in the corner of one of the more ornate headstones and realized that this might be the clue they were looking for.

"Matthew, come here. I think I may have found something."

He walked over and looked at an exceptionally nice memorial stone. At the lower corner was the name of the person who made this beautiful work of art. The name Frank Barnes stood out, beckoning them to study it in more detail.

As their eyes focused on the upper right-hand corner there was a sun formed into the bronze with sun rays radiating from it.

"This has to be it, Matt," she said excitedly. "Now what was the next line in the riddle?"

He thought for a moment, and, as his eyes lit up, he said, "In the stone by hook or crook, is the place of the book."

"I think we should take a couple of pictures with your cell phone and study them tonight when supper is done," she told her brother.

Once the camera work was done, the two headed home where they were greeted by both parents in the kitchen. Supper was on the stove and the aroma of fish was in the air, permeating from the oven.

"Smells good, Mom, I can hardly wait to taste it," Matthew said.

"How was your day, Dad? Is the home-based consulting doing well?" Elizabeth asked.

"As a matter of fact, things are really falling into place. I have jobs coming in from various contacts, and it looks like things are going to be good for us. How is school going for you two?"

"I'm making friends, and the classes are easier than they were back in Des Moines. I'm really glad we're here," Elizabeth said.

Leonard looked at his son, who replied, "The auto technician's course is teaching me a lot. I'm glad I got into it. The instructor says that this is probably one of the best fields to get into. There will always be cars driven and, with them getting more and more complicated, the average person can't work on them anymore. This means, that, if you are good at your trade, you can have a job almost anywhere you live."

"That's important, nowadays. It's hard in this modern world to find employment in a well-paying field and work steadily at a job," Leonard said to his boy. "How about you, Elizabeth, do you have any ideas as far as a career goes?"

"I'm leaning toward the financial end of things— maybe banking or financial officer in business."

"That's a good idea too," he said.

Once supper was done and family time over, the two

detectives headed upstairs to load the cell phone pictures on to the computer. Just to clarify things Elizabeth looked up the definition of both "by hook" and "by crook." She found that crook had more than one meaning. It could mean bend, curve, or flex.

When the photos were loaded, they expanded the view and found several interesting things that would need to be investigated more closely. There were a number of queer-looking designs on a rectangular piece near the bottom of the stone and bronze headstone. It was difficult to make out things, exactly, so they would have to make another trip to the cemetery in order to make a closer inspection.

While they were on the computer anyway, Matthew grabbed the camera and loaded the photos from the funerals. Upon inspection of the pictures, they found that three people attended both the first and second funeral. The third funeral had two who were at the first and second burial.

The faces were printed on paper. After going to a couple more of these unpleasant gatherings where the sad parents placed their children in the ground, they hoped to find just a single repeat attendee. The information for the funerals of both Anna Krause and Rebecca Jacobs was found, and each would be buried far enough apart that it should eliminate at least one of the suspects. If neither man was at these two funerals, they would have to find another way to locate a person of interest.

"Have you checked the clock to see if John is available to give us a ride to the burials?" Elizabeth asked.

With this, Matthew checked to make sure that neither Mom nor Dad was nearby and headed into the clock room. He came back a few minutes later, carrying a note.

"Well, it would appear that John can drive us to Anna Krause's funeral. We'll make the trip as soon as we have some alone time. Maybe we can get Mom and Dad to go out on the weekend. In the meantime, we can check the headstone tomorrow after school. Is that all right with you?" Matthew asked.

"Yes, I'm up for that, I'll meet you at the ferry landing in Edgartown again."

After school, they met up and headed for the cemetery. Once they were sure there was no one observing them, they studied the headstone. From the top, they worked their way down, examining every aspect of it.

"I think that if there is a hidden pocket in here somewhere, the activation mechanism will be part of the bronze. Stone over time will break down, so it makes sense to me that this is where we need to look first," Matthew said as he studied the headstone.

Running his hands over the metal, he poked and prodded, looking for what would be considered a hook or crook as the riddle had indicated. When his hands were near the bottom, there was a stone section with what looked like it could be a small handle. Just above this were a number of curved metal pieces that very well could have been handles or levers. He was about to start testing his theory when a familiar sounding voice called out.

"I see you have found what you are looking for," the priest said.

Matthew jumped up, startled, with a guilty look on his face. Elizabeth, having seen a shadow in her peripheral vision, was already thinking of an excuse for being here.

"Oh, yes, we have. You see, I am doing a project at school that deals with interesting history, and my subject is about how headstones and cemeteries have changed over time. I know it sounds like a silly thing to write about, but I wanted to be a little different than everyone else. I really hope you don't mind, Father, but it's important to me," Elizabeth said with a disarming little smile.

The priest thought for a moment and was trying to determine whether or not the pretty young lady was pulling his leg or not. In the end, he decided to give the two the benefit of the doubt because, if they were here to be disruptive, they would already have done it. He considered asking the girl to show him the finished paper, but that might be pushing things too far. "That sounds like an interesting project. Good luck with it. I hope you do well in class and, if you would like to attend our services, you are more than welcome. You probably should bring a notepad with you next time you come to gather information," he said.

"We have a cell phone to take pictures with, and I can also record with it, so we don't really need a notepad, Father," Elizabeth explained.

"My goodness, how the world has changed," he said as he started to walk away.

When they were alone once more, Matthew looked at his sister a little incredulously. "How in the world do you come up with this stuff so fast? I didn't have a clue as to what to say. He startled the heck out of me, and I couldn't think straight."

She didn't bother telling him that she saw the man coming and was already prepared with the little lie. Sometimes it was better to let someone think you're super smart, even if you were really just more prepared than they were.

Checking all the little protrusions and things that might trigger release mechanisms, he finally felt one of the curlicues move slightly. It took a bit of work to get it to move more than just a tiny bit. Over the years, dust and dirt must have gotten in the working parts. After about five minutes, and with Elizabeth pulling slightly on the stone handle lower on the headstone, there was a movement.

"Matthew, I think it just came loose, this section of stone is coming out."

"Before we pull it out, I think we should make sure no one is watching us. If the priest were to come back, he may very well demand that we give him whatever we may have found."

"Good idea. Let's walk around the cemetery," he suggested.

Making a slow circuit, as if they were looking at other headstones, they stopped for a moment to survey the grounds and the windows of the church. No point in having anyone see what they were up to and have them report to the police what had been going on.

Seeing the way was clear, the two went back to the gravesite. Elizabeth pulled out a section of stone revealing an inner compartment measuring approximately eight inches wide, three high, and five deep. Matthew reached inside and withdrew a small, old, plain metal box with a clasp on it. There was dust and dirt, creating a film all over it. Giving it to his sister, he asked her to keep it out of sight. He replaced the stone, after taking a last look inside the opening to make sure they hadn't left anything behind.

The pair walked back to Matt's truck and headed for home. Elizabeth turned the box over, studying it as she did. There was a small opening for a key, but no key had been in the headstone. Thinking back she remembered something.

"When we opened the hidden compartment in the dresser, I think I remember hearing something besides the book drop. I didn't think anything of it at the time because the noise was so small compared to the book dropping. I think it might have been a key."

"That's great, sis, I would hate to have to ruin the box just to get it open," he said.

She slid the box under the seat as they continued on their way home. They decided to leave the box in the truck until they could get it into the house without the possibility of drawing any unnecessary attention to it.

Mom was at work that day, being Thursday, and she would have to work Friday afternoon and most of the day on Saturday too. But their dad was at home.

Leonard greeted his kids as they came in the kitchen door. "Hey, guys, what's new? By the way, I'll be leaving for two days, starting tomorrow morning."

"We're good thanks. Where are you going?" Matthew asked.

"I have a meeting in Providence, and it will keep me pretty busy so I'm going to stay in town, completing the work late Saturday afternoon."

"Don't have a girlfriend do you, Dad?" Elizabeth asked teasingly.

"What would I want with a girlfriend when I have your mother? Ha, ha, ha."

"I'm not worried, Dad, we know you better than that."

Elizabeth helped her father make supper while Matthew retrieved and cleaned the box and snuck it into his room. He went back outside and walked to the newly repaired garage. Inside, he swept the floor and looked at the rough concrete.

He wondered if he and his dad could get the floor refinished. The way it was, it would be difficult to use one of those creepers that you laid on to roll under a vehicle. It was also going to be quite cold in there, so he'd have to ask his dad to keep a lookout for a used wood stove and start gathering firewood to use. Matt remembered seeing some on his way home from the ferry. He'd pick it up the following day.

Another thing that was needed in the garage was electricity. He was unsure of how to go about running a line from the panel in the house so would ask for help from his dad.

When they were eating supper, Matt asked his father about the things he would like to have done in the garage.

His father nodded. "I think we need a professional for the floor and the electrical work, but I'm sure I can locate the stove and piping, and we can install it all ourselves. I'll look into getting the floor fixed up next week and contact an electrician to find out the cost of running power to the garage. I am quite impressed with the paint job you and your sister did on the garage, in case I didn't tell you before."

"Thanks, I'm glad you like it. As far as the work goes, I hope it doesn't cost too much to have those things done. I found some firewood being given away at the side of the road on my way home from school. I'll pick it up tomorrow. That will give us a start," Matt said.

"The truck is coming in handy already," Leonard replied.

Leonard went upstairs early with Kate, in order to pack, getting ready to leave in the morning.

"It's nice having you home more of the time. Do you miss being out in the oilfields at all?" Kate asked.

"Not at all, being home with you and the kids makes me really happy," Leonard said as he hugged his wife and gave her a long kiss.

Once the packing was done, they let the two kids know that they were going downstairs to make hot chocolate and asked if they wanted any. Neither one did because they wanted to open the dresser/desk to see if they could locate the key for the box found in the headstone.

When the way was clear, they opened the secret compartment and, after a short search came up with the key.

Matthew got the box, the key was inserted, and after a bit of key wiggling, the little box was opened, revealing a letter inside. The letter was opened, and Elizabeth read another riddle.

> "'Through the stones, you will see
> The place where you need to be
> Only when they do align
> In a beam of SS sunshine
> On the shore, two oaks will grow
> In this spot, you will know
> When it is right, the rocks so big
> Will show you where you should dig
> Military point the two do stand
> Overlooking a view so grand
> When in the spot you are to be
> The entrance to EGP you'll see.'

"Oh, my goodness, what the heck does this mean?" she said exasperatedly.

"Wow, the person who wrote it sure didn't want anyone to easily guess what he meant by this. It was probably Frank Barnes. He's the one who made the desk and headstone and seems to have a flair for this kind of thing."

"Do you really think it was him? How do you know?" she asked.

"His initials are on the bottom of the page."

At this, she laughed and realized he may have gotten her back without knowing it. "I'm not sure how we're going to be able to figure this one out," she said.

"Oh, I'm sure if we look at it properly, we'll be able to find out what it all means. We just have to look at it the right way."

"I'm not so sure about it this time. This looks like it

will be a lot more difficult to crack than the last one, and that was already hard enough," she replied.

"We have to figure out the plans for Saturday. We're going to be home alone, so we should try to get as much done as possible. I think that I'll go to bed early because we'll be spending a quite a bit of time away."

"We gave John the dates of the funerals. I just hope he or Alice can drive us to the town. By the way, you said you would get him some information to help him be a success with the bakery. Have you come up with anything?" Elizabeth asked.

"Not yet, any ideas?"

"I'll look online, and see if I can get it for you."

After a little browsing, she came up with two she thought might work. "Here you are. First, there is an Italian cookie called biscotti and, second, we have the good old chocolate chip cookie. These are fairly popular in the nineteen twenties and make it pretty big later on," she informed her brother. "I'll print off the recipes for both."

Saturday arrived with both Mom and Dad having gone their merry ways. The two siblings got the things they needed and prepared for the trip. In West Tisbury just off State Road was a small cemetery where little Yvonne Routar was to be buried. Because John was able to drive the pair to the address they picked their time of arrival and didn't need to allow extra time. The clock was set, and the two were on their way at the top of the hour. The room once again eerily clouded over.

Chapter 17

They were on their way down the stairs, letting John know they had arrived. A short time later, they were on the ferry and soon landed in Edgartown. The three got to the cemetery just as the ceremony started. This time, in order to remain obscure, they had dressed totally different and separated. The camera was in a bag with a hole in the side and had been in a position to still be able to see the screen.

Elizabeth took pictures of everyone there without being obvious about it. One man was there with an old style camera too. It looked similar to the type used by reporters. While she was taking the photos of the people there, she didn't even look at the faces, and so she didn't recognize anyone. Matthew and John stayed outside the group of mourners and didn't know if the two men they were looking for were there or not.

When she was done taking photographs, they headed back to the car, unaware that a pair of eyes was following them. The face the eyes were in was frowning in concentration, as if he was trying to remember where he had seen the three before.

John had the date of the next funeral and said he would leave a note in the clock again, letting the two know if he or Alice could drive them.

Back home, the young sleuths changed clothes and then read the new note that John had left in the clock. Unfortunately, neither John nor Alice would be able to drive the two to the funeral of Alison Mason at Oak Grove Cemetery on West Spring Street.

Matthew figured out that the distance from John's home to the cemetery was around eight miles and, with the ferry ride would take a good hour and a half. With the funeral and riding to and from the burial, they were looking at a four-hour stayover. Packing a lunch and drinks, plus a few items he might need, he had set the time for six hours.

"Why the extra time, Matt?" she asked.

"Just in case there's a problem, I want to make sure we can get the bikes back to John's."

The trip was made, and the two grabbed the bikes. An hour and twenty minutes later, they were at the gates of the cemetery. They were the first there and, after looking at his watch, Matt realized that the procession would be arriving in mere minutes. This would give them no chance to change into their disguises.

"Do you think we should leave here and find a place to change? I really don't like the idea of having the man seeing us and remembering us from the Cassandra incident. We were in the bushes for a while, but we were seen by several of the drivers. We had no disguise on then and, if he has a good memory, he'll recognize us," she said to her brother.

"Ahh, how would he remember us after four years? I think we'll be safe."

"I hope you're right, Matt. If you're wrong, we could have a big problem," she told him.

The procession started coming through the gates as the two found cover. The casket was followed by the priest and the parents, who were weeping. There was a small group of people at that gathering, and only a few shots were required to catch the faces of everyone who was suspect.

When they had what they wanted, they walked away and headed toward their bicycles. From the mourners, there was another person who left, too.

Chapter 18

The man, who was at all the funerals, including the last, eyed the siblings, thinking that something was wrong. He remembered the two youngsters from another time. The problem was that they looked exactly like they did when he took the child in Edgartown. He saw them while he had been driving past the home of Cassandra Boothe, scouting the area. This was, of course, impossible because that had been four years ago. He meant to find out who they were and why they were there. He suspected that they were at the last funeral too but couldn't be sure, so he followed them.

The two got on a pair of bicycles, so it would be easy to keep up with them. If he was careful, he should be able to keep them from spotting him. The car he was driving started easily with the first crank, and off he went. He turned onto side streets and then went back onto the road again now and then, which reduced the chances of being spotted. The nosy little brats ended up getting on the ferry and went to Chappaquiddick Island.

On the ferry, he took great care to remain hidden from the young man and teenage girl. Once the ride was finished, the two young people pedaled down one of the long open roads. He waited for the right moment and then made his move. Checking all around and seeing no one anywhere, he picked up speed closing the gap quickly.

Chapter 19

The two had had what they wanted and then had hopped on their bikes, heading for the ferry. It didn't take too long before they were cruising along on the water.

"Let's have a bite to eat and a drink while we're waiting to get to shore," Matthew said.

"Good idea, I'm getting kind of hungry and thirsty."

When the ride was over, they were back on the road again, pedaling their butts off so they'd get back in plenty of time. The mirror on the bike vibrated so hard, Matt could hardly see anything in it. It sure was a funny looking thing, being clamped to the handlebars and having a long bent arm. The two were on the right side of the hard-packed road with grasses growing on the edges of a small ditch. The sun was warm, and the breeze created by their swift travel along the road helped to keep them cool. Every now and then, they had to swerve to miss a pothole.

Elizabeth was in the lead, and Matthew thought about passing her. The only reason he didn't was that she had no mirror on her bike and couldn't see what was behind her.

There had been something in his mirror that he saw occasionally between the vibrations. It seemed to be an old automobile coming up quickly on them, and it was far too close to the right side of the road. If it didn't move over, he was sure it would hit him and his sister too.

The closer it came, the more he thought that the driver was purposely going to hit them, so he swerved off the road through the grass while he shouted at the top of his lungs at Elizabeth.

Chapter 20

"Okay, kid, time for you to be taken care of, then blondie and I can talk," the driver said to himself. He sped up, driving right on the edge of the road. He had planned on knocking the nosey boy into the ditch hard enough to eliminate him so he could have a chat with the girl, whose long hair was blowing behind her in the breeze.

"We'll find out why you two are spying on me and just who you are. The girl is a little older than I like, but that doesn't mean I can't have some fun with her. I'll kill the boy, and then do away with the girl when I'm finished with her," he said, smiling.

He closed the gap and was only about thirty feet away from impact when the kid looked back and pedaled off the road into the ditch, yelling at the girl.

Damn.

Chapter 21

As Matthew yelled and veered off the road, he headed right into a shallow ditch. Hitting the other side, he came to an abrupt stop, throwing himself off the bike.

Elizabeth heard the shout and, seeing what was transpiring, went into the ditch too.

The car flew by them, slamming on the brakes and skidding on the fine gravel with a plume of dust in the air.

While he was still lying in the ditch, Matthew opened the bag and pulled out what he wanted.

The man exited the car and was running toward Elizabeth, holding something in his hand. When he was about twenty feet from her, Matthew let loose a shot. The marble, traveling at approximately three hundred feet per second, struck the man in the shoulder.

There was a scream. The man dropped what he had been holding and placed a hand on the injury, looking to see if he had been shot. Matthew loaded another marble into the pouch of the slingshot and got ready to fire again.

The man, seeing this, turned and ran back toward the

car. He hadn't gotten there fast enough to avoid being hit by a second marble in the center of his back. The pain was intense, and he screamed yet again. Fortunately for him, he was wearing a jacket which reduced the impact slightly.

The automobile raced away, leaving the two youngsters scrambling to get their bicycles back on the road.

"Are you all right?" Matthew asked his sister.

"Except for a scratch on my knee, I'm okay. How about you?"

"I'm fine," he returned.

On the road, he walked to where the marble dropped after hitting the attacker and picked it up. He then went and picked up the other one farther away. On his way back to the bike, he reached down and grabbed the rag the attacker dropped when he was shot. He sniffed it and quickly pulled his nose away.

"Holy crap, I think what I smell is Ether. I think he was going to knock you out and take you with him," he told her.

At this point, she started to cry. This had almost turned into a real disaster. Thank god, Matthew had the skills necessary to get them out of the situation. "I thought taking your slingshot was a bit of overkill, but you saved the day with it. Thank goodness you saw him coming and had the instincts to do something about it," Elizabeth said as she hugged her brother.

Looking at his watch, he said, "We better get moving or we won't get back to John's in time."

The siblings checked the bikes and peddled quickly to their destination. All the way there, Matthew kept an eye out to make certain that they hadn't been followed. Just in case, they did a couple of double backs and stopped to have a good look, making sure they were alone.

They had twenty minutes to spare so Elizabeth wrote a

note informing John what had happened. Matthew checked the bag of things he had brought back with them and found the printed photo of the man that had tried to kill him and abduct Elizabeth.

He left it for John to see if he could find out who the man was. It came back to him that John knew someone who, in turn, knew a policeman. If they got lucky, they might just have been able to have the man identified. Chances were probably slim, but who knew?

Matthew double checked the note and added a few minor things, then the two signed it and left it and the photo in the clock room, along with another note in the kitchen letting him know to look for the main note.

Chapter 22

A few minutes later, the very tired time travelers were back home and, after having a quick discussion, checking on Buddy, and setting the alarm, they were in bed, drifting into a shallow sleep. Elizabeth and Matthew both had very disturbing dreams.

She dreamt of being abducted by a crazed man who did horrible things to her. And, no matter what she did or said, there was no reasoning with him. He laughed as if this was great fun for him. She woke up with a scream, perspiring terribly.

Matthew dreamt of lying in a ditch, bleeding and seriously hurt, all by himself with his sister gone. He, too, woke up but with his cheeks wet with tears. He quickly went to the bathroom to wash his face.

Real men didn't do the tear thing, at least not anyone he knew.

He heard his sister scream and ran into her room, without knocking, to make sure she was safe. "Are you okay, sis," he asked.

"I just had a horrible nightmare. I dreamt that the man who chased us caught me and was torturing me like he had done to all those little girls. Oh, Matthew, we have to stop him. We just have to.”

“Yes, we do, I’m going to put all my thoughts into solving this mess. I don’t know how yet but there has to be a way to stop that man. Maybe John’s friend can get the policeman to find out who he is and where he lives.”

“I need a shower. I’m all sweaty, and I see by the clock that Mom will be home soon.”

She got out of bed, straightened the sheets, and headed to the bathroom, still feeling a little shaky. By the time she was finished, she felt better. She also hoped that they wouldn’t have to confront the man in any way. This thought made her whole body tremble.

Matthew saw this when they met in the kitchen. “Don’t worry, I’ll figure something out,” he said. “You won’t run into that man again, I’ll make sure of that. If we have to deal with him, maybe John and I can enlist Sam’s help. I’m sure the three of us can handle him.”

“I guess so, maybe that will help. What happens if he has a gun?”

“I sure hope he doesn’t,” he said with a worried look.

A short time later, Kate got home. The siblings put on a brave face and helped get the evening meal together.

“What time is dad getting home?” Elizabeth asked.

“He should be here around seven-thirty, so we’ll eat ahead of time and save some for him,” Kate replied.

“I think I’ll take Buddy out for a short run. We’ll be back in half an hour,” Matthew told his mother.

The two took off toward the beach and went for a slow jog. Matt was still somewhat tired from the latest incident. Buddy ran back and forth along the sandy beach, periodically chasing a gull. Matthew let his mind drift here and there, allowing thoughts to come and go. He tried to determine how a parent would feel when their child was taken and abused the way the children had been by the man who had almost taken him out that same day on their trip back in time.

Matt was sure that the father would do whatever it took to save his child. A thought crossed his mind and was gone as fast as it came. Trying to retrieve it was like attempting to unscramble an egg, useless. He continued letting his thoughts go hither and thither but didn't come up with anything useful.

By the time they got back home, Buddy was in need of a rinse and shook himself off vigorously before he was allowed back inside. Before going in, Matt made a mental note to practice his martial arts moves later in the evening. He always liked to watch the cage fighters and had learned plenty from imitating them.

Supper was done, and Dad back home. The family spent some time together before the youngsters excused themselves and allowed the adults to catch up.

"Have you had a chance to think of anything so far, Matthew? I figured that's why you went out with Buddy."

Buddy, hearing his name, perked his ears and looked at them.

"No, nothing yet, I'm at a loss as to working this one out. I'll plug away at it, maybe something will come up. John may get an idea if he can find out who the man is."

Having only a short nap in the afternoon, they went to bed early, because tomorrow was a school day. The week rolled by fairly quickly. Matthew and Elizabeth had put last weekend's episode on the back burner.

They had learned to do this because they knew they could go back in time to any moment they wanted at any time, except to the times they had already visited. This had taken a lot of stress off them because there really was no need to enter any situation prematurely.

This had happened more than once with almost fatal

results, so they had learned their lessons well—hopefully.

In order to divert his attention so his subconscious could work independently, Matthew thought about the second riddle now and then. While he went for another walk with Buddy, he looked at the little rhyme and read it to himself as he stood on the shore.

> *Through the stones, you will see*
> *The place where you need to be*
> *Only when they do align*
> *In a beam of SS sunshine*
> *On the shore, two oaks will grow*
> *In this spot, you will know*
> *When it is right the rocks so big*
> *Will show you where you should dig*
> *Military point the two do stand*
> *Overlooking a view so grand*
> *When in the spot you are to be*
> *The entrance to EGP you'll see.*

The first four lines meant nothing to him, so he put them aside for the time being. Lines five and six seemed to be fairly straightforward. Line seven and eight were tied in with the first four and didn't make sense at that point. Lines nine through twelve appeared to describe a place, and they could have a chance to discover where it was by looking at a detailed map of the island.

Actually, it could be on either island or even the mainland near the two islands, but it seemed more likely that the place being described would be on one of the two islands. The reason for this was the fact that three of the robbers came to the island and met up with the fourth. It was thought that they were meeting up in order to retrieve the hidden jewelry.

Too bad one of the officers prematurely intercepted

them, and the shootout commenced with all four being killed.

Matt would have to pull up maps of both Martha's Vineyard and Chappaquiddick Island and go from there when he got the chance.

He thought of all this when he was on a walk with Buddy. It was a good thing he kept a copy of the riddle in his wallet.

His pet barked at him as if to say, "Hey, what about me. I thought we came out to have some fun."

"Sorry, Buddy," Matt said as he threw a ball for the dog to fetch.

While he was playing with his pet, an elderly couple strolled along the beach. The man was stooped over, walking with a cane, and the little lady had her arm looped through his for support. They looked like they were at least in their late eighties, but, for Matthew, it was hard to tell. It looked like they had just come out of a small, year-round cottage very nearby. When they were near the boy, they stopped to watch as he and the dog interacted. Matthew, seeing them, smiled and said hello, introducing himself to the pleasant old folks. Buddy immediately loved the old folks as they talked to him and patted him on the head.

Matt found out that they were Martha and Fred Johnston and that they had lived there for many years. There was something that the little old lady was on the verge of saying but she seemed to think better of it, and so they continued on their walk.

Matt and Buddy played till it was time to go back. When he and his sister were alone, he told her about his thoughts concerning the riddle. She thought that studying the maps was a good place to start, and they walked up the stairs.

"Hey, kids, your dad and I were thinking we'd like to

play a few games unless you have something better to do?"

"No, no, that's great. We haven't played anything in quite a while," Elizabeth replied, even though the riddle was on her mind.

The games were played and, despite the fact that he wasn't caught doing anything underhanded, Matthew came out on top most of the time.

"How can he win all the time? There must be something fishy going on. No one is that lucky, and he isn't really that smart, so he has to be cheating," Elizabeth complained.

Matt laughed. He liked winning. "Sorry, sis, but when you've got it, you've got it, and, unfortunately, you don't got it. Not tonight at least, ha, ha, ha."

It took a few days to get to the task of looking for maps online and, by the time they did, it was Friday. The next day, they had several hours to themselves and decided to try and do something about the man who tried to kill them.

Matthew looked in the clock to see if John had left a note for them and found that he had, indeed, done just that. Carrying the note back to his sister's room, Matt read it to her.

"'My friends Matthew and Elizabeth,

"'I have contacted Gregory, and he has spoken with his friend Danny, the police constable. He has been looking into identifying the man in the photo. Danny says he may have a lead, but at this point, there is nothing definite. I will discuss all this with you when you arrive here. He did ask where the photo was obtained from. It is not the type that is common nowadays.

"'I look forward to our next meeting, John'

"So far nothing yet, which means he isn't a known criminal. It may be a little harder to find him. Maybe if we showed the picture in Edgartown and a few other towns on the islands, we might get a hit. I'm worried about involving John or Alice in this any further. That man tried to kill us, and he'll have no hesitation in doing the same to our friends," he said, extremely concerned.

"You're right. I don't want that to happen either. I sure hope we lost him when we returned the bikes to John's house."

"We'll have to really think this all through and prepare ourselves well. I wish there was a way to warn John without having to go back in time," Matthew said thoughtfully.

Each thought things over in their own rooms. Matthew lay on the bed and wondered if there was a way of locating the man without involving John or Alice and Sam in it. He knew that the man would do whatever it took to eliminate anyone who interfered with his practice.

If Matt and Elizabeth went to any more funerals, they would surely be spotted. All of a sudden, an idea popped into his head. He had just thought of the way they needed to find out who the dirtbag was. If all went well, they might find the means of stopping the deaths of the girls, maybe, just maybe.

The next morning, he filled Elizabeth in on what he had come up with. She thought about it for a minute and smiled.

"I think you have made some major headway here, Matt. We'll have to arrange things with John, and if we can get Mom and Dad to go out this afternoon, we can go back today."

Checking the dates of the funerals, the pair decided to skip the next two and go to Margaret Thorne's burial instead. There was a six-year gap between this death and the last one. The two had thought that maybe the man had moved away for a while and then come back to live in the area once more. The address in Oak Bluffs was obtained, and the dates were written down. They wrote down the route to take to get to Old Lighthouse Road and would take a practice run there, in order to find remote places to observe from.

"Hey, kids, your dad and I are going into town, do you want to come along?" Mom asked.

"I have some homework I'd like to catch up on," Matthew said.

"Me too, Mom," Elizabeth added.

"All right, we'll be back in three or four hours. See you then," Kate told them.

With the parents gone, the siblings got things ready and, after taking care of Buddy, the clock was set.

The room clouded over, and they were gone.

Chapter 23

The two had picked a Sunday afternoon to appear in the past. John, luckily, was home, and they explained what they were up to. John was free, and the three were soon on their way to Oak Bluffs. John had been given the recipes, and Elizabeth asked how the bakery was doing.

"Those recipes you gave me are a big hit. A lot of my business is brought in because of the demand for the cookies. Thank you so much."

"Glad we could help. We'll see if we can find a few more to help the bakery succeed," Elizabeth told him.

They got to the cemetery and drove around the area, trying to find suitable places to survey the burial from. They found several places that they could hide and view the people as they parked their vehicles and walked in.

The funeral was going to be in two weeks, and John told them that he would make sure he was available. They drove back to John's home, with Matthew watching the rear to make sure that no one followed them.

"It feels rather strange that no matter how many years pass for me, you are always the same age. I know why, but it's still difficult to put in perspective," John said, shaking his head.

Back home, the two siblings gathered up what they thought they would need, including the two pairs of binoculars and both cameras. One of the binoculars was quite powerful. Matthew had purchased them while still in Des Moines, knowing they would come in handy. The one camera had a telephoto lens on it and could take shots from quite a distance.

The clock dials were set, and the two were yet again on their way. As promised, John was waiting for them, and Matthew, wanting to be careful, asked him to take along a good disguise too. This done, the group headed to Oak Bluffs and the funeral for little Margaret Thorne.

They got there an hour early and were already dressed in clothes that groundskeepers would wear. That way, if they were spotted, they would be mistaken for adults. They placed themselves in the grove of trees, far out of sight. The binoculars were in their hands, and Matthew had the camera with the telephoto lens hanging from his neck inside his jacket.

The trio chatted for a while to pass the time but found that John's interests had changed as he had gotten older. This was, of course, not surprising as he was now in his late thirties. He mentioned that he met a girl he really liked who stayed at the resort. She, however, lived quite far away and communication was done through letters only.

The thing that tied Matthew, Elizabeth, and John together was the common goal they had—that, and the fact that the two siblings had saved John's life as well as Alice's and their Uncle Robert. This had happened many years ago for John but only a few months had passed for the time travelers. Matthew asked John questions about the war that ended five or six years ago. Matt didn't mention it was WWI. Otherwise, John would have asked why it was called number one.

The time passed, with the occasional person entering the cemetery, and, then finally, the procession began. The people arrived in vehicles of various sorts, ranging from automobiles to old trucks and even a couple of horse-drawn carriages. John and Elizabeth looked through the binoculars while Matthew peered through the telephoto lens.

Elizabeth was the first to spot the man they were after and told Matthew where to look. He found the man as he exited his automobile. Matt took several pictures of both him and his car. To their surprise, he also was in disguise, but not one that would fool anyone who already knew what he looked like.

The man looked around, searching everywhere trying to see if he was being watched. The three ducked completely out of sight as his gaze started to swing in their direction. By the time, they felt safe enough to look again, the service had started, and the man was standing amongst the mourners.

At this time, the three left their hiding place and went to John's Tin Lizzy. He had had this vehicle for quite a while because cars were not traded in for new models every few years in that time period. They parked in a spot where they could see when the man got back in his vehicle. They had to wait just over half an hour and, when they saw him, he had a smile on his face as he started to drive away. The trio followed him back to Edgartown staying as far behind as they could without losing him. Luckily, there were other cars leaving the cemetery and their car blended right in.

It would not do to be spotted by this guy. He was far too dangerous. When they got to town, the gap was closed, and they had to follow much nearer in order to see where he was going. Much to their surprise, he doubled back and headed toward them. John pulled into the first driveway he could and walked with a limp into an open garage door, leaving Matthew and Elizabeth to duck down in the car.

Luckily for John, the person in the garage was pleasant enough to give him directions to the ferry.

The man they had been following glanced at the car where the two siblings were hiding. Having noticed the limp and seeing nothing suspicious, he continued on his way and headed around the next corner.

Matthew jumped out at that point, ran full tilt to the corner, and looked to see where the car was headed. John pulled up beside him. Matthew jumped back in, and they took off down Cooke Street, following his directions. When they got to where the man turned, they saw him pull into a driveway and, after getting out of the car, he walked up a set of steps. He put a key in the front door, unlocked it, then walked in.

The group waited for ten minutes, and Matthew walked past the home to get the address. When he got there he was shocked to find a sign near the steps reading, *Harmon J. Williams, Attorney at Law, 68 School Street.* When Matt got back, he told Elizabeth and John what he had found out. Just to make sure that the man was actually the attorney, they waited as long as they could. After two hours, they felt they had the right man and went to the ferry.

They did a couple of double backs too, just to be absolutely certain they weren't followed. When they arrived at John's home after doing a few more double backs at Elizabeth's insistence, they went inside to make plans. Nothing concrete was decided before the familiar beep sounded and the two made a promise to John that they would be very careful.

Chapter 24

As soon as the two were back in their own time, Elizabeth got online to make sure that nothing had happened to John.

"I'm really worried that Harmon Williams will find John and hurt him, trying to get information about us," she said to her brother.

She looked up the information and sighed with relief when she found nothing out of the ordinary.

"Wow, I'm so glad that he's all right. It really is weird thinking of him this way. He's long dead, at this point, but to us, he's alive because we can go back and see him and Alice anytime we want," she said, laughing a bit.

"Fixing this is going to be hard. We managed to set things right during the summer vacation by working outside the law ourselves, but I don't think it will be that easy with the lawyer. He knows the law and how to use it in his favor."

"Do you think you'll be able to come up with something? He almost got us on the road back to John's house, and I don't want that to happen again," she asked.

"I'll try as hard as I can, but it may take some time.

While I'm working on that, we should look at the maps of these two islands. We might find something to help us with the riddle. That usually helps me come up with solutions to other problems."

Elizabeth brought up a detailed map of Chappaquiddick Island. Matthew took hold of the sheet of paper he had written the riddle on. The lines of the riddle were spaced widely apart so notes could be added between the lines.

"The first eight lines of the riddle have no meaning to me, at this point. We'll have to find the place the writer is talking about before we can decipher them. The last four are…" and he started reading them.

"'Military point the two do stand
Overlooking a view so grand
When in the spot you are to be
The entrance to EGP you'll see.'"

"Okay, 'military point the two do stand.' I assume that he is talking about the two oak trees. It doesn't say how close they are to each other or if you can see them from a distance," she said.

"The next line says that they overlook a view so grand, which I take it to mean that they are in a high place. Otherwise, they wouldn't overlook the view that is so wonderful," Matthew informed her.

"Yes, you're right there."

"Then it says when we are in the right place the entrance to EGP we'll see," Matthew said as he studied the map on the screen.

"What do you suppose EGP means."

"It's probably an abbreviation for some thing or place. Maybe we'll find it on the map," he said.

They studied the map of Chappaquiddick Island from

one end to the other and found nothing to help them. Elizabeth was just loading the map for Martha's Vineyard when Buddy barked a few times.

"Oh, boy, I forgot all about poor Buddy. I'll go and take him outside for a while, and you see what you can find on the map you were about to bring up," Matthew said to her.

He was just going toward the beach with his pet when Elizabeth noticed that their parents were pulling into the driveway.

"This will have to keep till later," she whispered to herself. She shut down the computer and headed downstairs. "You guys are back pretty quick. Did you get done what you wanted to do?" she asked her dad as he walked in the door.

"We really didn't have that much to do. Can you help mom with the rest of the groceries?"

This she did, and after they were put away, the three had a root beer soda together. Dad asked where Matthew was, and Elizabeth let him know that he was walking Buddy along the beach.

"Matthew tells me school is going great. Is that what he says to you too?" Leonard asked his daughter.

"Yeah, as far as I know, he's doing really well in his classes."

"Good. I thought he would. He has a real aptitude for mechanical things. I'm sure he'll become an excellent auto tech."

"We're so proud of him," Mom added. "You, on the other hand, are a bit of a disappointment," she said, laughing hysterically. "I'm only kidding, dear. We're very proud of you both."

"Yeah, *sure* you are. Matthew has always been your favorite." With this, she walked out of the room in a huff, leaving her mother with a shocked look on her face. As soon as Elizabeth was out of sight, she turned around, stuck her head around the doorframe, and laughed loudly too. "Ha, ha, you're not the only one with a sense of humor."

"You brat, for a second I thought you were serious."

With this, all three had a good laugh.

At this point, Matthew entered the kitchen asking what was going on.

"Oh, Mom was just telling me how I'm her favorite, and we were laughing at you," Elizabeth told him.

"Yeah, right, as if that would ever happen."

He walked out of the room with a smile on his face too. He knew his sister was trying to pull one over on him, the way he had done so many times to her.

This left the three others sitting in the kitchen with a stunned look on their faces.

The first one to recover was Leonard. "I think he is a little too quick to be taken in by that line, Elizabeth."

Nodding her head, she got up and followed him upstairs. Going to her computer, she loaded the map of Martha's Vineyard and called out to her brother. The two searched the map, working their way across the island from left to right. There was nothing that jumped out at them most of the way across. Then Elizabeth enlarged a section at the bottom of the map south-west of Edgartown.

"Look at this, Matt. That body of water is called Edgartown Great Pond. I think the letters EGP refer to the pond."

"You're right, sis, enlarge the whole area and focus on all the shorelines."

This she did, and as they studied the map, Swan Neck Point and Bold Water Point crossed the screen. Then there was King Point and Butler Neck Point. Near the southern part of the pond on the east side, was the place that caused Matthew to jump up, "That's it, right there. It has to be that place. West Point has to refer to the line, 'Military point the two do stand.'"

"Yes, that has to be it. There's a West Point, and it's a military academy. The two oaks must be there and, if we can find them, we may be able to figure out the rest of the riddle. This is getting really exciting, I wish we could go now to look, but it's too late and too far away. We'll have to wait for a time when we have a few hours to spare for the search," she exclaimed.

"We also have to come up with a way to take care of Harmon Williams, the lawyer. He can't be allowed to murder all those children and get away with it."

"I have an idea poking around in the back of my head, like you usually do, Matt, but I can't, for the life of me, think of what it might be. It does give me the willies when I get close to grasping it, so that means it will be something that could be dangerous for us."

"If it comes to you, let me know, maybe I can help you with it," he said.

"All right. I wouldn't mind checking with John to see if he has noticed anyone watching him. I have this feeling that the lawyer may have an idea as to where we were headed the day he tried to run you down."

"I'm sure we lost him, but if it's bothering you, we'll go back and check just to make sure as soon as we get a chance," he told her.

With this, the two headed down for supper. The meal was pleasant, and, when it was finished Leonard and Kate suggested a walk on the beach. The family had a pleasant time playing and talking about the week's events.

At the end of the evening, Matthew lay on his bed, thinking of ways to handle the case of the disappearing children. He wondered what motivated the lawyer in this aspect of his life. There had been a period of six years where there were no abductions. Why did he stop, or did he move away and do it somewhere else. How this can be investigated was a question that went through his mind.

He also wondered if it would be a good idea to search the man's house to see if there were any incriminating pieces of evidence hidden there. Of course, if they were caught, it would present a real problem. He would know they were onto him. If he was a meticulous person, he might even notice things had been moved, and then would make a concentrated effort to find them or John.

Matt had to discuss it with Elizabeth and John next time they saw him. With this decision made, Matt fell asleep, waking the next morning rested and ready for school. On the drive to class, he told her his plans for dealing with the situation.

"That sounds like it might be something that could backfire on us if we were to get caught in his home. Last night, when I was in bed, it came to me what was in my mind for the last day or two. What do you think about writing a letter to Cassandra's father, explaining what is going to happen to his daughter? We can let him know that the police won't be able to help with the problem, but he may be able to keep her safe if he is ready for Harmon."

"I don't know if that will work or not, let me think about it. What could he do besides keep her inside and not give the lawyer the opportunity to grab the girl? I think it would just force him to take someone else like he did when he spotted us watching him."

"I suppose you're right. I just don't like the idea of entering his house. It really scares me," she said, obviously frightened.

"I'd like to know why the killings stopped from 1920 to 1926. Do you think it's possible to check online as to his whereabouts during that time?" he asked.

"I'll look tonight and let you know."

Matt dropped his sister off at school and continued on to the college. This week went by fairly quickly, and the two made plans to see John on Saturday or Sunday if they had the chance. Saturday came and Mom had to work and their father had to go to Providence to meet with a client. This gave the siblings the opportunity they had been waiting for.

Buddy was looked after and, because this had happened so many times already, he knew he was being left behind for just a short time. The preparations had been made, and the clock dials were all set. Matthew started the pendulum swinging, and they waited for the clock to send them back in time.

Margaret Thorne was taken August 29, 1926. They decided to go to this date, instead of one of the earlier ones, thinking enough time had passed to make Harmon less wary. They went to a time a few days before that so they could talk to John. The clock made its familiar sound, and the two were on their way.

Chapter 24

The situation was explained to John and, as it happened, he was able to help them in a few days. The two disappeared an hour later and came back the day Margaret was taken. All three went into Edgartown and took refuge near the lawyer's home, which was on School Street. Half an hour before the girl would be abducted he came out of his house, carrying a small leather satchel similar to a doctor's bag.

"I think he has a rag and a bottle of chloroform in the bag," Matthew said.

"How do you know that?" John asked as he turned toward Matthew.

"He tried to take Elizabeth this way when he followed us back on our way to your place, but we managed to thwart him."

"You mean he could have found out where I live?" John asked rather fearfully.

"No, we took great precautions to make sure that didn't happen. Don't worry, John, we would never let anything happen to you," Matthew said, trying to ease his fears. Watching John's facial expressions, Matt realized that he had only been partially successful.

The three waited for ten minutes, and then with Elizabeth remaining on guard, the two would-be detectives made their way to the rear of the lawyer's residence. The door at the back of the house was locked, but they gained entry through an unlocked window.

The home was immaculate with everything neat as a pin. The two searched all the drawers in all the desks and dressers in the home. The closets were then gone through with no results. Matthew having watched many detective movies looked behind paintings on the walls. Behind a rather large painting in the office, he found a wall safe.

"What made you think of looking there?" John asked.

"I don't know it just came to me. I don't know how to get into it though, do you?"

John shook his head, and the search was continued. In a locked desk drawer, which Matthew managed to force open, they found several photos of young girls. Matthew recognized two of the girls that were victims of the lawyer.

"This clinches it. These are some of the girls that are taken by him. This isn't evidence, and the police couldn't do anything with these except question him, so we aren't any further ahead at this point. I wish we could get into the safe," Matt said, more than a little frustrated.

They left the house the same way they entered, making sure they weren't observed. They told Elizabeth what they had found and then got out of the area, making sure they weren't seen.

Back at John's home, the three discussed what had transpired. They agreed that the only thing that would be accomplished if they informed the police about what had been found in the desk would be to cast suspicion on the lawyer.

Nothing of any consequence would happen, and John

would be accused of breaking and entering. Another solution would have to be found.

"Maybe we should have waited for him to abduct Anna and tried to follow him," Elizabeth suggested.

"He is far too wary for us to be able to do that, I'm afraid," Matthew said.

"Yes, we'll have to come up with another plan of attack. What it can possibly be is beyond me, though," John added.

The moment had come for the siblings to be transported back to their own time and, as usual, their vanishing before his eyes left John with the memory of his being trapped in his past all those years. He had told his friends that he wished he had had the nerve to try it again. He knew that if he could do it once more, his fears would have been calmed and he could join his friends in the future now and then. He dreamt of what the future held and hoped he would one day get the courage to make the trip.

Chapter 25

Many hours later, after he had done what he needed to do with young Anna Krause, Harmon J. Williams entered his office. He had felt a slight regret at having done what he knew was wrong. Unfortunately, the deep-seated need he had overpowered any of the real feelings of remorse he ever had. After the episode with Anna, his craving had been quenched and could be put aside for a time. It never actually went away but was at least controllable.

Living a normal life had then been possible, and he could get on with his career as an attorney. He sat at his desk and sensed immediately that something was wrong. He pulled open the desk drawer and saw that someone had forced the lock. There were marks at the mechanism that showed the damage created by an object used to put enough pressure on the lock to damage it. The photos were not in the same place as they had been when he left. He was meticulous about how he placed his possessions.

He felt violated and rushed to the painting behind which his wall safe was hidden. He examined the safe carefully to see if anyone had done anything to gain entrance to it and found nothing. There was an anger flowing through him as he spun the dial and opened it. Pulling out his prized possessions, he looked at the photos he had of the girls he had spent time with. This relieved some of the resentment he felt as he relived the moments spent in his secret place.

Locking the safe, he headed to the back of the house to see where the intruders had gained entry into his private life. It became obvious to him that he had made a grave error not making sure all the windows were locked before he left the house. This he vowed would never occur again and he thought about setting a few traps as deterrents against that happening in the future.

He headed toward a corner of the room, pushed a handle that blended into the bookshelf, and opened a door that was so much a part of the wall that no one had ever suspected it was there. The door opened into a small room that served as his darkroom for developing the pictures that kept his memories alive. In the back of the room was a file cabinet where he had a great many mementos that he cherished.

His anger subsided as he saw that the room remained undiscovered. He had toyed with the idea of asking the neighbors if they had seen anyone lurking about but had quickly discarded the thought. Why have the dolts living near him, wonder why his home had been targeted and not anyone else's? The last thing he wanted was undue attention. What would have happened if the police became involved and wanted to look for clues in his home? No, no, this could not happen, he thought as a shiver ran through him.

"Is it possible that I've been careless and was followed home one day and, if so, by whom? Could it be those two youngsters I tried to eliminate on the road? That happened six years ago, so it seems highly unlikely," he muttered. "But then again, being an attorney, I have seen stranger things happen. How can I check this when I don't know who they are? Do they now have an automobile to get around with? Pity, it would be far easier to deal with the pair if they still used the bicycles, unless there is someone else to blame.

"Of course, there have been some unsavory characters that I have been involved with. It's always possible that one or more of the ones I shortchanged wants to get even. Hell, I've convicted a few people in court and sent them to prison. Maybe I should look into this and see if any have been released lately."

His mind continued to ponder the dilemma. He decided to start keeping an eye out for the possibility of someone watching him. With any luck, he would catch a break and be able to track down the culprits.

Chapter 26

John sat at home and fretted about the possibility that the lawyer would find out that he had been involved in the attempt to implicate him in the children's disappearances. He had thought that he should keep an eye on the man now and then. He had wanted to see what transpired or to see if he could have learned anything on his own.

He talked with Alice who thought it was a bad idea. Sam became involved when he noticed that his wife had been a little on edge. He also thought that taking too much of a part in the escapade was a mistake. He, of course, knew nothing of the fact that the two people John was in partnership with had a refuge that no one could get to. He didn't know anything about the clock and what Alice knew about it. She had been sworn never to reveal anything about it. She took that oath very seriously because the two from the future had made it very clear what would happen if the clock were ever to fall into the wrong hands.

John weighed the advice he was given but felt that if he did nothing to help, he would be considered part of the problem, and he had liked this even less. He decided to wait for his friends to return and see what they had to say about it, maybe.

Chapter 27

Matthew and Elizabeth were then at a point where they hadn't a clue as to what to do next. He told his sister that he and John had most certainly given the lawyer cause for concern. He would undoubtedly by now know that someone suspected what he had been up to. He was also concerned that involving John may have put him at risk. He felt that their friend from the past cared too much about the children and might have taken it upon himself to attempt to correct the situation in some way.

"I don't think he will do anything rash, but if he is found out, the lawyer will surely retaliate. Being capable of killing all those children and trying to kill me, he won't hesitate to do what is necessary to extract information about us in any way he needs to."

"Do you really think John would make a move without us?" she asked with a fearful expression on her face.

"What concerns me, even more, is the fact that Harmon saw us years earlier. If Alice is with John since the time we broke into his house, he may mistake them for us. You and the older Alice look enough alike to be mistaken for each other and it is possible that John may be mistaken for me, especially since half the time we were only somewhat disguised."

"Oh my goodness, it never occurred to me that anything like that could happen, but now that you mention it, it makes perfect sense. We need to warn John about it as soon as we can. We still have a bit of time left today, don't we?" she asked.

He looked at his watch. "If we can set the date quickly, we should be able to do it now."

The dials were set to two hours later than they left John on the last trip and off they went into thin air again.

Chapter 28

Back in John's house, the two called out for him. There had been no answer to indicate that he was there. They ran over to Alice and Sam's home and knocked on the door impatiently. Sam came to the door and, after being asked about John's whereabouts, let the pair know that he knew that John was considering going to town, but he and Alice had talked him out of it. Alice was over at the church they attended regularly with her friend and would be back shortly. John went to the church too but not as often as Sam and Alice did.

The two had known that their friends were churchgoers. It was a common practice those days in the past. Elizabeth wondered if it might be something her family would be interested in. The friends she had who went to church seemed to be much better adjusted and kept out of trouble more than the kids with no moral compass guiding their decisions.

"You're sure that John took your advice?" Elizabeth asked, forcing her thoughts back to the task at hand.

"I'm fairly certain, but who can be sure what he will do. You know what John is like."

"I wish we could find him and talk to him. If you see him, can you let him know we were here, and that he is not to do anything without us?" Matthew pleaded.

Sam agreed, but it was obvious that he wanted to ask for more details. Before Sam could ask them anything else, Matthew and Elizabeth walked back to John's home. He was wondering why the two never got any older and had been about to ask them when they turned away and left.

They wanted to check, in case he had come back while they were gone. They looked in the garage and found his car wasn't there, but the bicycles were. Back in the house, the two tried to reason things out.

"I doubt he will try to catch the lawyer himself, so we're probably worrying for nothing. We'll come back at first opportunity and see if we can get hold of him. In the meantime, Sam will relay our message and that will take care of that," Matt said, more confidently than he felt.

Chapter 29

A short time later, they were back in their own cottage, feeling very tired. It had been an exceptionally long day, and both found themselves badly in need of a nap. This would not happen today though, as their father was pulling into the driveway.

"You're back early, Dad. Did everything go well?" Elizabeth asked.

"Yes, it did. We finalized the plans faster than I anticipated, and it's all a go. This home consulting business is doing better than I could have hoped for. You guys weren't bored by yourself today, were you?" he asked.

"No, no, we found things to occupy ourselves," Matthew said offhandedly.

It was obvious that Leonard wanted to ask what, but had thought better of it. He didn't want to intrude in their affairs. Besides, if it had been anything important, they would have come to him, wouldn't they?

"Mom will be home for supper soon so why don't we get things ready, guys?"

After supper, everyone sat in the living room in front of a fire that burned brightly, warming the room.

Both Elizabeth, relaxing in a soft, Lazy-Boy-style chair, and Matthew, on the couch by himself, fell asleep before long.

"What's going on with these two?" Mom asked softly. "They seemed really tired, and it took no time at all for them to fall asleep."

"I don't have any idea. They must have had a pretty hard day, but neither mentioned it to me," Leonard replied, whispering.

A short time later, the two teenagers climbed into their beds and were out for the night. They woke up refreshed and were questioned by their mother as to why they were so tired.

Elizabeth, as usual, was the first to collect her wits. "We went exploring the area by the caves that we took you to before, and we just wore ourselves out climbing and playing with Buddy. It must have looked funny with both of us passing out in the living room like that last night."

Kate looked at the innocent expression on her daughter's face and the look of relief on her boy's and knew this wasn't quite the truth, but couldn't question them more without insulting them. Inwardly, she smiled, thinking her girl was so much like her father. That man could think on the run like no other person she had ever met. Matthew was a little more innocent in that respect but was sharp as a tack too.

The family all made plans to go out for supper that day at the seafood restaurant in town. This was a place they went to during their summer vacation, and everyone had loved the meals there.

At first opportunity, Elizabeth checked online to make sure nothing had happened to John. There were no stories concerning him, and, when she informed Matthew about it, he asked, "Where do you suppose he went? Do you think he could have been spying on the lawyer but was lucky and never got caught, or maybe he went somewhere else?"

"I wish we could go there and check in with him." An idea popped into her head, "Why don't you check the clock to see if he left another note?"

This Matthew did and came back with a note in his hand. There was a noise on the stairway, so he tucked the note into his pocket. She brought up the map of Martha's Vineyard on the computer. The door was pushed open, and in walked Buddy, wagging his tail. He seemed to feel that the two siblings needed to be reminded that he was still here. They breathed a sigh of relief and patted the dog vigorously.

"Don't worry, Buddy, we'll take you out for a run in a little while, okay?" Matthew told his pet.

After looking out the bedroom door to make sure they weren't overheard, he pulled the note out of his pocket and read it, speaking softly.

"'Dear Matthew and Elizabeth, I went to Edgartown and watched Mr. Williams, with no results. I am sure that he has no idea that he is being watched, so I should be safe. Sam gave me the message about your concerns and, rest assured, I will be careful. Your friend, John.'"

"I don't like this," Elizabeth said anxiously. "I really don't think that John realizes just how dangerous this man is. If he is caught, he will be tortured for any information he may have about us. What happens if he finds out about the clock? He could easily use it to commit murders all through time."

"On top of that, I think we would lose access to the clock, because I am sure he would move it, and it would disappear from this cottage. Would it undo everything we've done so far or would it stay the same? I don't like this at all, not one bit. I don't think John has thought this through properly. We have to warn him, any suggestions as to how to go about it?"

"I think we have to get back there as soon as possible and tell him the danger he is in and what will happen if he is discovered by the lawyer," she said, obviously frightened.

"Absolutely, you couldn't be more right," he stated emphatically.

"We're supposed to go out for supper with Mom and Dad late this afternoon. When do you think we'll be able to go?"

"Maybe we can get them to go for a walk along the beach after lunch. That will give us more than enough time to make the trip there and back. We only lose a few minutes on this end, no matter how long we're back there. If necessary, I could go by myself, if the only way to get them out for a walk, is for you tag along," Matthew said to a sister who was already shaking her head.

"Not a chance, I'm going with you. He has to be made to see just how dangerous the situation is. I'll go downstairs and see if I can guide the conversation in a direction that will make them think it's their idea to go for a walk."

She headed to the kitchen where her parents were chatting. She included herself in the conversation and eventually brought it around to suggest they get a little fresh air by going for a nice long walk.

As they got to the water's edge with Buddy bounding up and down the beach, Leonard smiled. "Do you think she was subtle enough? If we hadn't left when we did, I'm sure she would have pushed us out the door."

Kate laughed. "What do you suppose they are up to? I know they have something in mind because this isn't the first time they've done this."

"I'm sure it's nothing to worry about. They'd tell us if it was. Moving here has been one of the best decisions we've ever made. The kids have never been so happy," Leonard told his wife.

"For the most part, yes. There have been a few times, though, that it looked like the weight of the world was on them. Remember the times during the vacation this summer? I thought Elizabeth was going to burst into tears."

"Now that you mention it, I do remember that. Do you think we should head back and check to see what they're up to?" he asked.

"I don't know about that. I'm tempted, but I think we need to trust them to make the right decisions. After all, they have grown up into very responsible young adults," she said with a look on her face that indicated that she hadn't been entirely convinced of this remark.

The parents continued their walk, with Buddy soon distracting them. They strolled along the beach, looking at homes and wondering if this is the way things had always been. There had been a thought in the back of their minds that some of the things they were seeing had changed somewhere along the line. It was almost as if not everything was the same as it had been during the summer vacation. This was, of course, not possible so the feeling had been dismissed.

As they walked, they saw an elderly couple walking toward them. Recognizing Buddy, the people called out, "Hello, Buddy," and he ran up to them wagging his tail, obviously thinking of them as friends.

The elderly couple introduced themselves as Martha and Fred Johnston. They chatted for a while letting the Janssens know that they had met Matthew on an earlier walk and thought that he was a fine young man. A few more minutes of talking and the folks were on their way.

Back home, the clock was set, and the brother and sister were waiting for it to send them on their way.

Chapter 30

I wish these binoculars were a little better," Harmon muttered to himself. "It's a good thing I have them, though. I would never have spotted that man hiding down the street without them. He must be one of the thieves who broke into my house."

Anger filled him, and he was determined to find out who the person was. He watched from a second story window, being extremely careful not to be seen himself. The man hiding was mature but the clothes he was wearing made it difficult to make out any details. He looked like he was in disguise. In case a confrontation happened, Harmon would make sure his pistol was handy because the man appeared to have prepared himself well in order to keep his identity secret.

"There he is walking down the street away from me. He must be going back to his automobile. Now is my chance," Harmon said to himself.

He reached into the drawer, picked up the revolver, and ran out the door, determined to follow the watcher.

Chapter 31

The two siblings reappeared the morning of August 30, 1926, the day after the break-in and their attempt to give John the warning. Calling out, they were relieved to hear John answer back.

"John, why did you spy on Mister Williams? I thought we asked you not to do that?" Elizabeth asked.

"I felt that I couldn't just sit around and do nothing."

The three sat down.

Matthew had a worried look on his face. "John, this man is so dangerous and smart that it won't take much for him to put two and two together. He knows the general direction we were heading when he tried to run us down. If he saw you, he would follow you back here and torture you to find out who we are. If he were to find out about the clock, he would kill you and then take it to his place. He might even disappear and use the clock to travel to other times to murder young girls in other cities. Then he would just keep moving around the country. The clock would disappear from our cottage, and we could never find him."

Elizabeth looked into John's eyes. "Is there any possibility that he could have seen you and trailed you back here?"

John had a faraway look in his eyes as he thought back to when he was leaving his hiding place and heading back to his automobile. Sorting through the images of the day in his mind, he began relaying what had gone on. "When I left my hiding place and was walking back to drive home, I turned around and took a quick look at the lawyer's house. I thought I saw a curtain in the upper room window move. Seeing this, instead of going to the car, I ducked out of sight and stripped off my extra clothing. No longer being in disguise, I threw the clothes behind some bushes and walked away. Right after I did this, the lawyer drove by rather quickly looking in all directions as if he was looking for something.

"Now that I think about it, I'm certain that he was looking for me. How he saw me is a mystery. You're right, he must be very smart. I had my suspicions yesterday but wasn't sure."

"So the question remains, did he follow you back here?" Matthew asked.

"When I saw him drive by, I waited for quite a while before returning to my automobile and going home. First, I walked to the city center and stayed there for an hour or two. Then when I returned to the automobile to drive home, it was getting dark, and I walked back from a different direction that kept me away from his home. I didn't see any lights following me, so I doubt very much that he knows anything concerning me."

"We certainly hope that you're right. You will have to stay away from him and promise not to watch him anymore, all right?" Elizabeth asked.

John nodded his head and soon it was time for the return trip. The two siblings felt a little better, but John felt worse. He remembered seeing a pair of headlights in his mirror now and then last night on his way home. They were there only occasionally, and so he thought that they probably were several different vehicles, but now he wasn't so sure.

Matthew caught the look on John's face just as they disappeared.

Chapter 32

Driving down the street, Harmon couldn't see any-one walking or driving away. He circled a few times, driving around the neighborhood trying to find the man. There were a few automobiles that were unfamiliar to him, and he made a mental note to check the area later to see which were gone.

This, of course, wouldn't give him any solid leads, but he had found things in his court cases with less to go on, so he remained vigilant. He wondered why he couldn't find the man. Could he have given himself away at the window and spooked him? If so, was the man hiding somewhere? Harmon's head swiveled back and forth in an attempt to locate him.

Later in the evening, he spotted a man he was unfamil-iar with getting into a car he hadn't seen before that day and didn't ever recall being in the area before. His clothes were different than the man watching his house, but that didn't mean too much at that point. On a hunch, Harmon followed the man to the ferry and boarded near the end of the line. He stayed in his car and sat low in the seat. The man stayed in his vehicle too and drove off without looking around. He was totally unaware of Harmon.

Harmon followed at a safe distance so as not to raise any suspicions. He even made a few turns and returns to the road, trying to drive without lights, but this threatened to put him in a ditch as he had hit the shoulder of the road more than once.

In the end, as Harmon was halfway across the island on Chappaquiddick Road, the car ahead had made a series of turns, and he had lost his quarry. The area was not too far from a popular resort hotel known as Mariner Lodge. There was any number of places the driver could have gone to, and he could even have been a guest at the lodge and been visiting someone in town. So Harmon felt he was no closer to finding his quarry than he had been before. There were just not enough facts, at that point, so he drove back home and had tried to figure out his next move.

Chapter 33

As the time travelers got back home, and the door to the secret room had been relocked, Matthew looked at his sister. "When we were just about to travel back here, John had a look about him that indicated he didn't tell us the whole truth. There was something worrying him."

"Do you think that he may just have thought about what might have happened to him and felt bad about it?" she asked.

"I don't know. It could be, but my first instinct is to believe there is something he didn't tell us. I'm just as worried now as I was before we went to see him," he said.

"What can we do about it? It's not like we can spend all our time going back to protect him. If we go back too often and keep an eye on the lawyer, I'm sure we'll be spotted too, and then things will really escalate."

"We have to come up with a plan to handle him ourselves, but I'll be darned if I know what it might be," he said.

With this, they went downstairs and headed out to the

beach. As they walked along, they saw what they assumed was their parents a long way off heading toward them. The giveaway was the dog that they had with them.

Buddy with his keen eyesight noticed them a few minutes later. He barked and ran full tilt toward his friends, knowing that playtime had just been ramped up again. Matthew, having thought ahead to bring the Frisbee, now tossed it as their pet approached. The dog detoured in order to catch the toy in mid-air. His body twisted as he reached for the spinning disc. Then he ran to his owner and required to be patted vigorously before he released the toy.

Elizabeth thought that this was just what they needed to take their minds off the problems they faced. With her parents approaching, she didn't want them to see there was something troubling her so she too got into the game of tossing the Frisbee. The conversation came around to the old couple, and Matthew smiled as he remembered talking to them.

It hadn't taken long for everyone to get in the spirit of the game and, before they knew it, the time had come to get ready for the trip to the restaurant. The drive there was uneventful, and soon they were enjoying fish and chips all around.

During the meal, Leonard and Matthew discussed a possible remedy to smoothing out the floor in the garage. It was decided that a concrete mixer would be rented and the two would pour a new floor over the old one. Wire mesh would be used to strengthen it, and the existing floor had to be cleaned so the new one would adhere to it properly. It would be a fairly large project, but Leonard felt that it was doable.

"Why don't you price the cost of the rental and all the materials and get a couple of quotes from contractors?" Kate suggested. "You may find that the cost to have a professional to do it may not be much more."

"I guess I could do that. I'll check into it this week, and we'll go on from there," he said with just a bit of disappointment in his voice. He had been looking forward to the project but saw where it might be much easier that way.

The rest of the meal was enjoyed by all and, by the time they got back to the cottage, it was bedtime. Matthew fell asleep quickly, but Elizabeth lay awake for a while. She had been worried that John might be found out. She checked online to make sure nothing had happened to him but found nothing to indicate a problem. This, of course, could change easily enough if when they went back in time, another path was taken, and the three gave themselves away.

She drifted off and dreamt of being trapped in a dark place, not able to get out. The next morning, she remembered the dream and, after trying to analyze it, came up with a thought. It most likely just meant that her thoughts had been so gloomy, they were affecting her sleep. It would have been nice if she could turn off the worrying part of her mind, but unfortunately, this was how she was wired, and that was that.

On the drive to and from school, each day the two siblings discussed things that they could do to deal with the lawyer. On Tuesday, Elizabeth thought that they should inform the police about the photos. Matthew thought that he would rather try to come up with a better plan.

"Too many things can go wrong with calling the police in. He is a lawyer and will be able to stall them long enough to get rid of the evidence," he said. "We would have to do it anonymously too."

Wednesday on their way home, Elizabeth made a suggestion as they drove along the gravel road. "I think we need to get our minds on something else, because we aren't making any headway with plans for stopping that horrible man, anyway."

At home, with their father busily working on a consulting job, she had brought up a map that showed West Point protruding into a body of water. Having noticed earlier with Matthew that the body of water was called Edgartown Great Pond, they had realized that was what EGP meant. They were certain that had to be where the two oak trees stood. The entrance to the pond was to the southwest of the point and shed light on at least part of the riddle.

She searched for a way to get to the spot where the trees were and saw that they had to drive to the end of Crackatuxet Road and then hike in the rest of the way. The point was close to a half mile walk from the end of this road, and somewhere near seven or eight miles from Edgartown.

In order to undertake this trek and make a thorough search, they needed at least half a day. Their mother didn't have to work that coming Saturday, and their father wasn't going anywhere in the near future either, so this looked like it would have to wait unless Matthew wanted to go anyway taking the chance of being questioned by their parents.

Even if that happened, she was sure that they'd be able to come up with some viable answers.

Getting up, she had left her room to go look for her brother so she could tell him the news. Locating him in the garage, she had found that he was fiddling around with the radio in his truck.

When she let him know she had found a way to get close to the location of West Point, a big smile came on his face. "Good work, sis. This will put us a lot closer to finding out if the jewelry is buried somewhere out there. This is every bit as good as looking for pirate treasure."

"Suppose we do find it, what then? Do we see if we can collect the reward?"

"Gosh, I haven't thought that far ahead. What do you think we should do? I bet the reward would be a lot. It would probably pay for all our tuitions," he said, grinning from ear to ear.

"How would we explain finding it? Would we have to tell mom and dad about the secret space in the dressers? It makes me wonder if they would put two and two together and find out about the clock."

"I see what you mean. This has the potential to open a real can of worms. Besides, do we actually deserve to collect a reward for finding the treasure? I think using the clock is its own reward, and we should wait to make this decision about it when we have had more time to ponder the ramifications of it all."

"Besides, we haven't found anything yet and may not ever," she said laughingly.

Later in the week, Matthew suggested that they take a closer look into why there had been a six-year interval between abductions from 1920 to 1926. "We need to find out where he was during that time or if he just stopped for a while. When John and I were in his house, I saw a name on a letter. Look up and see what you can find out about Edwin Fitzpatrick," he asked.

"How did you remember that name so long? I would have forgotten it long ago," she said.

"The only reason I remembered it is because I had a friend back in Des Moines by the name of Edward Fitzpatrick which is almost the same."

She typed in the name and received several hits almost immediately. There was one that dated back to the 1920s. There was a photograph of a man and a story accompanying it, which she read aloud.

"'Mister Edwin Fitzpatrick has been arrested in conjunction with a raid taking place in Falmouth, Rhode Island. A major bootlegging operation has been in business in the port for some time, and Mister Fitzpatrick is one, of several people involved in the smuggling of illegal alcohol into the area. It is suspected that there is an entire network of people involved in the smuggling and distribution of the contraband liquor.'"

"Unless I'm mistaken, the letter I saw the name on was addressed to Harmon, but he lived in Falmouth at the time. This must have been during his absence from Edgartown. I'll bet he was involved with the smugglers," Matthew said, bunching his eyebrows together as he thought.

"Do you think that he stopped stealing children during that time?" Elizabeth asked.

"That would be hard to say. He may have done it somewhere else, and unless we knew where to look, we could never know for certain."

"What I really want to know is how we can stop him?" she asked. "I was thinking that we could do something similar to what we did with those men during our summer here."

"That worked great, but we put ourselves in jeopardy during that episode. I'm not sure that I want to take that kind of chance again. If that guard had been armed, we might have been shot." Matthew said with a bug-eyed expression.

"This is turning out to be harder to figure out than I would have thought," she said.

"Yeah, you're right; I just don't know where to go from here. How do we go about stopping a child killer without putting ourselves or John and Alice in harm's way? I wonder if John has any ideas that may help us."

"Do you really want to get him deeper into this? He has already been in a position where he could have been followed back to his house. There's something he hasn't told us, and adding more may just get him to do something dumb and get him caught. I couldn't live with myself if we were to be the cause of him being tortured by that maniac," she said fearfully.

"I guess you're right again. It seems that this problem has fallen into our laps, and we're the ones that have to come up with a way to deal with it. I'll put on my thinking cap and try to solve this."

At supper, while everyone was at the table, Leonard made an announcement. "I've been doing some cost comparing. After speaking with a few contractors, I've found out that hiring someone to do the concrete job in the garage is almost as cheap as doing it ourselves. Your mother was right again and deserves a pat on the back for saving Matthew and me a lot of unnecessary work."

He started to applaud her, and the kids joined in.

Kate smiled and accepted the cheer with a bow. "When do they start?"

"They'll be here on Saturday and asked us to keep the driveway near the garage clear so the equipment can be brought in and the concrete truck will have room to maneuver," he said.

"Do they need any of our help, Dad?" Matthew asked.

"Actually, you and I are going to tie into the septic system by the house here and build the forms for a concrete pad for the mud room. When the concrete cures, we'll build the mudroom your mother wanted. The contractor wants to have a quick look at our work, and discuss a few things. After that, it will be best if we stay out of the way."

Kate smiled happily at the thought of the mudroom and asked what the youngsters would be doing.

Matt shrugged. "Elizabeth and I are planning a little hike and wondered if we needed to postpone it. What are you and Dad going to do?" he questioned.

"We thought we'd go shopping and have a day out. If we didn't need to do that, maybe we would have come with you, or weren't you offering?" Leonard asked.

"I was just wondering. We can take Buddy with us. He'll probably like to go for the hike. You guys go out and have a nice time."

After supper was over, Elizabeth took Matthew aside. "Why did you tell them about the hike? What would we have done if he said they'd come along?"

"Then we would have all gone together. We would have searched the area without telling them that we were actually looking for something. After all, we're only looking for the two oak trees at this point. The other part of the riddle doesn't make any sense to me. Maybe we'll see the rocks the riddle talks about, and then it may clear up the rest of it."

"I guess you're right. It wouldn't have hurt anything to have them along. Are you planning to take anything with us?" she asked.

"It says something about digging, maybe a shovel will come in handy."

The rest of the week went by quickly with the work outside the kitchen door done. Before they knew it, Saturday had arrived. Leonard and Matthew met the contractor at the garage at eight o'clock, and he was told exactly what they wanted to be done. The workbench was quickly unattached from the wall and taken outside, leaving the floor free of obstacles. The forms and rebar for the pad outside the kitchen had been checked and found to be suitable. With this out of the way, the siblings headed out toward the ferry.

The drive and ferry ride took about an hour, and they picked up a few snacks and drinks on their way to the end of Crackatuxet Road. The hike was started with Buddy running ahead, and as the excitement started to build, they saw far ahead of them, several groups of trees. To pick out the right ones may be a little harder than they first thought. Maybe they'd have some luck and find the place they're looking for.

The pace was picked up as they made their way toward the point. It was a long walk, with the terrain going through gullies and over hills. The two found themselves walking through many small groups of trees, but not in a spot that overlooked the water. Most were located in the gullies they had to walk through. On they went, working up a little sweat but getting closer to what looked like a rise high above the water.

"I see a high spot over to our left, about three hundred yards in front of us, do you see where I'm pointing?" Matthew said.

"Do you mean the spot with the trees on it?"

"Yeah, that's the one. There are some trees at the top. With any luck, two of them will be oaks. Let's go, sis, I think we're getting closer to solving the riddle," he said, laughing with joy.

Down a slope, they ran and quickly reached the bottom. They started up an incline that would take them to the top of West Point. This had, of course, been slightly more arduous for them, but not for Buddy. Ten minutes later, they reached the top, catching up to their pet, very much out of breath.

"Hey, Matt, do you see what I see?"

Chapter 34

W hat to do is the question," John muttered to himself. "I have to find out if that lawyer knows anything about us. I have to see if he found out where I live. I can't take the chance of him being here one night and taking me by surprise."

John made a decision he knew would displease his friends from the future but felt that he had no choice. He had some time off and, after gathering some clothes in order to disguise himself, he was on his way. The binoculars were on the seat beside him and, as he steered the vehicle toward his destination, his hands began to tremble.

He knew he should not be doing this, but the thought of being caught off guard worried him even more. It was two in the afternoon, and his employee could handle the bakery by himself for the rest of the day.

Soon, he was in position and watching the front of the house where the lawyer both conducted his business and lived too. John had found himself a place to hide and felt fairly safe. The only way he could possibly be seen was if the lawyer was also watching with a pair of binoculars, which John doubted very much. He knew the man had to be a total paranoid to be always on his guard. John really had no idea how accurate this statement was, in describing the person he had been spying on. He wasn't even sure that watching the man would give him any useful information, but he was there nevertheless.

He sat waiting for an hour, getting stiff in his joints. He got up and stretched then went for a short walk, making sure he hadn't been seen. As he got back to his position, he looked at an upstairs window and thought he saw a curtain moving back into a hanging position.

"Crap, has he seen me?" he asked himself. He quickly grabbed the spy glasses and trained them on the window. There had been nothing to see, but he looked for a long time, trying to keep his hands from shaking. "Has this been a mistake? Have I just given myself away?" he asked himself. He switched from one window to another and then another.

There, in a lower window at the corner of the house, he saw a glint of light being reflected from what was probably a pair of glasses or binoculars. *Damn, why did I come here? How can I get back to the vehicle without being seen and followed?* He actually started to panic.

Quickly as he could, he left the hiding place in the bushes in which he thought he had been so safe. Making his way around the corner of a home, he quickly went down an alley. Down the next street he ran and hopped into his car. Once it started, he drove away as he removed the excess clothes he had been wearing.

Just to make sure he hadn't been followed, he drove around the town several times, constantly checking the rearview mirror to see if anyone was tailing him. When he was certain that there wasn't any car behind, he headed for the ferry, and, as he drove on, he breathed a sigh of relief. He looked casually at some of the cars on the boat to see if the lawyer's car was there but saw nothing obvious. Too bad the car the lawyer drove was pretty much like all the cars there.

Chapter 36

"It's fairly slow, today being the middle of the week. I think I'll look through the windows and see if one of these busybodies is still watching me," Harmon said to himself.

He looked through the sheer curtains in the back of the house one by one. Finding nothing, he moved to the side windows and searched with his spy glasses. He had been doing this at every opportunity since he had found out someone had been observing him after his house had been broken into.

He found nothing on either side and took a quick look out the front windows, moving to the upper floor in order to gain a better vantage point. There, across the street behind a number of bushes, someone was getting up. Harmon moved the curtain slightly to get a better look and just as quickly let it go. He knew that it would have let the man know that he had been seen if it had been pulled back.

He had moved to the left so he wouldn't be obvious and peered through the edge of the curtain to see if the man had noticed him. The man looked just as the curtain came to rest and he could see that he had aroused the man's suspicions. *Darn it, why did I move the curtain?*

The character stretched and went for a short walk working the kinks out. He must have been there for a while. Soon he was back, but Harmon had moved to a window in the lower portion of the house. This time he took no chances and sat in a chair well back from the window. He watched as the man took his position once more. The sun had moved slowly in the sky to a point where it was low enough to be reflected from the glass of a passing car, through the window hitting him in the eyes. Momentarily, he had been blinded and had to lower the glasses to regain his vision.

When he could see once more, he looked through the curtain, but the watcher was gone. Harmon looked around the area and spotted him running past the corner of a house. Harmon knew he had given himself away and quickly gathered his coat and a hat he seldom wore. Two could play the incognito game, he thought.

He ran out the house, got his car out of the garage, and drove down the street where he suspected the guy's car was parked. There was nothing to be seen, so he stopped and tried to reason out the best plan of action. He could have driven around hoping to spot the man, but that, he knew, would probably yield no results. He knew that the jerk lived on Chappaquiddick Island because that had been where he went the last time Harmon followed him. Too bad he had lost him that time. It would have saved him several sleepless nights.

His best chance was to park his car near the ferry dock out of the way and wait for the jackass to hightail it home again. This guy had made a bad mistake coming back to spy on him again. He would have been home free if he'd stayed away.

It took a while, but his hunch paid off. It hadn't been

long before he'd seen the car that he suspected was carrying his quarry. He was sure that this was his man, and if things worked out, he knew he'd be able to find out where he lived. Then he'd be able to deal with him at the appropriate time.

His target drove on the ferry near the head of the line. Fortunately, there were quite a few cars to be loaded, and Harmon managed to be close to the last car boarding the boat. His quarry looked around at the cars traveling across the water but didn't see anything to alarm him, so he sat down in the driver's seat again.

"This is going well so far and, with a bit of luck, I can take care of the situation and resolve it to my satisfaction soon," Harmon muttered as a smile crossed his face.

The ride was short and, as everyone disembarked, Harmon took his position as far back from his target as he felt safe. He hadn't followed too far back because this had been how he lost him last time. They made their way down Chappaquiddick Road across the island where the car he was following turned onto Jeffers Lane. The route took them to Mariner Lodge and, in his eagerness, he started to go a little faster and had closed the gap between him and the man he considered a nosy jackass. The car made a couple of quick turns and came to a stop.

Harmon stopped about fifty feet to the rear of the vehicle and quickly exited. He caught up with the man who now knew he had been found out. Harmon struck out at the person who had had the nerve to invade his privacy.

Chapter 37

Boy, I'm glad to be on the ferry ride going home. How could I have been so stupid? Why did I come back here to spy on that murderer? I sure hope I lost him," John said, chastising himself.

His hands had been shaking and as he drove off the ferry. On his way home, he tried to keep an eye out for anyone who might be following him. There were several cars on the road and so nothing, in particular, had aroused his suspicions. It was tourist season, and so there were always people driving to the lodge for a holiday.

When he turned down Jeffers Lane, he became aware of a car behind him. As he pulled over and got out, the car had pulled over too. As soon as he saw the man, he knew it was the lawyer he had been watching.

Panic had been about to set in, but he had thought that if he played it cool, he might be able to feign ignorance and dissuade the man from accusing him. The man came up, and, without saying anything at all, slammed his fist into John's jaw.

Luckily, John saw it coming and, having been in a few fights before, managed to slip the punch enough to light-en the power that struck him. He backed away and prepared himself to strike back.

The man weaved back and forth as he came at John, and John knew instinctively that he was outmatched. This man had fought many fights before and probably won most of them.

John was hit twice more, and, as he realized that this was going to end badly, he heard a voice coming from nearby. He hadn't been able to make out who it is because he was already in a daze but had been glad someone was there. Stumbling back, avoiding any more punches, he saw that Sam was confronting the lawyer.

Sam blocked a punch and returned a haymaker. The lawyer now knew that he was in a real fight. Sam, being much bigger and stronger than John, had also been in many fights during his youth.

The fight stopped, as the lawyer shouted, pointing his finger at John. "This man has been spying on me, and I want to know why?"

"I don't know what you're talking about," John said.

"You're lying. I saw you. You're probably the same guy that broke into my home. Admit it because I know you are," Harmon yelled.

"Unless you have evidence, you better be on your way, or we'll have you charged with assault, mister," Sam shouted back at the lawyer.

"We'll see about that," Harmon said. He turned, walked back to his car, and drove away.

"John, is that the man Matthew and Elizabeth asked you to stay away from?"

"Yes, he is. I was worried that he might know who I was and went to check."

"Well, that really worked out well for you, didn't it? Now he knows for sure who you are. What on earth were you thinking John?" Sam asked incredulously.

Chapter 38

Harmon drove away very angry, rubbing his jaw. He was angry at the man who had interfered with him and the beating he would have given the fool. Harmon was also angry at himself for confronting him before it had been necessary. That hadn't been the first time his temper had gotten the better of him. During his involvement in the bootlegging industry, he regularly had gotten into skirmishes.

As he drove, he quickly regained control and turned around, heading back on a different street. He parked out of sight and watched as the two talked about what had just transpired. He was too far away to hear what was being said but that didn't matter. He knew what they were discussing.

He waited till his quarry got into his car and drove away. The second man that had interfered went to another vehicle and left too. Harmon managed to catch a break and had seen where his target had driven to. The dope had parked the car in a garage and then walked into a nice-looking cottage.

"Great, now I know where you live. We'll have a talk when the time is right, pal."

There was a smile on the lawyers face as he thought about what was undoubtedly going to happen soon. He would wait for a while before doing anything. That would lull his target into thinking things had blown over.

After that, more than ever, Harmon had to watch his back. He had no idea how much was known about him at that point. He had a hiding place that no one knew about and couldn't be traced back to him, but he was going to have to safeguard himself as much as possible anyway.

"Better get on this right away," he said to himself.

Chapter 39

John was back in his house and visibly shaken. There had been considerable pain from the impacts of the lawyer's fists. If Sam hadn't been at the scene, the lawyer would have hurt John badly. He never suspected that the man would be as tough as he was. It was a good thing Sam came from a rather rough upbringing too. John hadn't approved of Alice's choice in suitors at first, but Sam's pleasant demeanor had won him over soon enough.

"God, what am I going to do now? I'm in big trouble and living alone puts me at the lawyer's mercy," he said out loud. "I have to let Matthew and Elizabeth know what I've done. I'm pretty sure they're the only ones who can help me now. I'll write a note and leave it in the clock again. Gosh, I hope they think to look inside it."

He wrote the letter with trembling hands and described what had transpired. He had included an entire paragraph letting them know that he should have heeded their warnings and that he was so sorry he hadn't.

After making several corrections and crossing out things that made little sense, he went to the clock room and placed the letter inside the clock. As he left, he secured the locks in the closet so no one could gain entry to the hidden room.

Matthew had warned him to do this on several occasions. John had taken offense when Matthew repeated the instructions before but was glad he did. Just to ensure that the clock room wouldn't be discovered, he placed a number of items in the closet. That should help to hide the true purpose of the extended interior.

He had, at that point, been unaware that Sam had told Alice what happened, and she had wanted to have the three meet to discuss their options. It had been too bad that Sam couldn't ever know about the clock and what it could do. Alice wanted desperately to include him in her confidence. The secret weighed heavily on her.

"Maybe Matthew and Elizabeth can help. After all, John wouldn't be in this predicament if it weren't for them," she said to herself. She immediately corrected the thought. She was well aware that John could have prevented this from happening, if only he had heeded the warnings.

Chapter 40

So what do you think the kids are up to now," Kate asked her husband.

"I have no idea. Matthew did ask if we wanted to come along, so it can't be any big secret."

"I guess not, but then again they seem to be preoccupied with a lot of things that we have no inkling of. It's a good thing they have each other. By the way, is either of them interested in dating? I hear them talking about people at school, but that part never seems to come up," she asked.

"I haven't heard anything, and I'm actually glad. We haven't been here all that long, and this dating thing always seems to have consequences. At least it did for several of our friend's kids we knew back in Des Moines," he said, thinking back to a time before they had moved to the cottage.

Chapter 41

atthew looked to where his sister had been pointing and gazed at two massive oak trees and some smaller elms. The oaks trees dominated the scene, and another piece of the puzzle fell into place.

"This is great, do you have the riddle with you?" he asked. "I seem to have left mine at home."

At this, she pulled a piece of paper out of her backpack and read out loud.

"'Through the stones, you will see
The spot where you need to be
Only when they do align
In a beam of SS sunshine
On the shore, two oaks will grow
In this spot, you will know
When it is right the rocks so big
Will show you where you should dig
Military Point the two do stand
Overlooking a view so grand

> When in the spot you are to be
> The entrance to EGP you'll see

"Okay, so the trees we've just found. The view so grand is down below us and the entrance to Edgartown Great Pond is over there," Matthew said, as he pointed to a narrow separation in the shoreline exiting to the ocean.

"What I don't understand is the thing about the stones and looking through them. How can you look through a stone?" she asked.

"I see what you mean. Plus, what the heck is a beam of SS sunshine? I've never heard of such a thing, have you?"

"No, I never have. Maybe we should try to find these stones and the mystery will clear itself up. That's the way we've found out pretty much everything else so far," she said, quite puzzled by it all.

"All right, but how big are the stones we're looking for? Can we hold them in our hands or are they something much larger?"

"I think they will be pretty big because if we are to look through a stone to see where to dig, that will mean it has to be something that can't be moved. If they are small and got moved out of position the spot to look at would no longer be in view, right?" she asked.

"Hey, you're pretty smart thinking of that. Okay, let's look for some big rocks."

The two separated and started searching the area, first covering the place that overlooked the water. Buddy walked along watching the two crisscrossing back and forth. Nothing much was found in that area, so they had turned their sights to a direction away from the water. Walking past the two trees, they discovered that the hill sloped down somewhat, revealing several large outcroppings. Past the rocky area, the hill sloped down more rapidly and, about fifty or sixty yards downhill, the land leveled off and then rose rapidly forming a cliff of sorts.

Part way up the cliff face there had been the entrance to a small cave. The bottom of the entrance was about four feet off the ground. If they decided to explore it, it would take a bit of climbing to enter the cave itself but nothing the two couldn't handle.

They saw several large boulders and rocks that were part of the hillside. The rocks were fairly smooth and reached quite high in the air. There had been nothing that would indicate that one could see through the rocks. After discussing what to do next, they felt that the best plan of attack was to take a close look at all the boulders and then the stone outcropping.

At that point, they felt a break was in order and sat down on soft grass, leaning against one of the oaks. A drink was first on the agenda and then a bite to eat. Elizabeth took a granola bar, and Matthew started on a donut.

"Yum, nice and sugary and really good for you too," Matthew said.

"Ha, ha, ha, sure, Matt, you just keep telling yourself that. Maybe one day you'll actually believe it if you have any teeth left."

The sky was almost free of clouds, and there was a gentle breeze blowing off the water, cooling the two siblings off. They chatted for a few minutes and finished what they were eating, with Buddy eager to help. Getting up, they went to the nearest of the boulders. A close inspection was done on the one and then the next. There was one large boulder that was just where the slope started downward. It had been the bigger of the boulders and had an odd shape to it.

The rock had a large base and was quite wide as it extended upward. Looking from the side, about three-quarters of the way up, it became quite slender, where it was close to a foot thick near the middle of the stone. Toward the edges, it had quickly flared back out. Looking from the front and back, there was a rather large depression on both sides.

"That looks rather odd. If you get close you can see weathered chisel marks where someone hollowed out the two sides, in order to make it thinner, three feet from the top," Matthew told his sister.

"Why would someone go to all that trouble? It must have taken hours and hours to do."

"There has to be a really good reason for it, that's for sure. Let's take a good look at the depression, maybe it will give us a clue," he said.

The two got on either side of the rock and inspected it closely. In the center of the depression, Matthew, with a fist-sized, round stone in his hand tapped on the larger rock. Everything sounded solid till he hit it at the deepest point. There was no longer a slight ringing in the stone, but it sounded more like there was something loose in the stone that had been hit.

"I might have found something," he said excitedly.

She walked around the boulder quickly and studied the place he was pointing to. He gave the spot another rap, and the same sound was heard again.

"It sounds like there is a loose piece here. I need to find a tool to pry around and see if it is loose enough to get out," he said, looking around for anything that might work.

"How about using the tire iron in your truck, Matt?"

"It's quite a walk back, but there isn't anything around here, so I guess that will have to do."

"I'll stand guard so you won't have to worry while you're gone," she told him, smiling.

"You're a real hoot, sis."

He ran down the slope, heading in the same direction

they had come from originally with Buddy running be-side him. Going downhill was easy, but, when the lay of the land changed and went uphill, he was forced to slow his pace considerably. It took almost half an hour for him to return, holding the tool. He had had to sit down for a time to recuperate. He had a drink of water and five minutes went by before he was ready to get to work. Buddy, of course, hadn't been tired at all and would have liked to run a little more.

Elizabeth had been poking around, with little to show for it. Matthew looked closely at the place he thought may yield the best results. There was a build-up of debris and dirt, most of which he had already cleaned out. He took a deep breath and blew, causing some of the dust to hit him in the face. Luckily, he closed his eyes just before impact and didn't get anything in them.

Wiping his face off, he looked closely, noticing what appeared to be a circular line in the recess of the rock. Using the sharp end of the tool, he poked and prodded at the center. Suddenly there was a bit of movement, and a section loosened, rattling in the larger rock.

With his fingertips, he took hold of a well-fitting stone around two inches in diameter and pulled it out of the hole. The stone was close to four inches long and had a very slight taper.

"This taper is what made it so hard to pull out of the hole," he told her.

Lowering his face, he looked into the hole that went through the boulder, front to back. There was a down-ward angle to the hole, but all he saw was darkness. Us-ing the tire iron, he pushed it into the hole and hit bottom.

"This hole is manmade, and there is no reason for it unless you put something in it or it goes straight through the rock," Matthew said.

"Maybe there is another stone plugging the hole at the

other end. Do you want me to look there or is it better just to hit it harder?"

"Let's take a look first. We can always hit it harder if we have to. Just in case, let's take a look around to make sure there isn't anyone in the area. We don't want any company while we're doing this," he said, looking around.

They walked around the top of the knoll and, after a visual inspection, saw that they were alone. At the backside of the rock, they cleaned the spot at the deepest area of the second depression.

There was a similar circular line and, with this information, he walked to the first side and lightly tapped the bottom of the hole. When he hit a little harder, he felt movement. One more impact freed the stone on the other end of the hole.

"Excellent, Matthew, you got it. Look through the hole and see where the second stone is. That has to be what it's for, according to the riddle."

He bent down and peered through the opening. Looking through the hole, what he saw was another large rock farther down the hill toward the cliff face. Because of the short length of the hole he was looking through, he saw considerably more than just the rock.

As a matter of fact, he could actually see three big rocks through the hole.

"Elizabeth, can you walk down the hill and stand in front of the rocks and move to the one I direct you to?"

"Sure thing, tell me to stop if I go to the wrong one."

She started down the slope and continued past several smaller rocks, when Matthew didn't say anything. When she came into view, he directed her to the rock which was closest to the center of his line of sight.

She was on a slight rise where the rock sat, elevating it above the rest of the boulders in the area.

"Okay, stay there, that's the one most likely to be the second stone," he told her.

Making his way down to her, he noticed other people hiking in the distance. Walking quickly after telling his sister about them, he headed back to the first rock. When the hikers disappeared in a low spot, he put the tapered stone back in the hole and tossed some dirt on it. Heading to the other side, he did the same thing and walked back to where their backpacks were on the ground.

Acting very nonchalantly, they sat on a stone overlooking the large pond and enjoyed the sight.

"Darn it, why did they have to come here? It's a nice spot, but their timing stinks," he said with a slight edge to his voice.

"I guess we should count ourselves lucky that we had this much time. At least we found some of what we're looking for. The riddle is making more sense all the time."

At that point, the hikers came over the rise and noticed they weren't the only ones there. The newcomers chatted with them for a moment and continued walking. It took almost twenty minutes for them to get completely out of visual range.

Another look around and the siblings found themselves alone once more. They walked back to the second rock and found what they were looking for much faster than they had on the first stone. Once they cleared the hole in the rock, they took turns looking through it. That hole was much shorter than the one in the first rock, and so their field of view was quite large. What they saw was a big portion of the cliff face with the cave entrance a little off center.

"Do you think that the hiding place of the treasure is in the rock face of the cliff? Frank Barnes was quite the stone mason so he could have made an opening and fit a stone in place easily. Look what he did with these two rocks and the headstone," Elizabeth stated.

"It's possible, but if it was me, I'd do something in the cave. That way the hiding place wouldn't be exposed to the elements."

"We've figured out everything in the puzzle except for that one line, in a beam of SS sunshine. I still don't know what that means," she said.

"The beam of sunshine is obvious, but I know you already know that. So what is confusing us is the SS part of it, right?"

"Yeah, that's it. Do you have any idea at all what it could possibly mean because I don't have a clue," she said shaking her head.

"Let's plug up this hole too and go home to think this over."

Putting the stone plugs back in and camouflaging them, they then picked up their packs, took a drink, and headed back to the truck.

The ride home was fairly quiet as the two were lost in their own thoughts. The dog, as usual, had his head hanging out the window enjoying the breeze. Each was trying to make heads or tails out of what they had learned in the last few hours. By the time they got home, nothing much more had been discovered.

As they pulled into the driveway, they saw that their father was standing by the open garage door with the contractor.

The rest of the crew had already gone.

Parking the truck, the siblings headed to the garage and looked inside at the newly poured concrete floor.

"Nice job. This is going to make it a lot easier to work in here. Where should I write my name?" Matthew said, chuckling.

"No names in the concrete please," Leonard said as

the contractor just smiled. It must have been a common occurrence for him.

A short time later after the mudroom pad was checked out too, everyone was gathered around the kitchen table eating supper. Buddy, having had his dinner, lay near Matthew, hoping for some morsel to drop.

"How was your hike today? Did you see anything interesting?" Kate asked.

"It was really nice. We went on quite the pleasant walk and saw some spectacular scenery. There are quite a lot of interesting places around here. Which reminds me, do you think we'll ever get ourselves a boat? Not rushing you at all, just wondering," Matthew asked.

Elizabeth suspected that it was just a tactic to prevent their parents from asking to go with them to the hiking spot.

Leonard smiled inwardly, thinking the same thing. Kate actually thought that a boat might be a nice thing for more family time. With the kids growing up so quickly, it was only a matter of time till they became involved in other things.

Playing a board game passed the time. That was a pleasant way for the group to unwind.

Elizabeth thought over what she had learned about her friends in the past. "Say, Mom and Dad, have you ever thought about maybe going to church now and then?" she asked.

"What, where is this coming from?" Mom asked, just a little surprised.

"Oh, I was just wondering. I have some friends at school who go every week and seem to think it's great. They seem to be much more, well-adjusted than most of the other kids, so maybe there is something to it."

Kate nodded. "I went to church as a child but got out of the habit when I started university. I think a lot of the professors are atheists and steer the youth away from religion. What about you, Leonard?"

"Yes, I went to church when I was a kid too. As I recall it was a big part of my parents' life as they grew up. I really liked it and had some good friends who went too."

Elizabeth looked at her parents. "Do you think we could look into it sometime? I'd like to see what it's all about."

"I don't see why not. It might be good for us as a family," Mom said.

Inwardly, she was pleased with her daughter. She recalled all the wonderful excursions and happy picnics growing up in a church environment. What was that pastor's name who baptized her as a teenager?

The two siblings went upstairs to do a little research to see if they could figure out what that SS sunshine line could possibly mean.

"So how come you asked Mom and Dad about church? Is it because Alice and Sam go to church a lot?" Matthew asked.

"Yeah, I thought it might be good for us too. What do you think?"

"I know a couple of guys at school that go too, and they seem like good guys, so what the heck? You know you'll have to quit swearing all the time if you go, sis." Matthew laughed as he said this.

She giggled. "Oh yeah, like I swear at all."

"I just thought of something. Maybe I'll check the clock in case John has left any more notes for us. I did ask him to give some thought to the problem with the lawyer," he mentioned.

After looking into the hall to make sure they were alone, Matthew walked into her closet and, at the far end, searched for the locking mechanism. He felt along the edge near the corner and pressed the lever, unlocking the door. Inside, he turned on the light in the dark room and walked to the clock.

The panel hiding the dials was closed as it should be. He unlocked the door and reached inside to where John always left the notes intended for them. To his surprise, there was a note that had been written many years in the past.

When he thought about it, it seemed funny that someone long dead was able to communicate with him as if he were alive today. Having the clock able to transport him and Elizabeth back to John's time whenever they wished made it as though John and Alice were as alive as the two siblings were. A queer feeling came over him as he thought about it.

Locking the clock and hiding the key, he walked back to the door and turned out the light. Locking the door was standard practice for the two. This being done, there was no chance of the clock being discovered, which would have, unfortunately, stopped the trips from being a part of their lives. He carried the note over to his sister and, after checking the stairway, read it to her.

The two were shocked by what John had written. This had just complicated their plans a lot. John, confronted by the murderer, had now opened himself up to a world of trouble. It had become far more important to find a solution to deal with the man. Why did he do this? He was warned against it and was told what would happen. The siblings were sick at the thought of what might well happen to their friend and, if the lawyer found out about the clock, would that be the end of it for them?

If the lawyer were to kill John and take the clock, it would no longer have been in the cottage. How would that affect everything, or them? The consequences were too horrible to spend much time on. A solution absolutely had to be reached.

Chapter 42

Two weeks had passed, and Harmon thought it was time to pay a visit to John Fielding Smith. Through his contacts, he had found out who the owner of the cottage was. After following him home, it had been easy to find out his name. Being the owner of a bakery required the man to be away from home most days, leaving the cottage empty for Harmon to search.

Having no clients that day gave Harmon the opportunity he needed to put his plan into action. Packing the items he felt he might need and deciding to follow John's example, he brought along a disguise of his own. It took a short time to get to a street not too far from the cottage. He parked his car and took a route through the woods and across the small sand dunes in order to get to the water's edge, remaining hidden from view. Another fifteen minutes got him into position, and he took out his field glasses, surveying the rear of the property.

He was in a grove of bushes near the water that offered him concealment. From that vantage point, he saw a kitchen and entertaining room on the lower level. There was a slight drizzle coming down which helped keep anyone who might notice him indoors but made the sand stick to his shoes. The driveway and the garage were on the other side of the cottage as well as the road.

When the way was clear and he felt safe, Harmon cautiously made his way to the home. Living so far away from the city must have given people there a feeling of safety because Harmon found that the door had a very inferior lock. This had surprised him as he had top of the line locks on his doors and windows. Of course, this hadn't prevented a break-in at his home either.

After stamping his feet in order to remove the sand, he entered the home, being careful to listen for any sounds that indicated someone was there. After a moment, he was sure that he was alone and proceeded to look through the lower portion of the home. He didn't find anything of consequence so quickly made his way up the stairs. There was a landing at the top and from there a series of short stairways that lead to a number of bedrooms and bathroom. He had heard of this type of architecture before. It was called a good morning stairway. Well, good morning it soon would not be for Mister Smith.

He headed toward what appeared to be the main bedroom and walked into the room a little too fast, knocking into a vase sitting on top of a slender stand. The vase started falling and, despite a desperate effort on his part, the vase fell to the floor and smashed into small pieces.

"Damn, why did this have to happen? Now he'll know that I've been here and the element of surprise will be gone," Harmon said out loud, letting out a long sigh.

There had been no use cleaning it up and hoping for the best, so he left the pieces where they were. Being a rather large man did have its disadvantages in situations like this, but it had helped during confrontations with some of his former associates.

The search continued with nothing too much being

discovered. There had only been one thing that bothered him at that point. Having an eye for detail, he noticed the layout of the rooms was not quite right. He was certain that all the upstairs space was not all accounted for by the rooms that he saw. He had a hidden space in his own house, and so that was the reason he saw it so readily in this one.

He looked for an opening in all the most obvious places but came up with nothing. He had been sure there should have been an entrance somewhere, but he was unable to find it. Could it be that he had been mistaken?

Having found nothing of any importance that would indicate why this man would have cause to be spying on him, Harmon left. The door he entered through was re-locked, and he made his way back to his car. While driving, Harmon thought about seeing John Smith and getting from him any information he had concerning those two snoopy kids.

Chapter 43

After five o'clock, John came home from a long day at the bakery. Inside, he sat at the kitchen table thinking about how badly he had made a mess of things. He was concerned about the lawyer coming back and beating him up worse than he did when Sam had intervened. The man was very strong and knew how to fight. That was something John had never felt comfortable with. His hands trembled slightly at the thought.

Looking around, he noticed that there was a little sand here and there on the floor. He was always careful to clean his shoes when he came into the house, and so it was not normal. His suspicions were raised as he grabbed hold of the ax handle he kept in the broom closet. Carefully he searched one room after another. Not finding anything out of the ordinary, he started up the stairs with the ax handle in his hands, ready to swing.

His breathing was rapid, and his pulse had quickened. At the top of the stairs, he waited for a moment to listen for any sounds. All he heard was the blood pulsing through the veins in his ears. Fear took hold of him as he imagined the worst case scenario taking place. He desperately wished that Sam had been here. The two would stand a far better chance together.

No longer feeling he had a choice, he continued the search. As he entered his bedroom, he almost panicked when he saw the broken vase on the floor. There was no longer any doubt that someone had been in his home. Anxiety came close to immobilizing him. He had to talk himself into finishing the search and, despite the fact that he found nothing, he was almost in a state of shock.

No longer able to contain the fear in him, he ran out of the cottage, past the lilacs, and made his way to Sam and Alice's home. He banged on the door several times, hoping Sam was home. It seemed to take an eternity for the door to open.

"What's going on John?" Sam asked.

"Someone broke into my house. I'm sure it has to be that lawyer. What am I going to do Sam?"

"For the time being you better stay with us. We'll have to tell Alice all about what has been going on too. This is getting completely out of hand, and we better figure out a way to deal with the man."

Alice was informed and almost started to cry. John apologized again and again for not listening to the warnings. After an hour, when things had settled down somewhat, Alice asked Sam to get her a drink from the kitchen.

While he was gone, she asked, "Have you checked the clock room, did he discover our secret?"

"I don't know. I ran out before looking. I'll check later when I feel a little safer."

At Alice's insistence, Sam and John went back to the cottage with a rifle to make sure everything was in order before it got dark. The two went through the entire house and, except for the broken vase, things seemed all right. While Sam was busy elsewhere, John quickly checked the closet and the hidden door. After taking a quick peek inside the room, he relocked it and made a mental note to pack a few more things in the closet as a deterrent against discovery.

He was talked into spending the next few days at Sam's home. Sam was a hunter and had several rifles and a shotgun and gave John a few lessons in shooting. John was a little reluctant at first but had been persuaded after he was told that he didn't actually have to kill the man, just scare him off by shooting near him if John was threatened.

Chapter 44

On Tuesday, after school, Matthew took a walk along the beach with Buddy. He needed to come up with a way of handling the lawyer before something terrible happened to John. Buddy bounded up and down the sandy shoreline, chasing gulls when the opportunity arose.

When he was near the spot where he had seen the elderly couple, Buddy barked, as he saw them coming out of the rear door toward the beach.

When they heard the bark, they looked up and waved. The little lady, Matthew noticed as they got closer, was carrying a flower in her hand. When they were within talking distance, he asked how they were doing.

"Oh, we're fine, thank you for asking," she said with a sad expression on her face.

Noticing that the flower was a rose, Matthew inquired, "Are you sure you're all right, ma'am?"

"This is the day that my older brother Bobby disappeared in nineteen forty-one, and we have a little ceremony on the edge of the water, commemorating it. That is why we are a little sad today."

"I'm sorry to hear that, ma'am, were there any clues as to what happened to him?"

"He had a diary in which he named some people he was afraid of. When the authorities tried to find the men to question them, they were never found. Nothing was found that connected anyone to his disappearance," she told the boy.

"Do you still have the diary? I might be able to check online and see if anything was ever found out about these men. I doubt I could come up with anything new, but you never know, maybe a clue will surface," he said and immediately realized that it was a dumb idea. Why raise hopes when there couldn't possibly be anything that could help them after all that time? He was about to express his doubts when the old man spoke up for the first time.

"I recall seeing it in the trunk where we store all the old photos and things we no longer use. I'm sure it would be of no use anymore, but you are welcome to look at it nevertheless. It has been in the trunk for forty years at least," he said with a faraway look in his eyes.

"We'll see if we can find it and next time you happen to be walking this way, please do drop by. It will be nice to have company, it's been so long. All our old friends have passed away, and Bobby was my only sibling, you know. We never had any children of our own," she said with a tear in her eye.

Taking this as a cue, Matthew said goodbye and continued his walk. He wondered what had happened to her brother for a moment, but this was short lived as Buddy was in a mood to play. The time passed. Matt found himself quite a distance from home and realized that he hadn't thought about John's predicament yet.

He had no idea what to do. Realizing that he couldn't deal directly with the lawyer, he had to come up with a plan to have someone else take care of him. The police were already involved when Cassandra had been taken. Things were complicated when they tied up the cop by mistake, so contacting them probably won't do any good.

Buddy got distracted by a gull, and Matthew had, for the moment, been oblivious to everything else, triggering a thought. John had a friend named Gregory who had a friend Danny, a police officer. Maybe Danny could be brought into this affair. The wheels turned in Matthew's head refining the idea further. Calling his pet, he started running back to the cottage.

"Where have you been, Matthew? It's time for supper. We were going to start without you if you were any longer," Kate told her boy.

"Sorry, Mom, I lost track of time playing with Buddy. What's for supper, meatloaf?" he said, smiling.

Matthew had wanted to talk privately with Elizabeth, but Leonard took him to check out the new garage floor after they ate.

"So what do you think of it, Matt? Looks pretty good, doesn't it?"

"It sure does! How long before we can start working in here, Dad?"

"The contractor said we should allow the concrete to cure for at least a week before driving on it. I think that we should wait two weeks just to make certain. I would hate to have it crack just because we didn't want to wait a little longer. I'm going to pick up the materials with your truck this week, so we can build the small mud room. It will just be an area for us to wash up before we enter the house. What do you think about that?"

Matt agreed, and the two walked back to the house. Elizabeth was talking with her mother but, at Matthew's signal, she cut the conversation short and headed upstairs, following her brother. He explained his idea to her and, after a bit of discussion, the plans were made. At first opportunity, they would go back into the past and talk to John, filling him in on what needed to be done.

"Check online, sis, to see if anything has gone on with the situation back then."

This she did and, when they saw the story, they were shocked once again.

With her hands trembling she read aloud. "'John Fielding Smith has disappeared from his home on Thursday of this week and hasn't been heard from since. Alice Berger Anderson, married to Sam Anderson, cousin of John Smith is beside herself with worry. She has accused a prominent lawyer residing in Edgartown of being involved. The police have questioned the accused, who vehemently denies the allegations. Further investigations have confirmed Mister Williams's whereabouts at the time of the disappearance. It has been discovered that he plans to sue for slander those who have accused him, but this is unconfirmed. There are no clues as to the whereabouts of the missing man.'

"My goodness, Matthew, how could this have turned out so badly?"

"What I don't understand is why would the lawyer do this if he wants to keep a low profile? He had an alibi for the time John vanished, but that doesn't mean he couldn't have had someone else kidnap John."

"I don't understand any of this, Matthew. Why didn't John just leave the man alone like we asked? What do you suppose that horrible man will do or has done to him?" she asked as she cried and the tears rolled down her face.

"I don't even want to think about that. We have to get back there as soon as we can and see if we can change things back. I doubt very much that we can correct it all, but maybe we can at least help John somewhat."

"How can we get some alone time to make the trip there without raising suspicions with Mom and Dad?" she asked frantically, drying the tears with a tissue.

"I don't see how we can before the weekend. Mom has to work Saturday, and Dad will be on a trip, starting later in the week. The only possibility is if Mom has to work a little late between now and Saturday."

As luck had it, Kate did have to work late two days later and phoned home to let the two siblings know when they got home from school. The building materials had already been picked up and stored in the garage, freeing up the kids.

"Let's get ourselves ready, I already put everything we need in my closet, and the date is already written on this piece of paper," he said as he handed her the note.

The clock dials were set, and the pair waited eagerly for the timepiece to do its work. They had planned to arrive shortly after they gave John the original warning. Once again the room clouded over, and they were gone.

Chapter 45

The two siblings appeared in the room and, after unlocking the closet door from the inside and moving a few things out of the way, stepped into the hallway.

"Hey, John, are you here?" Matthew shouted down the stairs.

There had only been silence in the home many years in the past. Walking into the kitchen, they saw by the clock on the mantel that it was five-thirty and that John should already have been home by this time.

"Do you suppose that he disregarded our warnings this quickly and didn't tell us in the note he left in the clock?" Elizabeth asked.

"At this point, very little surprises me. I hope we haven't wasted this trip and our time?" he said, shaking his head.

"We're here for an hour, so why don't we go see Alice, and ask her if she knows where he is. Maybe she knows how to get in touch with Danny, the police officer, without going through Gregory," she suggested.

After talking to Alice, the pair found that they were no

further ahead than they had been before they had arrived.

"Are you still keeping notes on all the trips we've made?" he asked.

"Yes, every detail is written down, so we don't accidentally overlap any trips, and go to the same time twice."

The hour passed slowly as anxiety overwhelmed them. Finally, the two siblings reappeared in their own time. Going to the kitchen for a quick drink and to check on Buddy, Elizabeth noticed that the door to the clock room wasn't closed all the way.

"Matthew, did we not close this door properly?"

"I thought you did it, seeing as how you were the last one to enter," he answered.

Thinking back to when she last came into the room she said, "I can't remember closing it so I guess it was me that left it undone."

"We'll have to be careful about that in the future. If Mom or Dad finds this room, we'll have a lot of questions to answer."

Matthew looked at Elizabeth's journal which had all the dates, times, and duration of the trips the two had made. There were little side notes highlighting what had happened each time.

"This is quite impressive, sis. I doubt I could have done this well."

The clock was reset for a time immediately after they left when they first warned John about spying on the lawyer. As the time approached, they discussed what to do when they arrived.

The room clouded over and the trip was made. Down in John's kitchen, the pair found that John had already left and was nowhere to be found.

"What the heck is going on? This is twice we've missed him. How can this be fixed if we can't talk to him.

I'm running out of ideas again," he said.

"If we can't find him and warn him, we won't be able to save him from Harmon. We could leave him a note, but he hasn't heeded our direct warnings up to this point, so why would he now? You males, you take too many risks," she said angrily.

"I know you're upset with John so I won't take it personally," he returned gently. "I think I may just have come up with another plan. It may not work either but we will have to make another trip to put it into action."

The time passed very slowly for the siblings as they felt the next part of their plan would determine whether or not they would be able to prevent John from being abducted.

Finally, the beep sounded in his pocket and the return trip was made. Matthew relayed to Elizabeth the contents of a handwritten letter that would be given to either John or the only other person who could help them now.

"This will be our third trip today and will add four hours, making us pretty tired by the time evening rolls around," she said with a sigh.

The dials were once more set on the clock and soon they found themselves back in John's home.

"Hey, John, are you here," Matthew called out.

The two were rewarded by the sound of John's voice calling back to them from the living room.

"Boy, am I ever glad to see the two of you. I was hoping that you would find my note. I am so sorry that I didn't listen to you."

"We have some rather bad news for you, John. Things get a lot worse than having that lawyer breaking into your home," Elizabeth said to him.

A look of real concern crossed his face. "What do you mean by that? What's going to happen now?"

The two filled him in on what they had found out.

John almost seemed on the verge of collapse. After Matthew let him know of his plan and what would be required of him, John felt slightly better. It was imperative that John take care of the details himself and, if all went well, they may yet avert tragedy. By the time Matthew was finished, John's hands were trembling, and he had broken out in a sweat.

Whether or not they could save their friend would be decided by what transpired in the next few days. John said a prayer, pleading to have this trial pass him by and the lawyer's plans to have him abducted thwarted.

Although Matthew and Elizabeth had only another hour and a half left there, they relented to John's pleadings to accompany him on the ride to the city. Forty-five minutes later, they parked the car on the main street in Edgartown.

John had to perform this part of the task by himself as he walked into the police station and located Officer Danny Monroe. John filled in the officer, who had a very doubtful look on his face. The officer shook his head as he heard the story and was then handed an envelope. No promises were made, and John walked back to the car with a look of defeat on his face, just as the beep sounded.

The car was on the ferry when the moment arrived and the pair made sure they were well hidden to prevent anyone seeing them vanishing into thin air.

Chapter 46

There was a knock on the front door as Harmon was finalizing the details for a client wishing to make out a will. Harmon got up and saw that there was a police officer standing outside. From instincts developed long ago, he knew it would be best to get rid of the client.

"I'll be right there," Harmon said through the door and turned to the client. "I am working with the police on a case, so if you don't mind, I will contact you when I've completed your will."

The two shook hands, and the man left, walking past the officer.

"Please come in, Officer," Harmon said loudly for the benefit of his client. As he closed the door behind the policeman, he asked what it was the officer wanted.

"I have come to inquire about a break-in near the Mariner Lodge. It has been reported that you had an altercation with a young man and his friend. They believe you are responsible for the unlawful entry to his home shortly afterward."

"Are you actually accusing me of breaking and entering?" Harmon said, obviously shocked.

"No, sir, I am just checking as to your whereabouts on the day in question." He filled in the lawyer with the details and waited for an answer.

"I'm sure I don't know what you're talking about. Yes, there was an altercation, but it was the result of a driving mishap which almost ran my vehicle off the road. I would have no reason to break into anyone's home. Whose home is it, by the way? I don't know anyone who lives in that area."

"I am not at liberty to say at this time. Can you remember your whereabouts during the said time, sir?" the officer asked politely.

"I take great offense to this, but, in the desire to be helpful, let me check my calendar," he said. Walking over to his desk, he picked up a journal, and after studying it for a moment, he said, "I see here that I had appointments all that day and so could not possibly have performed the break-in. If you wish to verify this, I will ask my clients to contact you."

"Yes, please have them telephone me at this number and ask for Officer Monroe," the officer said, handing him a card. "Thank you for your co-operation, sir."

After the policeman left, Harmon made a call informing his cohort about what was required of him. "By the way, I think we will have to postpone grabbing the baker for a while. There has been an unfavorable development, making this ill-advised at the present time." Harmon hung up and thought about the situation. "Why the hell would the law be called in at this time? I'm sure that the baker realizes that I could have accused him of the same thing. He can't possibly have gotten wind of what was going to happen to him, so what the hell is going on?"

Harmon sat at his desk, very confused. He realized that he would have to be very careful for the next while. Maybe he should check into that Officer Monroe.

"There has to be more to this than is obvious to me. How can I get the information if I can't get hold of the buffoon? Is there someone else who has the answers? Maybe the guy who interfered with the beating knows something. No, this is too close to home. If he disappears, the cops will put two and two together far too easily and my other hobby will have to come to an end. I'll get rid of all the incriminating evidence and stash it somewhere safe tomorrow."

Harmon sat in his chair, rocking back and forth with his hands together and his fingers intertwined under his chin. He debated the merits of having one of his old cronies watch the baker to see if anything came to light. The situation had become far more complicated than it should have been. He did not need the attention that had been drawn to him and would have to lay low for a longer period of time than he had in the past. Maybe he should take a trip next time his special need arose and perform his task well away from there. Many thoughts came and went in his mind for the next several hours.

Chapter 47

Meantime, Matthew and Elizabeth reappeared back in their own time. After locking the door to the clock room and rearranging things in the closet, Elizabeth fired up the computer. She looked for the story of John's disappearance and found nothing.

"We did it, Matthew. We did it, John is now safe." Elizabeth said, laughing with glee.

"Wow, this sure is a relief. We should have checked the clock to see if there is another note. I'll do that right now." As he turned, Buddy barked several times from the kitchen.

"Better see what he wants. We can look later. Maybe Mom is coming home," she said.

Looking out the window, she saw it was exactly what had happened. The two went downstairs and let Buddy out of the back door to visit his designated place, so he could relieve himself. Mom walked around the cottage and came into the home through the kitchen.

"Hi, Mom, how was your day? We were thinking we'd let you decide what you'd like for supper, and we'll make it for you," Elizabeth said cheerfully.

"I have had a good day, thank you. I would love hamburgers and a salad for supper. We have the premade meat patties in the freezer and, while you're thawing them, I'll go upstairs and change. Are you sure you're up to it, you look a little tired? Did you have a hard day at school, dear?"

"I just had a hard time sleeping last night, but I'll be all right. I'll go to bed early and catch up on my rest," Elizabeth explained.

"All right, dear."

When their mother was upstairs, Matthew came in and helped get things ready. The table was set and the meat defrosted. While he cooked the burgers, the buns were thawed, and the salad was prepared. By the time Mom walked back into the kitchen, supper was ready. Later in the living room, Elizabeth chatted with her mother while Matthew went out into the shed to see if there was anything new to discover.

In a corner where there had been little reason to poke around, he saw an oddly shaped box underneath an old damaged table. Being under a torn sheet, the box had been well hidden, hence the reason it had escaped earlier detection. Lifting the box out of its hiding place, Matthew cleaned off the dust that had accumulated over the years.

"Wow, I wonder what's in here," he said to himself.

He looked the detailed wooden box over. There were many fine carvings on it, depicting scenes from the past. On the top, there was a sailing ship on a stormy sea and what appeared to be thunderclouds in the sky. Turning the box over, he looked at the front, noticing the key hole. Unfortunately, there was no key with the box to unlock it.

Searching the area where he found it, he didn't discover a key. "So how do I open it without doing any damage and just whose box is it anyway?" he asked himself.

He shook it, trying to ascertain what the contents might be. There was only a soft sound emanating from the inside, indicating that there were probably papers within. Because it was getting dark and he didn't want his mother asking about it, he decided to put it back in its original place. When he and his sister were alone, they could tackle the problem together. Who knew? It may hold something interesting.

On his way back to the house, his thoughts went back to the other riddle they were trying to solve. The riddle, as far as he could figure out, indicated that the sun needed to shine through the two holes, thereby showing a location where the jewelry was hidden.

Trying to picture things in his mind, he visualized the holes when they were in line with each other. In order for the beam of light to go through both holes, the sun had to be in a certain position. The sun was always at different heights in the sky, depending on the season. This meant that they had to know what days of the year the sun would be in the correct position to shine through both holes at the same time.

Maybe this was why the men who performed the heist in the first place were meeting at a particular time so many years ago. He decided to look online to find out the date of the incident when the men were shot by the police.

Heading back into the house, he saw his mom and Elizabeth in the living room. Elizabeth looked like she was drifting off to sleep. It had been a long day, and he thought that he might as well go to bed and discuss his ideas with his sister the following day.

Matthew hit the pillow and was asleep in no time, not waking up until the next morning. Elizabeth was still in bed when he went to the kitchen, where he found his mother was already awake and had the coffee on. He sat at the table and had breakfast with her. Buddy was wait-ing by the back door and made his wishes known by whimpering a bit. Getting the hint, Matthew finished and headed toward the beach for a stroll along the shore.

Looking back at the cottage, he visualized the scene and how it looked when he and Elizabeth visited John. The entire area surrounding the cottage was quite differ-ent in John's time. The homes that were near this spot were now no longer there because of fires and other things that had happened through the years. The land the cottage sat on was quite large, and this made him wonder if his parents might one day sell off a portion of it. He hoped not.

Matthew and Buddy had a good time as they played with a ball that Matthew tossed here and there. Buddy sometimes had to run into the water to fetch the ball, but he loved that part. As the two were playing, Matthew heard a voice calling to him. Turning around to look, he noticed little Mrs. Johnston waving at him.

"Yes, Mrs. Johnston, what can I do for you?"

"I thought that I would let you know that my husband and I found my brother's diary. You said that you wanted to look at it," she said, speaking softly.

"Yes, ma'am, I will certainly do that. I'll check things out for you, but don't be surprised if I don't actually find anything. It will take a bit of time, so if you don't see me for a while, try not to worry about it, all right?"

"We don't expect you to find anything at all, dear, but it is nice of you to try, thank-you," she said, smiling at the lad.

Matthew took the diary and said goodbye, heading back to the cottage. He tucked the book into his waist-band inside his shirt. He thought that it would be best to keep it to himself and his sister. By the time he got home, Elizabeth had gotten up and had had her breakfast. There were some chores to do around the home and Matthew, Elizabeth, and Kate made short work of it.

Groceries needed to be bought, and Kate asked her children if they would like to come along. Matthew had other things he would have liked to do but felt that it may be a good thing to go along with his mother. With their dad gone away, it might be a nice gesture to spend a little time together, so off they all went.

"When is Dad coming home?" Elizabeth asked.

"Not till Thursday. I have to pick him up after supper, so we'll have to eat early that day," Kate replied.

The three walked into the grocery store, getting the things that they needed. There was a special on steaks, and enough were bought to have a barbecue on the week-end. Matthew even managed to sneak in a little extra dessert, and the shopping was completed. Once they were back home and things had been put away, Matthew and Elizabeth headed upstairs.

There were several things that he wanted to talk to his sister about. First thing was what to do about the murderer in the past. The second was the issue concerning the stones with the holes in them. The third was the diary that the little old lady gave him and, finally, the beautifully designed box that had piqued his interest in the shed.

When they got upstairs in her room, Matthew informed her of all the things that needed to be addressed. Both came to the conclusion that the lawyer had been temporarily taken care of, but they still didn't know how to stop the man. They would have to find a solution before they could go back to deal with him.

As far as finding the hidden treasure was concerned, Elizabeth went online to find when Barnes and his cohorts had met. It might give them an approximate time that the sun would be in the correct position to shine through both holes and show them where to search.

The two would have to study the diary before any plan of action could be taken, so that would have to wait. Finally, they came to the box. Since they were upstairs already, it would draw unwanted attention to them if they went out to get it at that time of night. It would have to wait until the following day.

The only thing they were able to do at that time, was to check online as to the time of year that the robbers had gotten into the shootout with the police. Elizabeth typed in the name Frank Barnes, and the story was one of the items that came up. When they read the story about the shootout, they found that the incident took place at the beginning of summer. After a bit of investigating, they read on the screen that it was commonly known as the summer solstice.

"Hey, I remember taking this in class. This is the longest day of the year, and the sun is at its highest position in the sky, the first day of summer. Barnes must have figured this out and used it to safeguard the location of the jewelry," Matthew said excitedly.

"It being early fall means that the sun won't be in the right position in the sky for eight months," she said.

"I wonder if we can find some other way to see through those holes."

"What about a telescope pushed up against the first hole? Do you think we'll be able to see through the second hole and see the spot that the sun would illuminate if it was in the proper place?" she asked.

"It might work, but I'm not sure," he replied thoughtfully.

"I've got it," she said excitedly, "how about shining a flashlight through the holes and see where it hits."

"Excellent idea, that may just work, I've got a fairly good one. We'll try it out tomorrow after school. We'll have to be fairly quick, though, because Mom will get suspicious if we're too long coming home. I'll go to my room and get it ready for the morning," he said as he left her room.

The next day after school, Matthew picked up Elizabeth and had to backtrack in order to get to the area overlooking Edgartown Great Pond. With flashlight in hand, the two ran as quickly as they could to where the two rocks were standing. They took out the plugs in the holes and cleaned up any debris that might restrict the light beam. Giving Elizabeth the light Matthew headed to the far side of the second stone.

"All right, turn on the light, and I'll see where it points," he told her.

"It is on, don't you see it?"

Matthew held his hand in front of the second opening where the light was shining through.

"I see the light hitting my hand but it's way too light outside right now to see where it hits after it comes out of the hole," he informed her.

"I guess we'll have to come back when it's dark," she suggested.

"Yeah, I think you're right. Darn it I thought we had a good idea."

"Say, Matthew, I know I've asked this before, sort of. Do you ever feel that we should be telling Mom and Dad about some of the things that we do? I know we can't without losing access to the clock, but I sometimes feel a little guilty about kind of lying to them. Do you know what I mean?"

"Yeah, I know what you're getting at, but I also know that our chance to make a difference will be gone if we do tell them. I realize that we've had a number of close calls and that we could have been killed a few times. But our friends John, Alice, and their Uncle Robert would have been gone if not for our help. Plus Albert would be dead too. I think we can still stop Harmon Williams, and maybe we can do something to help the Johnston's too. So I think we have no choice but to continue our efforts to change the past," he stated rather emphatically.

With this, they got back to the truck and went home as quickly as they could. When they pulled into the driveway, Matthew asked Elizabeth to keep their mother occupied while he got the box and brought it into the house.

He stowed it in his closet when he managed to slip upstairs. This would keep them occupied until they had the opportunity to get back to the lost treasure problem. Going down to the kitchen, he was informed that supper would be in half an hour and that Buddy needed to be let out. The two took a quick run to the beach and had some fun.

After the meal was done and their mother was sitting at the table, balancing her checkbook, Matthew and Elizabeth went upstairs to have a look at the locked box. Having cleaned it off, they studied the designs covering the unique item.

"I wonder why the owner left this in the storage shed. It's a nice piece and would look good on a dresser," she said.

"I'm curious as to how to get into it without damaging anything. My locking-picking talents are minimal, so maybe we can go online to find a way to open it."

Elizabeth found a site that helped people open things that they had lost a key for. Trying a few different ones, they found one that actually showed how to open a lock similar to the type the box had.

"I'll have to go to the garage and make a lever like the one shown. It's a little late now so I'll have to do it tomorrow after we get home," he said. "It doesn't look all that hard."

With this, they started reading the diary written by

Bobby Shoals. Most of the diary was filled with ordinary things. It wasn't until they reached the last number of pages that anything of interest had been written. Bobby had joined the navy and was stationed in Woods Hole for training in the year 1940. There was a war being waged in Europe, and Bobby felt he wanted to be ready in case the United States became involved.

"If we need to do some investigating, at least we won't have to travel far," Matthew said as she continued to read.

Bobby had finished his training and was put in a position at headquarters where he worked as a file clerk. He wrote in his diary that the job, although somewhat boring, did give him access to more and more sensitive information as he started to rise in the ranks. He had been hoping to be on a ship, but the education he had made him more valuable in office duties.

At that point, things began to become more interesting. He went out with some comrades during off-duty times, and they ended up frequenting a bar called Ships Ahoy. He soon made the acquaintance of two men who insisted on buying him drinks. They did this on several occasions and, over a period of time, managed, more and more, to steer him away from his friends.

"These men tell me that they want to show me their appreciation for my efforts serving our country. I believe that, on occasions when I drank too much, I may have let them know of my having access to sensitive information. The war going on in Europe is spreading. These men say to me that they fear it will, in the near future, spread to the point where the United States will become involved."

Bobby went on to describe a developing relationship that became more and more intense. "These men, I think, are Europeans with blond hair, slender builds, and have an air about them that is starting to give me cause for concern. They are increasingly putting pressure on me to divulge information on plans that the navy has for dealing with the ever-increasing turmoil overseas. Canada, our neighbor to the north, is already heavily involved in the fighting, and these men want me to check and see if the navy has access to the Canadian's war plans. I am starting to realize that these men have befriended me for the sole purpose of having me pass information to them. Allan Beaumont and Frederick Jolson, I believe are fictitious names. I have no way of checking up on them and am becoming increasingly concerned about the part they insist I play in their plans. I have to go to my superiors and inform them as to what is going on," Bobby wrote.

Bobby went on to describe the two suspicious individuals and tried to investigate them, in the hopes that it would lead him to their true identities. As more time passed, he described the ever-increasing pressure being put on him, and he was, by then, thinking that it was time to involve his commanding officer.

Plans for a rendezvous with Allan and Frederick were made, and he intended to follow them afterward in order to discover where they went so he had something concrete to give his lieutenant when he reported the incident. Bobby was to meet with the men that coming Saturday and described his feelings of nervousness in the diary. He expressed his doubts about the wisdom of the move but felt it was too late to alter his plans. He didn't say where the meeting was to take place though.

"Maybe I should see the lieutenant before Saturday. I'll think it over between now and then." Bobby wrote.

"This is the end of the diary. I'll bet the meeting went badly. Otherwise, there would be more written," Elizabeth said.

"I think you're right. The old couple said that there was an investigation by the authorities but nothing was found. The police never located the men and, when they questioned Bobby's friends, they claimed that the boy had pulled away from them months ago. In the end, the authorities hit a dead end, and the investigation came to a close," he informed her.

"Just what do you propose we do next?"

"We can check online to see if there is any other information to be found that may have turned up later. Type in the name Bobby Shoals and see what comes up," he suggested.

They found there was a story about the disappearance of the young man. It said that there were no clues as to his whereabouts, even though his sister Martha believed he had met with foul play. She informed the authorities that Bobby had been under duress the last time she saw him but didn't know why. A search had been undertaken, but no clue had been found as to what had happened to the young man.

"I think that we will have to put this on hold for now. We still haven't figured out what to do about the lawyer or the hidden jewelry. I'll see what I can think of to solve those two problems during the rest of the week, and I'll make the little tool to open the box when I get home from school tomorrow. I'm getting tired. I think I'll go to bed now," he said as he yawned.

As he lay in bed, he thought over the situation that John was facing and how they could stop Harmon. He was a very dangerous man, and if Sam hadn't been there to interfere, John would have been severely hurt and maybe even killed. Matthew had no doubts that the lawyer would have found out about the clock. It was even then still a real possibility that he could still find out. After all, he broke into John's home once. What was to stop him from doing it again?

Matthew felt that it was a really good plan to have

Danny pay the lawyer a visit and ask him about the break-in. It may well have saved John's life. That, of course, wouldn't stop the man for too long. Matthew made a mental note to check online again to see if anything new had developed as far as the child abductions were concerned.

If Harmon were to find out about the clock and how to operate it, disaster would strike. There would then be absolutely no way of catching the man. The lawyer would move it and probably disappear to a new locale, changing his name, and he would then be home free to do as he pleased, where and when it suited his desires.

The direction of his thoughts caused Matthew a restless night's sleep. He woke the next morning a little the worse for wear. On their way to school, Elizabeth asked him if he was all right.

"I had a hard time sleeping last night. I was thinking about the lawyer and John."

He proceeded to explain his reasoning to her and, by the time he was finished, she too felt the pressure to find a solution to this dilemma soon.

"Do you have any idea of how to stop him? We've tried a number of times, but so far nothing has worked," she said.

"I have to confess that I'm at a total loss as to a solution, short of killing him ourselves. I doubt that I could do that. It would be nice if he had a fatal accident, though," he said.

"Now that it has become so important to work out something, I think that if you let your subconscious mind work on the problem, you may come up with it if you relax your efforts. This has happened many times in the past for you."

"I don't know. The other times, I had some inkling in the back of my mind, and that helped me work it out.

This time there's just nothing there at all. I can't think of a single thing," he said, obviously distressed.

He had been troubled all day at school. The two siblings had gone back in time and, when the police were warned about the impending abduction of a child, their interference had actually helped the criminal. They thought that they could plant evidence in the lawyer's house or break-in at an earlier time than they had already done to see if something incriminating could be found. Thinking it over, he didn't like that idea at all. The man was far too wary and too dangerous to fool with directly. Another method would have to be found. If only Danny Monroe could have been brought into their confidence, it would simplify things immensely.

On the way home, Matthew mentioned the last idea to Elizabeth.

"I don't like that idea at all, Matthew. If Danny knows about the clock, and I don't know how we could tell him everything else and leave the clock out, this whole thing will blow up in our faces. In the end, we will, one way or another, lose the clock and I, for one don't want to risk it."

"I guess you're right, I'm just grasping at straws."

"I'm sure you'll come up with something," Elizabeth said, patting him on the back.

At home, she went into the house as he headed for the garage. Taking a used hacksaw blade, he cut it in two and clamped them in the vise. He ground the strips of metal into the shape he saw online. He knew he would have to make a few modifications to them so he'd bring the file and a hard sharpening stone along with a pair of vise grips when he worked the lock. As he was working, he remembered that he should check the clock to see if John had left any notes to keep them abreast of any new developments.

By the time he was ready to try out the lock picking tools, it was time for supper, so he stuck them in his pocket and carried the other tools in his hand. He walked toward the cottage on the gravel driveway, looking up at the three dormers. Studying the one that he covered on the inside, he saw exactly what he wanted others to see if they looked up. He passed the lilac bushes along the side of the building and continued on to the rear entrance of the kitchen.

"What are you doing with the tools Matt?" Mom asked.

"Oh, there's something I need to fix," he said, caught off guard.

"Just what is it you need to fix?"

Elizabeth, seeing her brother caught unawares, jumped in to help. "He's just going to fix my desk drawer that has been sticking. Thanks for helping me out, Matt."

"Uh, no problem," he said, going quickly upstairs.

This hadn't been the first time she had bailed him out when he had been caught off guard with his mouth hanging open. He had marveled many a time at how quick her mind was.

"Supper will be in fifteen minutes, Matthew," his mother called after him.

"All right, Mom," he shouted back as he reached the top of the stairway.

Going straight to the box that he had taken to his room, he started on the lock. He fiddled with it for a few minutes as he mumbled to himself. "It looked a lot easier online than it is."

The trouble was that the tool had been a little too wide, so he clamped it in the vise grips and slowly used the stone to take some of the metal off. Removing the pliers, he tried it again and was rewarded when he felt the mechanism move a bit. Adjusting the tool slightly and getting a better grip, he continued twisting the tool. A little jiggling and the lock opened the rest of the way.

"Yes, this is great, who would have thought that it would be so easy?" he said as he smiled to himself.

Taking the tool out of the slot, he put things away and lifted the lid. He knew that he should wait for his sister because this was as important to her as it was to him, so he closed the lid again without looking inside. Sliding the box under his bed, he went to the bathroom to wash up and then headed down for supper.

"Did you get it fixed?" Elizabeth asked.

"Yes, I did, I'll show you after we eat," he answered.

She gave him a look, and he knew instinctively that she was asking if he opened the box and looked inside. When he carefully shook his head no, she smiled with relief.

The evening meal was done and the day's events discussed. The youngsters went upstairs, claiming to have homework to do. They did have some to do, but it would be done in no time. Entering his room, Matthew reached under the bed for the box just as Elizabeth entered. Placing it on the bed and with a flourish of hand movements, he lifted the lid. "Aw, what the heck is all this stuff? These look like a bunch of letters," he said, obviously disappointed.

"They could be important letters, you know."

They each took a few and, after opening them, they started to read. Matthew groaned as he went from one to the next.

"These are love letters that John wrote way back when. Why would he write these? He never got married, did he?" he asked.

"No, I don't believe he ever did. Maybe if we read them all, we'll find out why."

Matthew looked through the rest of the contents and

found nothing of interest, so she took the box to her room, and he started his homework. He closed his door, got to the task at hand, and was soon finished. After washing up for bed, he went downstairs, gave his mother a hug, and said goodnight.

Lying on his bed, he thought about solutions to the situation with the lawyer. He wondered if maybe they could discover something with which to incriminate him. Some evidence they could plant somewhere and then send an alert to the police. As a smile crossed his face, he made up his mind to run it by Elizabeth in the morning and see what she thought. Once the plan was made, sleep came to him.

On the way to school, the idea was put to Elizabeth, who mulled it over for a time.

Once he explained exactly what it was that he had proposed to do, a horrified look appeared on her face. "There is no way that I can possibly do it. You and John will have to be the ones. It's already making me ill just thinking about it."

"I know what you mean. It will be difficult for me, too, and I'm not sure I'll be able to handle it either."

The rest of the ride took place in silence as each thought about the magnitude of the task.

Chapter 48

Harmon wondered again for the umpteenth time why he had confronted the baker and beaten him up. It would have been so much wiser to have followed him, found out where he lived, and dealt with him there. He started to talk out loud to himself, muttering angrily.

"Now the police know about me, and that's the last thing I wanted to have happen. If that stupid baker disappears now, I'll be the first one they suspect. I'd like to have one of the boys from the mainland keep an eye on him, but even that may backfire on me. Damn, I should learn to keep my temper under control."

Looking at his appointment schedule, he saw that it was almost time for his next client to come. He settled himself down and took a deep breath, trying to relax. He was sure he would come up with an idea as to how the fool could be taken care of.

He knew that the man suspected him of foul play, and Harmon was desperate to find out just how much he knew.

Harmon wondered if the baker had been involved with

those two kids on the bicycles. The ones he tried to run off the road all that time ago.

He knew from past experience that things like that were in one way or another tied together, and he had to find out how. He also knew that his freedom depended on it. Maybe he should just have moved across the country, change his name, and start a new life. That was the simplest solution, but he really hated to be ousted by a bunch people he felt were totally inferior to him. Maybe he could take care of the man, make it look like an accident, and get this information at the same time. He'd have to have an ironclad alibi though, one that would completely exonerate him.

Since the encounter with the baker, Harmon had not spotted anyone watching his home. He had spent many hours with the binoculars up to his eyes and now felt safer, at least in that respect.

Chapter 49

Thank goodness for Matthew and Elizabeth," John muttered. "How they came up with the idea to have Danny visit the lawyer and let him know that he is known to the police has been a stroke of genius. Even Sam was impressed with the ploy."

John found that he had been talking to himself more and more lately. It certainly had to be an effect of the strain he was under. This had caused him to overbake some cookies and bread. Some of the customers had asked about the burnt smell in his store. So far he had been able to find an excuse, but it was getting to be an all too common occurrence, and he had to get a grip on himself.

Deep down, John knew that the episode with that murdering man was not over. He was constantly looking over his shoulder and was afraid to spend the night alone in the cottage. He had slept over at Alice and Sam's home, but that had only postponed the inevitable. Another concern was the fact that his home had already been broken into and, if it happened again, he was afraid that the clock would be discovered.

He had taken great care to prevent that from happening, but he couldn't seal it up completely or Matthew and Elizabeth wouldn't be able to get out of the room when they came again.

Even though the panel covering the dials on the clock was always closed, the simple fact that the room was hidden and so well protected against discovery showed the importance of the clock. That alone would be an indication to Harmon Williams that the clock was not ordinary and may be worth closer inspection.

John decided then and there to write another note to his friends, explaining his fears, and leave it in the clock. He thought he could change all this by using the clock himself to go to another time. He would do this, but was desperately afraid because of what had happened once already, but then again, would it really matter?

"Why didn't I listen when they told me to stay away from that man?"

Chapter 50

That evening, on a whim, Matthew checked the clock to see if there had been a note left by John. He was almost pleased when he saw the note hidden in the clock, almost.

He knew that John was in a predicament and was writing because he had a problem.

Closing up the clock and checking that the panel was closed up tight, Matthew locked the clock room door inside the closet.

"I found a letter from John in the clock," he said once he knew they were alone.

"I hope it's not bad news. Read it, Matt."

This he did, and, when he was finished, they were aware of just how frightened John had been.

"We have to follow through with the idea I had. I haven't come up with any alternate plans unless you've got an idea?" he asked.

"I can't think of anything else, short of killing the man, and neither one of us wants to do that. So I think we're stuck with doing what you suggested."

"You mean I'm stuck with it," he stated.

"Sorry, Matt, I'm just too squeamish to do it," she said, shuttering a bit at the thought.

Many thoughts went through his head, but he liked very few of them. Unless he could come up with another plan soon, they will have to follow through with the one at hand.

"Do you think we should go back and see John before collecting the item we need or just get on with it?" he asked.

"I would like to just get it over with. We know from the internet where each of the bodies is discovered. How do we decide which one to use?"

"I think we should try it with one of the first ones. There is no point in letting any more die than necessary. What do you think?" he asked his sister.

"Yeah, you're right, when do you want to go?"

"Mom is picking up Dad on Thursday after supper, why don't we plan to do it then?" he suggested.

The plans were made and dates written down. They both realized that a trip back to see John was necessary. His help was needed getting to the hiding place and then getting to the lawyer's home. It all, of course, had to be done at night and timing would be fairly important. If something were to go wrong, there could quite possibly be dire consequences.

The time slipped by far too quickly for the pair, with each attempting to come up with some other plan. Unfortunately, neither one did, so the original one had to be it.

Thursday came and, as their mother left, she asked if either of them wanted to come along to pick up their father. They both claimed to have a lot of homework and said that, although they would like to, the schoolwork had to be done.

As Kate drove away, they quickly got the items al-

ready stored in a canvas bag and headed for the clock
room.

Chapter 51

The two siblings appeared in John's home shortly after the disappearance of the Yvonne Routar, the third victim. Circumstances didn't allow the pair to come any earlier than that. With previous trips already having been made, they had to be careful not to go to the same time in history twice.

Calling down to see if John was there, they were rewarded by an answering voice. Everything was explained to John about why they had come at that particular time, everything except the part about John's predicament with the lawyer. Both felt it unnecessary to inform John of that because, if they were successful in that particular escapade they were there for, the future problem more than likely wouldn't happen.

John informed them that he did have an engagement that evening, but because of the severity of the situation, he would cancel it. The two let him know that they were there for only one hour as they had not known if they would catch John at home. When they went back to their own time, the clock would be reset, and they would come back as soon as possible.

John was given the details of where they needed to go and what tools would be needed.

The time came and went, and they reappeared an hour later. The three got into John's Tin Lizzie. None of them were eager about that part of the trip but realized they had little choice.

The trip took almost an hour and had forced them to drive along some very narrow ill-kept roads. The gravel clinked on the inside of the fenders, causing them to drive slowly. By the time they got to their destination, it was pitch dark. The lights on the car were nothing like the ones on modern vehicles and caused them much concern about whether or not they would even make it there.

Matthew had a modern flashlight with new batteries and lit the way to the burial site. Elizabeth stayed in the car, unable to bring herself to view the scene. The two found the body of Yvonne and were almost physically sick when they had to touch her in order to get what they needed. They got back to the car in less than thirty-five minutes, and it was obvious that both were visibly shaken by the experience.

The trip back to Edgartown had been made in silence as none of them was in a talkative mood. John parked the car on a street well away from Harmon's home. They were all dressed in dark clothes and made as little noise as possible on their way to the murderer's car on School Street. There was a garage on the property, but because it had been warm, the vehicle had been left in the driveway. Because of nerves, exertion, and the warm temperature, both Matthew and John had worked up a sweat.

The trunk was found to be unlocked and opened with only a slight squeak.

Matthew shone the light into the trunk for only a second to find the best place to hide the sweater that had been removed from little Yvonne. Seeing the bloody sweater caused Elizabeth to exude a soft sob.

The job was quickly done, and, after the trunk lid had been pushed closed, the trio was on their way back to John's home in no time. This had been a very somber evening, and they were all glad it was over. John would call the police station first thing in the morning from a call box. He would inform them of the contents of a certain lawyer's car trunk, saying he had glimpsed it as he had walked past, when the man had opened it. No, he won't give his name for fear of retribution.

Chapter 52

By the time Mathew and Elizabeth got home, they were absolutely exhausted. It had been a long four-hour trip, plus the hour before when they had informed John of their plans. Both hit the sack before their parents had gotten home at nine o'clock. Leonard and Kate were surprised to find that their children were already asleep when they got into the house.

"They didn't seem that tired when I left to pick you up. Maybe they had a hard time with their homework." Kate giggled a little at that.

They went to the living room to chat for a while before turning in themselves. Plans for the future were discussed, and Buddy lay on the floor in front of the crackling fire. Life in this new home was pleasant, indeed, and the parents felt they had made a good decision when they had moved the family there.

"I'm glad that the kids made the adjustment so nicely. Matthew is doing really well in school, and Elizabeth seems very happy too," Kate said to her husband.

"I am a bit curious as to why neither of them has been dating yet. I thought that this would have happened in fairly short order. Especially since Matthew has a mode of transportation."

"They seem to have something else that has kept them fairly occupied, ever since the summer when we came here for a vacation. They keep this to themselves but don't appear to be getting into any trouble, so I haven't bothered them about it," she explained.

"I know what you mean. They always seem to be up to something, but it hasn't had any adverse effects on anything, so I guess it must be pretty harmless. They'll probably tell us when they're ready. Besides, I feel we're really lucky. A lot of people we know are having nothing but trouble with their teenagers. The booze and the drugs are creating so many problems for them that they can hardly cope with it. A few have daughters who are pregnant, and they just don't know how to handle it. I guess we should count ourselves fortunate that our kids are as good as they are," he said, smiling.

The next morning, everyone was at the kitchen table, and Leonard filled the family in about the new developments that occurred during his time away. The business was going well and, although he had to go on work-related trips, he was managing to keep them to a minimum. That, in itself, was a cause for celebration, and plans were made to go out to dinner with the whole family to an Italian restaurant the next Saturday evening. Everyone was looking forward to that.

On the way to school, Elizabeth remembered that they hadn't checked online to see if the child murderer had been arrested and put in prison. Neither had any doubts about that being the case, but it was always nice to have actual confirmation. They would check as soon as they got home.

Later that afternoon, with the day over and the drive home completed, they ran up the stairs and to Elizabeth's room. The computer was started, and the information they were looking for came up on the screen.

Chapter 53

Harmon woke up in the morning a little earlier than usual. After a quick bite to eat, he headed to his car in order to run a few errands on the main-land. There were contracts to deliver and a few items to pick up. He put his briefcase in the back seat and, after starting the car drove away. He went around the corner just as two police cars turned around the corner coming from the main road in town. They stopped in front of Harmon Williams home, quickly got, out and surrounded the lawyer's home.

An officer went to the front door and knocked rather loudly. There had only been a housekeeper there to open the door and, when asked about the man's whereabouts, she informed them that he had already left for the day. No, she didn't know where he had gone. She was only here for a few hours a week to clean.

The sergeant was consulted and, although the police would like to enter the home and do a search, they had no warrant. The only thing they did have was a telephone call made anonymously by some unknown person accus-ing the lawyer of a deed that hadn't even been explained properly. The caller just said to check the man's car and all would be revealed.

"This is all most likely just a prank, but we'll leave an officer here in case he returns, and then we'll decide how to proceed," the sergeant had explained to his men.

Harmon, of course, had been totally unaware of the situation. At that point in his life, he didn't even know about John, Matthew, or Elizabeth, aside from seeing them in the bushes once. That was one thing that had worked in favor of the time travelers.

Harmon got on the ferry to the mainland and relaxed at the railing, watching the water go by.

After he landed, he drove to the place of his first meeting. The contracts were delivered, and he was on his way to pick up a parcel that contained a rare vase he had managed to procure. He decided that the safest place for it was in the trunk.

As he reached down to open it, he noticed a smudge that should not have been there. Being fastidious, he knew he did not leave the mark himself.

"Why is this here? I know I didn't put it there. It looks like someone was in the trunk, and that's where their hand was placed too close the lid," he mumbled, quickly looking around to make sure he wasn't heard.

He opened the trunk and looked around inside. In the far back portion of the flat area, he saw something that was not supposed to be there. His blood ran cold as he studied the item in his trunk. He knew for a fact that he did not leave the dead child's sweater in it. Someone who knew what he had done had placed the piece of clothing in his trunk to incriminate him.

"How the hell did this happen? Who is the son of a bitch that has found me out? Why wouldn't they blackmail me or call the cops? Maybe this is a prelude to letting me know that I've been found out and the blackmail is about to begin," he thought. "I have to get rid of this right now."

After finding a suitable place to dispose of the sweater, he headed back home. The vase was in the trunk, but for once it had been purchased honestly and so wouldn't cause him any trouble.

"I have to get rid of everything at home immediately. I can't leave a trace of anything that can be used as evidence against me. How the hell could this have happened? I'm the most careful person in the world, so what went wrong?"

He banged the steering wheel several times because he was almost beside himself with worry and frustration. He drove to the ferry and then toward his home, fretting all the way. When he got there, he was greeted by a police officer who asked him to remain in the vehicle after he blocked the car from any escape.

"What the hell is this all about officer?" Harmon asked, somewhat politely.

"My superior wishes to ask you a few questions, sir, he will be here momentarily."

At that point, another police car pulled up. A sergeant got out and made a request that he open his trunk just to clear up a matter. Harmon thought about refusing and asking for a warrant but knew the evidence the police expected to find wasn't there, so he did as he was asked.

The police searched the trunk thoroughly and found nothing of interest except the vase. Harmon produced a receipt for it, and all was well.

"Just what were you expecting to find, Sergeant?" Harmon asked.

"Obviously this has been nothing but a prank. Thank you for your co-operation, Mister Williams."

With this, the police left to have a meeting back at headquarters. This meeting was not a pleasant one.

"What a stroke of luck that I found the sweater myself. I'd be in jail right now if I hadn't. So the plan was to have me arrested and not to blackmail me. How do I find out who is attempting to implicate me in these murders? There has to be a way," Harmon told himself.

Chapter 54

On the screen, there were a few changes but not what the siblings were expecting. They thought they would see the arrest of a prominent attorney had taken place. Instead, there had been nothing at all about it.

"It's obvious that something went wrong, again. Another setback with this guy. How on earth can this thing be resolved? I'm out of ideas, I thought for sure this was going to fix things, but nothing seems to be going our way," Matthew stated, frustrated at this turn of events.

"I wonder if we can find out what happened. The police were alerted the first time, but it didn't work because we messed that up. Breaking into his place hasn't done any good. Checking in on some of the funerals almost got us killed. John almost got his, too. Planting evidence was a waste of time, and everything we've come up with has gotten us absolutely nowhere. We had the same trouble during our summer vacation, trying to save John and Alice."

"I think we have to tackle the whole thing in a different way. What way that is, I haven't a clue at this moment, but there has to be a way to get the job done," Matthew said, throwing his hands into the air.

"Too bad one of his crooked accomplices doesn't get into an argument with him and shoot him."

"That would be nice, but they made a lot of money bootlegging booze together, so the odds of that happening are slim," he said in return.

"So the only option open to us is to wait and, hopefully, we'll be able to find another solution."

Matthew nodded and headed to his room. Elizabeth continued the search for information on Harmon and any associates she could find on the internet. It wasn't long before they were called down to help with dinner. Matthew was asked to take Buddy for a quick walk, which he did.

As he walked along the shoreline, a gentle breeze ruffled his hair. The season was still nice and warm, although that would soon change. He watched as a power boat made its way across the water, far from shore. It met with another boat going in the opposite direction, and the two stayed there for a short time. Whatever the reason they met was soon over and, after the engine backfired, one of the boats headed back in the same direction it came from. The boat left behind made no move while Matthew was still on the shore watching.

Being time for supper, the boy and his dog walked back to the cottage. When they got there, the meal was ready. The group enjoyed the time together and chatted about the day's events. Matthew and his father made plans to finish a project in the garage as well as the mudroom the next morning. Seeing as it would be Saturday, it was decided that the girls would go and do the grocery shopping.

Upstairs, Elizabeth informed Matthew that she had read all the letters they found in the locked box. "It turns out that John was very taken by a girl named Jennifer. He met her while she was vacationing at Mariner's Lodge in 1921. John and Jennifer communicated by letters for quite some time, and he even went to see her on several occasions. It looks like John was about to propose to her when she met someone else. This broke John's heart, and he never wrote another letter to her. He also never got involved with anyone again."

"I wonder why he kept the letters?" he asked.

"They were probably the only reminders for him of when he was truly happy. I feel very sorry for John. If and when this is all rectified, the lawyer thing I mean, I'd like to visit John after he loses Jennifer. Didn't John mention another girl he met at the resort quite a time before he met Jennifer? I guess that one went nowhere too. If we go back at the right time, seeing the two of us might help turn things around for him, what do you think?" she asked, turning her head slightly as she looked at her brother, hoping he thought it was a good idea too.

Sensing that, he agreed that it would be a nice thing to do. He saw the kindness in her eyes as she teared up, thinking about their friend in the past.

"So when do you want to go to the rocks and shine the flashlight through them, unless you want to wait till next summer?" Matthew asked, changing the subject.

"I think Saturday evening is out because we're going out for supper with Mom and Dad and, during the day, you're working with Dad. What about tonight, it's Friday, we don't have to get up early, and we really had a good sleep last night, despite the fact that it was all for nothing. How do we go out without drawing Mom and Dad's attention?" she inquired.

"We'll go out right now and say we're going to meet some friends from school for a few hours."

"That will work, I guess. I still hate having to lie all

the time, but I guess we don't have much choice. If we do find the jewelry, we could always save a piece for Mom," she said, actually thinking about it.

"I doubt that's a good idea. If she ever had it appraised, the jeweler might recognize the value, and then we'd have some real explaining to do."

"Hmmm," he replied, not really sure about the decision.

With the good flashlight in a bag, the two let their parents know they were going out to see some friends and would be back in about around three hours.

"Finally, they're going to hang out with friends. I thought they were giving up the social life for a while there," Leonard said, actually looking a bit relieved.

The two siblings drove to the ferry and, once they landed, continued the drive to the place of the stones. The trek on foot was somewhat slower in the dark, and Matthew almost fell a few times, pointing the light more for his sister to follow than himself. Finally, they reached the rise where the rocks were standing. With Elizabeth shining the light, he removed the stone plugs and cleared the hole in the first boulder.

"Darn it, why didn't I bring two flashlights. I could use one to see where I'm going while you shine that one through the holes in the rocks," Matthew said, feeling a bit dumb.

"You walk, and I'll shine the light for you so you can see. Go to where you can see where the light is going to hit, and we'll do this one step at a time."

Matthew shouted to her when he got to where he needed to be. "All right, shine the light through the rock while I clear out the hole in the second stone." He worked for a minute and let her know that he was ready to see where the light hit. "Can you tighten up the beam of light by twisting the front end of the flashlight?" he called out.

"I'll try to get it to shine narrower. Here, this is as tight as it will go. How is it now? Can you see what the light is shining on?" she asked.

"Wiggle it around a little, slowly. I don't think the light is hitting the hole in this rock dead on. Either that or it's just not working because the light coming out the backside of this hole is diffusing before it gets to the place it's supposed to illuminate."

"Is this helping at all?" she asked, shifting the flashlight back and forth.

"Nope, the light just isn't concentrated enough. So, now what?" he asked, just a little perplexed.

Elizabeth took the light and used it to walk over to the rock where Matthew was standing.

"How about if I shine the light through the hole in the second rock only, Matt? It may give us an idea of the general area we need to look," Elizabeth suggested.

"Good thinking," he said, pleased with the idea.

She climbed up the second rock which was somewhat higher than the first. She slipped and scraped her shin a little. "Ouch, that hurt."

Reaching up the rest of the way, she shone the light through the hole, and Matthew looked where it hit the slope going back up on the far side of the gully in front of them. The light, only having to go through the hole in one rock, spread quite wide before it hit the lower end of the hillside across the gully.

There was a large area that the light illuminated. The cave entrance was in the lit-up zone.

"Come here, Elizabeth."

She handed him the light, and he shone it on the far slope showing her the cave opening.

"I'm not sure, but I think that the sunlight is so much brighter than this flashlight and when it's in the proper position, the beam of light shines directly into the cave. If we are in the cave when the sun shines through the two holes, it will be easier to see where it hits," he explained excitedly. "It makes sense that the treasure would be hidden in the cave. Everything would be too well lit to see where the beam of sunshine hit. The inside of the cave is bound to be considerably darker, so the beam would be at least somewhat visible."

"Yeah, now all we have to do is wait till next year, right?"

"I really don't like the idea of having to wait until next summer to find the jewelry," he said, a little letdown.

"I don't see where we have any choice, do you?"

He nodded his head in agreement and suggested that they go home. The ride back was not as jubilant as they had hoped for. Both did realize that this didn't mean that they had been defeated either. The treasure was still out there and, with any luck, it would be in the cave somewhere.

"Maybe we can come back during the day sometime and look around inside the cave. I don't know how big the interior is but we might just stumble onto something while we're in there," Elizabeth said, sounding more optimistic than she felt.

"I guess so. It just might yield some results, you never know. We've gotten this far, so why wait till next year before doing something," he said. "The treasure, I'm sure, is—or—was really important to the people who lost it, but it's not going anywhere and can wait a bit longer."

"I read that it caused huge problems for the family who owned the collection. They fell on hard times because of the theft. The museum was held accountable for the loss, and there was a scandal that cost several people their jobs."

As they lay in their beds, trying to fall asleep, each had different thoughts running through their heads. Elizabeth feared that the lawyer was unstoppable and thought that John would pay a high price for the mistake he had made.

Matthew knew there was a way to take care of the murderous person who had, up to now, evaded all their efforts to bring him to justice. The problem was in finding that solution. He realized that it had been a mistake to tell old Mrs. Johnston that he would look into the disappearance of her brother so long ago. How could they delve into that when they were so overloaded with the other two challenges?

Matthew woke in the morning to his father calling out to him.

"Hey, sleepy head, you want to get up and start the projects sometime before lunch?" he said, chuckling.

"Ha, ha, very funny, Dad, I'll be right down."

When father and son finished eating breakfast, they headed toward the garage. The tools were brought out, and they put the workbench back inside and refastened it to the wall. With this done, they started building the shelves along the back wall. The garage was deeper than average, so this allowed a normal vehicle to park inside with plenty of room left over, front and back.

"Too bad the garage wasn't built a little bit wider. We could get both our vehicles in here then," Matthew said.

"Yes, that would be nice, but, unfortunately, the style of the building won't allow us to expand it at a reasonable cost."

The team worked very well together, and the jobs in the garage and the mudroom were completed before lunch. Having a little extra time, they did an oil change on the car when Kate got home, even though the engine had been hot. The three-ton floor jack rolled easily on the new concrete, and the creeper helped, making the job much nicer. The two washed their hands with mechanics hand cleaner in the garage. The sink in the newly constructed outdoor cleanup area finished the job and would help keep the ones in the cottage from getting filthy.

Family time was always pleasant, and even Buddy got a word in here and there during lunch.

Matthew, Elizabeth, and Buddy ended up going for a walk along the beach. Because Matthew didn't want to disappoint the old folks with his lack of effort or results so far, they headed away from where the elderly couple lived.

"Did you hear the news, Matthew, about the body found in a boat floating offshore not far from here?"

"No, Dad and I were in the garage all morning."

"When Mom and I were in town, everyone was talking about it. There isn't a lot of information at this point, but it looks like there was a rendezvous out on the open water. The authorities suspect it may have been a drug-related incident. People were saying that this kind of thing has happened before. Someone buys a large shipment of drugs, and when the time for the exchange comes, one gets greedy and kills the other. This way the killer gets to keep the money and the drugs."

Matthew frowned. "Was the dead person shot?"

"I think he was, why do you ask?"

He relayed the story about what he saw yesterday when he and Buddy were walking along the beach. Both thought that he may well have witnessed the murder. Being so far away, no details were observed, so there was no point in telling the police about it.

Buddy's antics soon took their thoughts away from the event and games were the highlight of their time along the water's edge.

They had fun for almost an hour when Matthew asked, "Have you done any more research on the lawyer?"

"I have. I found some stories that hint at a connection

between Edwin Fitzpatrick and Harmon for several years, starting somewhere around nineteen twelve. It sounds like they were smuggling goods and booze into the harbor for a long time. We already knew about the involvement in the nineteen twenties, but it started much, much earlier."

"So, Harmon has been involved in criminal activities of various types and has gotten away with it all that time," he said thoughtfully. "Good work, sis."

By the time their walk was finished, it was mid-afternoon. When they got back to the cottage, Kate let them know that they would be leaving at five o'clock in order to get to the restaurant in time for the reservations. Elizabeth and Matthew went upstairs to do a little homework, just to get it out of the way.

When Matthew was done, he lay on the bed and mulled over ideas on how to handle the child killer. He knew that Harmon was an extremely dangerous and resourceful man. Whatever they tried had to be very carefully planned out. The consequences of another failure could easily become catastrophic. So far, they had been extremely lucky not to be hurt. He tried to put himself into the shoes of a parent who had had their child stolen and murdered. He felt that the mother and father would do almost anything to prevent it from happening.

The police had already been involved twice with no positive results, so that idea might as well be put aside for now. John, Matthew, and Elizabeth had attempted to deal with the situation and also failed many times. The only ones so far not brought into the equation had been the parents. He mulled it over and tossed it back and forth in his mind, trying to run through different scenarios.

He thought about it for a while but didn't come to any definite conclusions. Maybe he'd get Elizabeth's and possibly John's opinion on that line of thought. Looking at the clock, he realized that he should start getting ready for the meal out. The family hadn't been to this restaurant before, and his mouth began to water a bit at the thought of an authentic Italian spaghetti and meatballs dinner.

The ride was pleasant enough, but Buddy had been disappointed at being left at home, or so it seemed. They were shown to a table and seated. Kate ordered a glass of Malbec wine, and Leonard asked for a Corona. Matthew was asked what he would like as well as Elizabeth. Both had a large Pepsi. The menu was gone over, and it was decided on rather quickly by the youngsters and their parents. Leonard and Matthew had the spaghetti and meatballs, Kate had the lasagna, and Elizabeth had the ravioli with meat sauce. The garlic bread that came with the meal helped make it a fabulous dinner. It was enjoyed by all, and soon they were on their way back home.

Upstairs, Matthew relayed his thoughts on possibly involving the parents of one of the children about what would happen to their child. He thought that, if a mother or father of one of the earliest victims was made aware of the impending event, some precautions could be taken.

"I knew you'd come up with something. Which girl's parents are you going to warn? Do you really think this might help, and what do you think the parent will do? I think that's a good idea, Matthew, unless Harmon just takes another girl instead."

"I'm not sure yet how this will go. I'm hoping he'll be identified and arrested. I think we should start with the girl we think is his first victim, Cassandra Boothe. If we can stop that one, maybe we can have a surprise waiting for Harmon at that point or down the road," he said.

Elizabeth nodded. "I bet this jumping back and forth in time, seeing John at all sorts of different times, must be confusing the heck out of him."

"I'm sure it must, but we have no choice. We have to

stop this guy, one way or another. When do you think we'll be able to go?" Matthew asked.

"We'll have to see if Mom and Dad are planning anything tomorrow. If not, I'll try to get them out for a long walk along the beach. It's supposed to be nice weather. Monday a rainstorm is coming in. That may make it more imperative that they enjoy it while they can."

Elizabeth managed to persuade Leonard and Kate that a long walk with Buddy was in order. After they left, the two time travelers got ready for the trip back into the past. A note had been handwritten for Mr. and Mrs. Boothe, explaining what was going to happen. The time was set for one-hour duration several days before the two would need John to drive them into Edgartown. That way John would be able to arrange his free time and work it into his schedule. The clock was set, and the two disappeared from the room.

Chapter 55

J ohn, are you here?" Elizabeth called.

"I'm in the bedroom. Wait a minute, please. I'm not presentable."

Soon the circumstances of their visit were given to John and the preparations made. The two siblings disappeared a short time later and returned on the day the three had decided worked best for all involved.

The drive into town was uneventful, and the vehicle was parked not far from the Boothe's home. John carried the letter as he walked toward the house. There were children playing in the area and parents sitting on porches. The time was seven o'clock in the evening. Most people had already had their supper and were relaxing for a few hours.

On the sidewalk in front of the home was a white picket fence with Cassandra playing on the grass. Little did she know that her life would end horrifically in a short time unless something was done to change the situation.

Seeing John on the walk, she asked, "Hello, are you looking for someone?"

"Is your mother or father at home?" John asked in return.

"I'll get Mommy for you," she replied.

As soon as she went around the side of the house, John stuck the envelope in the fence by the latch so it would easily be seen and left very quickly. Matthew and Elizabeth peered from a safe vantage point and watched as the scene unfolded.

The lady came to the fence, looking around for the man who had spoken to her daughter. Not seeing anyone around, she noticed the letter, picked it up, and opened it. As she read the letter, the expression on her face turned from bewilderment to fear. Her gaze swept the neighborhood, and then she rushed inside the home with Cassandra, yelling for her husband.

John, Matthew, and Elizabeth made a beeline for the car and left as fast as they could. During the drive back, they discussed what they hoped would transpire in the next few days. It wasn't long before the siblings were back in their own time. Elizabeth went to the computer to see if they had met with success for a change.

Chapter 56

Elizabeth was just about to sit down when she heard Buddy bark near the back door of the cottage.

"Oh, well, I'm sure this will at least have stopped that abduction, if nothing else. I'll check later," she said to her brother.

The two were in the kitchen by the time Buddy and the parents reached the back door. There was still considerable time until supper, so Matthew said he wanted to study for a bit. Elizabeth, although tired from having been in the past for so long, sat at the table with her mother. Not interested in getting involved in a feminine conversation, Leonard headed to his office to catch up on a bit of estimating for an upcoming job.

Matthew couldn't wait for Elizabeth to come up. His curiosity had been piqued, and he just had to know if their last attempt had been a success or not. Sitting down in front of her computer he typed in the necessary request and studied the screen as he read the article.

"In an attempt to foil the abduction of his daughter, Manfred Boothe, husband of Susan Boothe, has been fatally stabbed. Cassandra Boothe has disappeared, and witnesses believe they saw the child with an unidentified man. All attempts to locate Cassandra have been unsuccessful. A massive search is being conducted. Further details will be provided as they surface."

Dumbstruck, Matthew realized that they had made things worse, not better. How could this have turned out so badly? He shut down the computer and almost felt like crying after he read a later article written when the body of Cassandra was discovered.

He intercepted Elizabeth coming up the stairs and told her they needed to go for a walk on the beach. When she questioned him as to why, he held his finger to his lips and walked out of the house. When the two were out of sight of their parents, he told her of his findings.

Elizabeth almost collapsed as she heard the news. Tears flowed down her cheeks as she sobbed at the turn of events. "Why did we try to stop that horrible man the way we did? I know it was the only solution we had, but why did it have to end this way?" she cried.

"I'm so sorry that I came up with the idea. I had no idea it would end this way. I can't think of any possible ways that we can fix things. We've tried everything we can to stop him. I think we've met our match. He is far too cunning for us to deal with, and we've run out of options."

Chapter 57

Harmon sat at his desk two days later and wondered. Had the girl's father actually been waiting just inside the back door, when he was about to grab the kid? Was it possible that he knew his daughter was going to be taken? No, that, of course, could not be. Only Harmon knew it was going to happen. The father would have had no way of knowing, and yet, there he was.

Harmon had no idea who could have possibly betrayed him, so he wondered if he was safe. He was determined to keep a wary eye on things and possibly make a few discreet inquiries to find out what the police knew about the guilty party. That hadn't been the first time he had committed this type of offense. The other bodies had been disposed of completely. He thought maybe he should go that route again, except for the fact that he would like to go to the funerals.

When he went to Cassandra's funeral, it had been like reliving the whole episode again. Seeing all the mourners sobbing the way they did had been extremely enjoyable. He had almost broken into a smile, but that, of course, would not do. Living in the general area, he had been able to attend the services and offer his sympathies to the grieving mother, another bonus. He would wait for a while before doing this thing again, but not too long.

Chapter 58

The time went by slowly for the brooding Matthew and Elizabeth. It got to the point where their parents asked if there was a problem they wished to discuss. This woke the siblings up to the fact that they had to move on. It had been two weeks since they read the details of their failed effort.

"I think we need to get our minds on something else. This isn't helping at all and is keeping us from any advancement as far as the other things we're working on is concerned. Let's focus on either the lost treasure or the disappearance of Bobby Shoals," Elizabeth said to her brother.

"You're right, of course. It's just been such a letdown, failing so badly. We've read the diary Bobby wrote, and there are a number of questions that come to mind. How hard did the authorities try to find the men he says befriended him? Did he actually have the authority to see the plans that those men wanted? They were obviously spies, so why weren't they on the military's radar? What actually happened to Bobby is the biggest and most important question."

"We've checked online to see what we could find, and there isn't much to help us. I think the only way to get information is to go back in time and find it ourselves," she stated.

"You're right again, except we have enough on our plate with Harmon, John, and the treasure. I really think we'll be taking on too much if we start investigating this too. I can't think of anything concrete at this point, but there is something in the recesses of my mind. It's something we said or thought of, but for the life of me, I can't fathom what it is. Maybe it's nothing at all and just another question with no answer. There have been too many of those lately," he said a little dejectedly.

"That only leaves the hiding place of the jewelry to come up with, any ideas as to how to overcome this obstacle?"

"Not so far, but I haven't really given it a lot of thought either. As far as I can see, the problem is that the sun isn't going to be in the right position to show us anything until next summer. We don't want to wait that long, and we can't make the time go by any faster unless we use the clock to jump ahead. I'm really afraid to do that. What if we run into each other or if we run into Mom and Dad when they know our future selves are somewhere else. It would open a can of worms I don't want to deal with."

"I see your point, why create more problems, we have enough already," she said.

"Let's put this on the backburner too, I'm sure we'll come up with something," he said as he walked out of her room and went down the stairs. He saw his father working on a project. "Hi, Dad, how's it going?"

"I'm doing really well, Matt. This home-based business is really coming together, much better than I had hoped it would."

Matthew sat on the edge of the desk and idly picked up a rather thick looking pen. Studying it, he saw one end had an opening for the writing part to come out of and, when he flipped it over to look at the other end, his father's voice stopped him from pressing the button in the middle of the pen.

"Don't push that button while you're looking at the end of the pen. That thing is a laser pointer and the light is so strong that it will damage your eyes. If you want to see it work, point it at the wall. I use it when I'm giving a talk, and I want to point out specific things on a wall screen."

Matthew did as he was told and was fascinated by the little contraption. He had seen these things before but hadn't had the opportunity to handle one. "This thing is cool, Dad, where did you get it?'

"I picked it up through an office supply firm. You can get other models at other outlets around any larger towns. Some of them are bigger and quite powerful. Those types don't have the pen in them because they use bigger batteries. They're really quite cheap, all things considered. I hope this one doesn't disappear on me," he said with a smile on his face.

"Who me? Would I do something like that?" Matt laughed as he walked away.

The wheels were turning in his head as he left the room and headed back to Elizabeth's bedroom. She was lying on the bed, almost falling asleep as he entered. Matthew explained his idea to her, and they were soon online looking for an item in particular. After a bit of hopping from one site to another, they found what they were looking for. Matthew wanted to make a phone call to the store and started to punch in the number when Elizabeth stopped him.

"Matthew, this is late Saturday afternoon. I'm sure the

store will be closing. Why don't you stop by on the way home from school Monday?"

"Oh yeah, that's a good idea, sis."

Kate called from downstairs. "It's almost time for supper. Could you come down and help set the table?"

Monday after school, Matthew stopped in at a store in Edgartown and looked over laser pointers. There were several types available. He tried to weigh the pros and cons and finally selected the one with the most intense beam and straight tubular body. It should do nicely for what he had in mind, and it really helped that it was on sale. He would have to be very careful when he used it and come up with a plan to safeguard himself against possible eye damage.

On the way home after picking up Elizabeth, he showed her the light and instructed her on its safe use. He demonstrated its abilities in the daylight and in the evening. The pair decided it would be in their best interest to keep this to themselves for the time being. There was no use in causing Mom and Dad any anxiety.

Later in the week, Matthew went to the place where the stones were and took a few quick measurements before heading out to pick up his sister. She had already been told that he was going to be late, so she occupied herself until he came for her.

He found her talking with a few classmates, and the two siblings headed for home.

It took a few days for Matthew to make a holder that was suitable for what he had in mind. When he had what he needed, he informed Elizabeth, and they made plans for the best time for them to attempt the experiment.

It was not until a week had gone by that they had the opportunity to try out their little device.

In the meantime, Matthew thought that he was getting close to finding one last solution for dealing with the child killer from the past. He explained to Elizabeth that it might be possible to create some dissension between Harmon and some of his associates. Matthew wasn't sure of how to go about it, at that point, but he felt they had run out of other options. He also told her that it could become dangerous for them and was unsure if they would require help from John and maybe even Sam.

At that moment, nothing concrete had been planned and, because of that, they would have to make several trips into the past in order to set things up. At least they should be able to create a viable plan of action.

Because of the risk of retaliation toward John from Harmon, both felt that that case took precedence over finding the jewelry. They made plans to start getting together a schedule of events that needed to take place and set up a timetable of sorts. Elizabeth started jotting down all the notes as they tried to organize themselves. Both became more nervous as the time came closer to the start of the reconnaissance.

Leonard and Kate had been asked to visit friends back in their old neighborhood. That would allow the youngsters the time they needed to implement their plans if the visit was timed properly. At least some things were starting to fall into place. Of course, if these things fell apart at the wrong moment, disaster could strike just as easily.

"When do you think that you'll be going to see your friends, Mom? Will it be during the week or on a weekend?" Elizabeth asked.

"We're thinking of leaving Thursday morning and coming back on Tuesday. Would you and Matthew like to take a few days off school and come with us? Elli and Richard would love to have you come along, and I know for a fact that Marita, Bill, and Maureen have missed you guys," she said.

"That would be nice, but I have an exam on Friday,"

she said quickly, wondering if maybe she had jumped on it just a little too fast.

"Oh, that's too bad, dear. I'm sure you will be missed. I'd ask Matthew, but I think it will be better if he's here with you."

Elizabeth told Matthew what was transpiring and both felt it to be a real stroke of luck. The absence would give them all the time they needed to deal with the problem or, it might just have dealt with them. Neither was unaware that the whole thing could turn out bad for John and themselves. They hadn't wanted to include John but felt that they had absolutely no choice.

As the days went by, the pair tried to ready themselves as much as they could. Matthew lay awake in bed every night, going over the plans in an attempt to refine them as much as he was able. Tools were prepared and checked over, and items necessary to the success of the mission were packed.

Mathew and Elizabeth studied everything they could on the internet. They looked for trends and lifestyles so they'd be able to fit in. Elizabeth took notes, copied down addresses, and literally compiled an itinerary of what needed to be done, when to do it, and what results were expected. It was going to have to be an all-or-nothing venture because everything that had been done up to then had failed so miserably.

It would probably be their last chance to take care of the lawyer because, in order to do what they intended, the three would-be detectives were going to be put in harm's way. Failure could quite possibly mean death or permanent injury.

As the time drew near, their nervousness was becoming apparent. Asked what was wrong, Elizabeth had to tell yet another lie. "Sorry, Mom, I'm just a little anxious about the exam. I shouldn't be, but you know how it is."

"Relax, dear, you usually do very well, once you sit down and start the test," Kate said gently.

"Thanks, Mom," Elizabeth said and gave her mother a lingering hug.

Elizabeth knew that all might not turn out well and actually wanted to express her true feelings but couldn't.

The day came when Leonard and Kate drove away. Matthew and Elizabeth were already on their way to school with neither looking forward to their upcoming adventure. The day went by very quickly, unlike times when they were looking forward to something.

Chapter 59

After a quick meal, they gathered the things required, set the dials on the clock, and were soon on their way. The first trip was for an hour only because John needed to be filled in on what had to be done. John had then only been about five or six years older than Matthew and Elizabeth. The memory of his encounter with the Dutchmen was still very fresh. On the second trip, the three went to Oak Bluffs and then on to Falmouth on the mainland.

Through the internet, Elizabeth had found out that Harmon and Edwin Fitzpatrick had had an import business together for several years before he murdered Cassandra and her father. The time the sleuths spent there had been far longer than most previous trips, in order that the surveillance would yield some positive results. The three got a room in town for a few days and started keeping an eye on the subjects.

Having found out where the headquarters for the import business was, they took turns keeping watch. What few people in this time period knew was that some of the imports were illegal alcohol and stolen property. Anything that the men could make money on was brought in. The year was 1913, and the month was August.

Harmon lived in a small home not far from the building that housed the business on the waterfront. Edwin lived near the wharf, but on the opposite side of Grand Avenue. A lot of boat and ship traffic went on in the waters there. This had probably been one of the reason's they chose the location. At night, the area was quite dark, and a person could stay hidden there very easily.

The three sleuths found a place to hide near a rear window on the backside of the building. There was a lot of scrub brush between the back of the building and a steep hillside. It hadn't been easy remaining there, but when Harmon and Edwin were away, John and Matthew cleared enough brush away to allow them to sit near a window in a low spot and still remain well hidden. Because of the undergrowth, no one ever went near the spot, making it ideal for them. The only thing they needed to keep in mind was to sit still, or the vegetation rubbing on their clothes and moving would give them away.

During the third day of eavesdropping, among other things, they learned that a big shipment of booze was coming in eight days and that the money would be brought in to pay for it two days in advance. Harmon did not like that way of doing business and made it plain that he didn't trust anyone with a large amount of cash. He and Edwin almost got into an argument over it.

"We don't have a safe here and bringing the money with us is inviting trouble. The revolvers we have are good against one or two people but, if there are more, we'll be in trouble," Harmon complained.

"Nobody is going to know that it's here, so stop your incessant worrying, will you?" Edwin returned angrily. "The money will be safe in the lockbox. We don't need a safe and, besides, it will only be here for two days."

"I'd feel safer if it wasn't here until the night the shipment comes in. Geez, it's a lot of money. Maybe I should stay here with it just to make sure."

"You're not getting any ideas, are you? I remember Benny's partner Jake, took off with both portions of their business loot a few years ago," Edwin said suspiciously.

"What the hell do you mean by that? Have I ever given you any reason not to trust me?" Harmon retorted angrily.

"All right, all right, take it easy, will ya? I didn't mean nothing by it. Let's get out of here. We're starting to get on each other's nerves."

At that point, the two men left the building and, a short time later, Matthew and John vacated their hiding place. They were careful not to leave the spot disturbed in any way that would arouse suspicion.

It had been a hot and humid day. By the time the lads got back to the rented room, they were soaked in sweat.

John filled in Elizabeth about what they had learned.

"Do you think we can make this work in our favor? How do you plan to get into the lockbox? That is what you are planning on doing, aren't you?"

"Do you remember the box with the letters in it? I got that open fairly easily, didn't I?" Matthew asked.

"Yes, but you had the box in your hands, so that made it easier to make the lockpick. You'll have to break into the building to get a close look at the lockbox ahead of time, won't you?" she asked.

"Yes, I will. I'm not sure how to go about that part yet. If I can pick the lock on the door, no one will know I was there. John and I will go back later tonight and see if we can figure out a way in. You should come along, too, so you can warn us if anyone is coming," Matthew told her.

"How will I warn you without letting the person know too?"

"I'm not sure yet," he said, giving her an eye signal when John wasn't looking.

Elizabeth knew better than to ask any more questions about it. Later, when John went to the bathroom, Matthew let her know that he brought the laser light with him and that he thought it best that John not know about it. That kind of technology had the capability to upset the future greatly, and he didn't want to take that kind of chance unnecessarily.

"I don't think John could figure out what makes it work unless he got a hold of the light and gave it to an engineer, but you're right. Why tempt fate?" she said.

At midnight, the three headed out and made their way to the building on the waterfront. Elizabeth stationed herself so she would be able to shine the laser light through a high small window while keeping an eye on the front entrance.

It was suspected that the lockbox was in that room. If it wasn't there, John would be in the doorway of that room and would see the light if it shone into the room. Matthew had his tools with him, and he and John made their way to a door at the end of the building, so there was little chance of being seen. Once they were there, Matthew took a look at the old style padlock.

He brought several different styles of picks he had made earlier in the week out of the bag. His hands were sweating, and there was a slight tremble in them. He tried to insert the first pick and found that it was too large to work properly. The next one was better but still not right. The third one was close but still a bit off.

He took a close look at the lock and the pick while John shone a very small flashlight on the lock. While he was doing this, his eyes kept scanning the vicinity for other intruders. This caused the light to waver now and then and Matthew had to ask him to keep the light still.

"Sorry, Matthew, I'm quite nervous doing this."

Matthew pulled out the vise grips to hold the pick firmly and, with a small file, proceeded to make a slight adjustment to the pick. Once he was done, he tried the pick again and was rewarded by the lock opening. There were a few light scratches on the lock where the picks had slipped, and this concerned him somewhat.

"I hope those men don't check the lock," Matthew said. "If they do, they'll see that it has been opened without a key and suspect that someone has broken into the building."

"I think it will be all right," John countered, trying to ease Matthew's concerns. "Why should they look at the lock, anyways? The main door they use is on the front of the building."

Matthew shrugged and slowly opened the door as it gave a squeak from hinges, indicating it was seldom used. They entered the building after he looked back to where Elizabeth was hiding. The two made their way through the open areas, using the flashlight. Checking the interior, they found their way to where the lock box was hidden inside a large cabinet. Luckily, the cabinet did not have a lock, and they found the heavily built box inside it.

Matthew told John to stand in the doorway of the room that the small window was in. If there was a very small red light that hit the wall opposite the window, he needed to inform Matthew immediately. He also warned John not to look toward the window at any time and not to stand between the window and the wall. John started to question him about it, but changed his mind, thinking better of it.

The box was a very sturdy type, but Matthew knew he

could open it using some of the tools he brought back into the past with him. High-speed steel or carbide drill bits could make short work of gaining entry. This, however, was not how the scenario is going to be played. He looked the lock mechanism over carefully and, after taking a few measurements with a pair of calipers, he pulled out a small digital camera. Taking several photos of the lock and box, he closed the cabinet door. As the two turned to leave the building, the red light started flashing on and off several times

John saw it out of the corner of his eye and alerted Matthew. There was a noise outside the building as a car pulled up. Damn, why would someone come here at this time of night? What would happen if they were spotted? What would happen if he had a gun? Crap! A key was inserted into the lock on the front door.

The flashlight had been extinguished as the pair quietly took cover in a small room near the door they gained entry through. If they had exited the structure, the squeaking door would have alerted the person who was coming in.

John's breathing was heavy, and Matthew had to put his fingers up to his lips in order to quiet him down. An oil lamp was turned on and, as Matthew took a quick peek around the doorframe, he saw that it was a younger version of Harmon.

John pulled his partner back into the room with shaking hands, afraid of being caught. Matthew wanted to whisper in his ear but didn't want to take the chance of being heard in the quietness that surrounded them. He took the occasional look to see what Harmon was up to. The door to the cabinet had been opened, and Harmon unlocked the box. Reaching inside, he withdrew a small bundle of cash as he muttered to himself. His hand extended back in the cabinet and, as he pulled it out again, there was a revolver in it. This gave Matthew real cause for concern. If they were discovered now, they would have no chance of getting away.

Harmon inspected the gun, making sure that all the bullets were in the cylinder. When he was satisfied, he put the pistol back and took several bills from the bundle of cash, putting them in his pocket. After closing the box and cabinet, he headed to the front door. Blowing out the lantern he left, locking the door.

Matthew and John both let out a sigh of relief as the door locked. Both were in a sweat, and the jitters made their entire bodies quiver. They waited for several minutes before exiting the building, sticking their heads out to make sure the way was clear before they went out. Matthew closed the padlock and looked it over. Seeing the tiny scratches, he reached down and picked up a small amount of dirt. When he saw that the color was very similar to the rust on the padlock, he used the dirt to cover the scratches.

The heat of the night was still oppressive, and the humidity once again made their shirts stick to their bodies. The smell of the ocean and decaying fish was in the air, and Matthew felt just a little queasy.

"I think the heat and the stink are making me feel a bit off. Let's get back to the room. I need a cool shower," he said.

John could not agree more. It had been more of an adventure than he would have liked to be a part of.

The three made it back to the room without incident, and, after cleaning up, all three were asleep in no time. In the morning, they left town and headed back to the cottage. There was still another day to spend there before the clock brought the two back to their own times. Plans were made and, by the time they disappeared, everything was worked out, or so they hoped. Things could well become very dangerous if anything went awry. These were both very violent men, and neither would have any hesitation in killing the three busybodies.

At home, the time had only advanced a few minutes. Having slept at John's house, the two were well rested, and so they got all the things they would need for the next trip. Matthew went to the garage and collected several items that he thought he would require. Buddy was taken care of, and the dials were reset on the clock. Both were quite apprehensive about what was going to transpire shortly. After so many failures, both wondered if this time would really be any different.

They had tried to take into consideration all the possibilities, but, as they knew through past experience, plans didn't always come together. The brother and sister team sat on the floor waiting for the clock to reach the top of the hour. A last look at the clock showed that the weights had not been pulled to their uppermost position. Jumping up, Matthew opened the door on the clock and stopped the pendulum.

He moved the weights to the top positions, so there would be no chance of the clock winding down before it brought them back.

"Wow, in my haste to get back to 1913, I forgot to rewind the clock," he said.

"I'm glad you noticed. I never even thought about it," she said with a nervous giggle.

The pendulum was restarted, and the time was soon at hand as they held on to their things, in order to make sure they came back with them, and they vanished into thin air.

Chapter 60

John had been expecting them and was in the room when they appeared before his eyes. He had been tempted to make a trip himself to visit his friends in the future soon. He was planning to do it if the three survived the operation they were about to embark on. He had made up his mind. Yes, he would do it. Enough of the fear of being trapped in a time zone not his own. He wouldn't say anything about this until after it was all over.

"Do you have everything we need?" John asked. "I have all the items you asked me to get."

"I think we have it all, John, thanks so much for your help. We couldn't do it without you," Matthew said.

"I wouldn't miss it for all the tea in China."

"The shipment comes in two days from now, and that means the money will be in the strong box either tonight or tomorrow night. Are we going to check it out this evening, just to see?" Elizabeth asked.

"I think it might be a good idea to break in again, but we won't touch the money yet. I need to know if the picks I made will work. If not, I may have to use your garage in order to fix one or two of them, okay, John?"

"Anything that you need that I have, you are welcome to use."

It had been decided that since it was two in the afternoon, they would wait for an hour or two before heading to Falmouth, Rhode Island. The three occupied themselves reminiscing about the way their lives had interacted. John was told about some of the things that were coming down the pipe. He was told nothing that would really affect the future because that could all change depending on whether they were successful or not. Soon it was time to go, and the automobile John had borrowed again was readied. A horse and buggy would not be practical at that time.

Alice walked up to them with a smile on her face and gave the two a big hug. She remembered what they had done for her and John and would be forever thankful. "What are you three up to? You haven't come here on another mission have you?" she asked.

"To tell you the truth, we are just on our way to fix something. I'll explain it all when we're back," John told her.

As the group drove away, Alice watched with a concerned look on her face. She had noticed that Elizabeth seemed quite worried and this, in turn, worried her.

Sometime later, the three were in the general area of the import business, but not in a place where there was a chance of being noticed. From errors in judgment made when dealing with this man, the two siblings had learned a few lessons, which they conveyed earnestly to John. This was a most dangerous man.

Darkness was starting to fall and, looking through binoculars, Matthew informed his cohorts as to what was happening. Edwin left about half an hour before Harmon. By the time they were both gone, it was already nine o'clock and the heat of the day was starting to dissipate a little. The humidity was still high and made it difficult to keep comfortable.

The entire neighborhood had become quiet and deserted. They had not planned to make a move until at least midnight, not wanting a repeat of the other evening. It was scary enough without having Harmon or Edwin coming back while they were in the building. Going to a restaurant and using the washrooms to get freshened up before eating, the friends sat and had a nice meal.

Elizabeth stood watch again, while the two snuck to the door with the padlock. Matthew looked the lock over very carefully to make sure that no one had discovered that it had been picked. All looked as it should, and Matthew managed to open the lock a little easier that time. Entering the back room, they made their way over to the cabinet. John stood in position so he could be ready to notify Matthew if the curious light flashed again.

Laying the small flashlight in the cabinet so that it shone on the lock of the heavy box, Matthew brought out the picks and proceeded to work on the lock. He took care not to leave any scratches on the outside. It would be a dead giveaway if there were telltale signs left behind. It was imperative that it looked like a key had been used to open the box.

It was not easy to open that one. Matthew had studied the lock online and seen demonstrations of a locksmith opening it, but it was harder than it looked. He had to file one of the picks several times over a rag to collect the filings. Finally, he switched to another pick and, after a few modifications, managed to unlock the box. Twenty-five minutes had gone by, far longer than anticipated. Sweat was dripping from his face as he worked. He was careful to have it land on the rag he placed in the cabinet for this purpose.

"I sure hope neither comes back right now. I won't have time to relock it if they do," Matthew said with a sigh.

"Is the money in there?" John asked.

Opening the lid, Matthew peered inside and nodded his answer. The box was closed and relocked, which went much faster, to their relief. It had been tempting to explore the contents of some of the crates, but that might leave a clue that someone had been there, and so it wasn't done.

Sticking his head out the door to make sure no one was waiting outside, Matthew beckoned to John. They exited and closed the padlock, securing the building once more. The drive back home was long and quiet. It had been debated as to whether or not it would be wise to just stay the night in town, but John had a few things to do in the early afternoon.

Matthew and Elizabeth spent their free time the next day wandering around the grounds surrounding Mariner Lodge and the neighboring area. Matthew wore a hat just to make sure no one remembered him from years past. Uncle Robert was seen talking to a guest at the lodge and the transformation in him was surprising. The grumpy old man was actually congenial. Memories of events passed came back to the time travelers as they saw the different sights. It was a strange feeling to be standing there, knowing that they were in a time period that occurred more than a hundred years ago. Elizabeth and her brother felt at peace for a few moments while their present task was put aside.

The guests walking along the shore were dressed in very conservative clothes compared to modern attire. The ladies had long dresses, and the men wore trousers and button up shirts. Those who were in the water had bathing suits that covered most of their bodies.

"I wonder what these people would think if they saw a girl in a bikini?" Matthew asked.

"I think they would be quite shocked by the sight. I must admit this time period has an appeal to it. I wonder if we would be happy living here if something went wrong with the clock and we got stuck here?" she said, thinking back to when the clock weights had not been at the top of the mechanism.

"Hopefully, we won't find out. It's one thing choosing to come back for a visit, but another entirely to have it forced on you because you can't get back to your own time. Look at how it has affected John." Matthew told her, also remembering the incident.

"True, I think we'll keep it the way it is."

John came back home, and they had supper together. It was almost seven o'clock by the time they got a room in Falmouth again. This time they stayed at another establishment, not wishing to become familiar faces. Again it was up to John to foot the cost and, as Matthew watched him pay it, a thought came into his mind.

The evening passed quickly enough, but the excitement caused their pulses to quicken somewhat as the time to leave approached. At ten, they gathered their things and drove to a location a few blocks from where they wanted to be.

Taking a position that allowed them to keep watch over the area, they settled in for the long wait. The entire area seemed to be quiet, but they were not going to take any chances by moving in prematurely. After the long two hour wait, they began to get ready. All had been silent, and it appeared to be safe. Matthew picked the lock on the door as Elizabeth kept a lookout.

Once they were in, the strong box was tackled once again. It still took a few minutes to gain entry but nowhere near as long as it had the other night. There it was.

A very large amount of cash lay in the box.

"Okay, the money is here. I'll put it in the bag and close it up again. Do you think we should take the paperwork too? There might be something incriminating here, just in case things fall apart again." Matthew asked.

"I don't think so. It will put one too many twists into the works and could backfire on us," John said.

"You're probably right. We can always come back for them if something goes wrong."

The money was taken and, as he started to close the box, he was tempted to unload the gun. This, too, could create another problem, so he resisted the urge. The box was locked up, and they vacated the premises. Back in the room, the bag was emptied and the money counted.

"Wow, just over seventeen thousand dollars, what a haul," John said.

"I would have thought it would be more, but then again, I'm going by circumstances in our time," Matthew informed him.

"Really, what would be a large amount of money for a transaction like this in your time?" John asked.

"I don't know, but it would be a lot more. Money in our time doesn't have the same value as it does now. Everything costs so much more, but we earn a lot more too, so I guess it all balances out."

"What time does the shipment arrive tomorrow?" Elizabeth questioned.

"Actually, it comes in tonight at four in the morning," John answered.

"Weren't we cutting it a little close by going in so late tonight?"

"Possibly, but I doubted that they would be up this late, seeing as how they have to be back here so early in the morning," Matthew said.

"You'd better set your watch alarm, Matt, so we don't

sleep in too late. You said we have to be there to see what happens and put plan two into effect if this plan fails to come to fruition," Elizabeth instructed her brother.

"Yeah, I'll do that now. Let's get to sleep."

But sleep didn't come before there had been a fair amount of tossing and turning. Before they knew it, the time arrived for them to go. The three were groggy as they took up their positions. They had picked places where they could see each other, but no one else could see them. It took great care to hide without being seen as Harmon and Edwin had already been in the building. There was an eerie silence in the air and, despite the still overly warm temperature and humidity, the trio found themselves shivering slightly. The time slowly passed as each was alone in their hiding place.

On the water, a hundred yards offshore, the sound of a boat, slicing its way through the water, was heard. The means of propulsion proved to be oars, which were used to push the vessel toward shore. The boat was docked on the sandy beach, and two swarthy men quickly disembarked.

No introductions were made, and the contraband was unloaded from the boat and brought into the structure. Lights were turned on only after the unloading was completed, and even then, only minimally. It was time for payment and Edwin went inside with one of the men. Harmon and the other man stayed outside, with neither one talking to the other.

Matthew had placed himself in a low position so he could see through the front windows of the building. Using his binoculars, he watched the proceedings inside. The cabinet was opened and the box unlocked, in order to transfer the cash.

There was a look of surprise on Edwin's face as he saw that there was no money inside. His gaze darted back and forth as he looked at the box and then at the man behind him. There was the sound of raised voices from inside, and the two headed outside, where Edwin confronted Harmon.

"Where the hell is the money, you bastard?" he shouted. He had brought the revolver with him and pointed it at Harmon.

"I didn't take any money," Harmon shouted back angrily.

The other two men had, at that point, drawn weapons too and backed away from Edwin and Harmon. Matthew decided to make his move while there was still a lot of confusion. He pulled out his slingshot, lined up his arm, then let go. There was a scream as Harmon jumped toward one of the men. This had been done only because he was hit in the posterior, and it had made him go in that direction.

The smuggler, thinking he was being attacked, fired his revolver, and shot Harmon, hitting him in the heart area, killing him instantly. Edwin started firing at that point and took out the man who had just killed his partner. There was wild firing as the two remaining men reacted instinctively. Bullets flew everywhere and finally, only one man was left standing, and he was wounded. Running away, the injured smuggler headed toward the town center, limping badly.

John, Matthew, and Elizabeth regrouped at first opportunity and, when they were together, Elizabeth almost screamed as she noticed that John had been wounded too.

"John, what happened? There's blood running down your side."

Upon closer inspection when his shirt was lifted, it was seen that he too had been shot.

"I got hit by a stray bullet when they were shooting wildly at each other," he said, grimacing.

"The wound is not too serious but needs to be looked after soon," she said, her hands shaking. You're bleeding quite badly. We have to get out of here."

The trio headed for the rented room, taking care not to let anyone see the blood on John's clothes. There were sirens in the streets as the police responded to the discharge of firearms on the waterfront. Elizabeth did her best to patch John up. It was a superficial job, but the bleeding had been stifled enough for them to go back to his house. Alice had nursing experience and would be able to fix him up right as rain, hopefully. Matthew drove the vehicle back to the cottage.

Alice screamed when she saw all the blood staining John's shirt and trousers. Composing herself, she gathered what she required and brought it to John's home. When she had patched John up, she demanded an explanation. Elizabeth filled Alice in as to what they had been trying to do. She was told how every attempt to bring Harmon J. Williams to justice had failed and how John's life had been at risk, and possibly the clock could have been lost also.

As the entire story was relayed, Alice found that she needed to sit down. "This is amazing. I don't know how the three of you have been able to bring this to a favorable conclusion. You all just saved an untold number of lives by dealing with this man."

"Now there is the question of what to do with the money. Matthew and I can't take it with us so we have to decide what to do with it here," Elizabeth said.

"I have been thinking about this," Matthew interjected. "Except for maybe two hundred dollars, the two of you should split it and use it to pay off any outstanding debts you might have," he suggested.

Before any objections could be raised, Elizabeth said, "I agree completely, and we won't take no for an answer.

John has helped us, and there have been costs incurred."

"We will be back on other missions, I'm sure, and we will need help from both of you. Take this as payment for services rendered and which may be incurred in the future, please," Matthew insisted. "The two hundred dollars will be used by us when we return to the past, so we can pay our way around, in case we can't get hold of you."

Alice and John looked at each other and saw the logic in Matthew's words. They all agreed, and the four spent as much time together as they could for the rest of their stay. The following day after a slightly tearful farewell, the two-time travelers returned home.

Chapter 61

As Matthew and Elizabeth reappeared in their own time, there was a great sense of relief in them. Although they had been through a lot, there was a great feeling of satisfaction. Elizabeth went online to check if the past had truly been changed.

She knew it had to be, but seeing it made a big difference. Typing in Harmon's name showed the face of a lawyer and his partner, Edwin Fitzpatrick, involved in smuggling and their untimely death as a criminal activity had gone bad.

There were no murders of young girls to be seen where there were many in the past.

"Oh, Matthew, we finally did it. That awful man has been stopped, all those poor children that beast hurt so badly have been able to live normal lives. I'm so happy we were able to make a difference."

"He sure gave us a run for our money, that's one thing for certain. I'm glad it's all over with too."

"Mom and Dad will be away for two more days. I guess we can rest up and take it easy for a while. What do you think?" she asked.

"I might just go for a walk with Buddy. I need to unwind a bit."

Once he was gone, Elizabeth lay down and drifted off almost immediately. Matthew and his pet had a bit of fun together along the shore. As he passed the Johnston's home, he had the feeling that he should, in the near future, make an effort to look into her brother's disappearance.

"Plenty of time for that, though. We just got back so it will have to wait awhile," he said to himself.

Despite her nap, both Elizabeth and Matthew went to bed early that evening. In the morning, both were refreshed and ready for a new day.

"Say, Matthew, I was just thinking. Seeing as how Mom and Dad are coming back tomorrow, do you want to have a look through those two rocks overlooking Great Edgartown Pond?"

"Sure, who knows? We may be able to find the solution to that mystery too. Lord knows we've been trying to solve that one long enough. Let's go after we eat. Remind me to bring a few tools with us. Also make sure I put the things we took with us to bring Harmon down, back where they belong."

Once the two had what they needed and chores were done, they hopped into the truck and were on their way. Buddy sat in the front between the siblings and barked his appreciation at being able to come along. It didn't take too long, and they were once again parked on the side of the road. After checking to make sure no one was around, they put on their backpacks and started walking along the trail, carrying a few tools.

Buddy ran ahead and was there before the youngsters. Sniffing at anything and everything that bore a scent, he ran to and fro. Matthew got to the top of the rise first and removed his backpack after laying down the pick and shovel. The sky was cloudy, which made things better for them. There were birds all over the place, chirping loudly, lending a cheery note to the scene.

"Maybe the birds singing is an omen that this too will come to a successful conclusion soon," Elizabeth said, smiling.

"I think that might be a bit fanciful, but then again, who can tell?"

The stones were removed from both of the rocks. Things were tidied up, so there were no obstructions in the holes. A quick look around had revealed that no one was in the area.

Opening the pack, he withdrew the laser and a wooden holder he had made at home. The holder was a round piece of wood that had a hole the size of the laser drilled through it lengthways. Pulling out a folded piece of black cardboard he walked to the rock nearest the bay. Turning on the laser, he slid it into the wood and placed it into the hole in the rock.

He and Elizabeth walked to the second stone, and he held the cardboard behind the second hole.

"Darn it, I think the laser isn't quite lined up with this hole. Can you go back and carefully adjust it until I tell you to stop."

"Sure, Matt."

Running back with Buddy alongside, she reached up and slowly twisted the wood. Matthew called to her saying he was going to place the cardboard in front of the second hole so he could advise her as to which direction to move it.

In a few minutes, they had the light lined up exactly right, and the next phase began. Matthew walked down the slope toward the place where it was suspected the light would hit. It had been too bright to see if the laser was striking any area on the far side of the gully. Matthew reached the bottom, and Elizabeth guided him to where she thought he should be heading.

"Okay, Matthew, hold the paper up at about chest level and walk to my left. Go slowly and while you're walking raise and lower it slowly so I can tell you when you're in line with the laser. Yes, that's it, keep going, and don't look this way, you don't want the light to hit your eyes.

Matthew walked slowly, making his way along the bottom of the gully. As he made his way in front of the cave opening, Elizabeth yelled out.

"That's it, Matthew, the light just hit as you had it about head height. There it is, Matt. Do you see it?"

"Yes, it goes right inside the cave. Stay by the rock with the light and check to make sure no one is around. If there is, distract them and turn off the laser. That way I'll know something is up."

As she headed to the rock, Matthew quickly entered the cave. He had to use his flashlight in order to see clearly enough inside. Once he was inside far enough, he turned it off and looked to see if he could find where the laser was hitting.

In the rear of the cave about two feet up the rear wall the red dot could be seen. He quickly went to it and marked the spot. Being careful not to be looking at the laser light, he made his way to the mouth of the cave and called out to his sister.

"Yes, Matthew, what is it? Did you find something?"

"Is it all clear?" he asked.

"Nobody's around. Did you find something?"

"Yes, take the laser out of the hole and turn it off, plug the holes, then come down here," he instructed.

When she was finished and put everything away, she headed down the slope and into the cave too. Matthew pointed to the spot he had marked where the red dot had hit. The rear wall was fairly smooth, with fractures here and there, which was usual in this type of formation.

Shining the flashlight on the stone, Matthew had examined the surface closely. Reaching into the pack, he removed a brush and proceeded to whisk dirt off the surface of the stone. The interior of the cave, especially the rear walls had not been touched very much in many years. A layer of fine material had, over time, accumulated, obscuring any fine lines in the rock.

"I think we need some water to wash the dirt away. There are a few lines in the rock, but I can't see them clearly enough to determine what's important and what's not," he said.

"I've got a little, but I doubt that it's enough. There's an empty pail in the truck, should we get it?"

"I'll go with you and drive down to the water where we can fill it," he suggested.

In three-quarters of an hour, they were back in the cave. Buddy was left outside as he didn't like it in the cave much anyway. The stones on the floor were sharp and hurt his paws.

Using the water sparingly, the two gently washed away the dirt. The last of the water was used to rinse away the rest of the residue and the light was then shone on the wall.

"There are a number of straight lines in the rock. Barnes worked with headstones, and I'll bet he used his talent to work in here. Do you see how these lines here form a rectangle? Right beside that, there's a bigger square formed by other lines with a few little chips at the edges. The fit of the stones is fantastic. Unless you were looking for it, you'd never notice this," he said, tracing his finger along the lines.

"I do see it. How do we open what has to be a cavity in the wall?" she asked.

"I think the trick will be getting the small stone out first, but unless I can find a place to start, I'm sure damage will be done, and that could create more trouble and make it that much harder to open."

"Let's have lunch first, then we might be able to think this through properly," Elizabeth suggested.

"Yeah, it's been here all this time, a little longer won't matter."

The two tried to make things in the cave look like they were before the work started. It was highly unlikely but neither wanted to take the chance that someone could come into the cave, notice the cleanup job, and start to investigate. While he was near the rocks on top of the knoll, Matthew threw a little dirt on the plugged holes in the rocks. He told Elizabeth that they were no longer needed, and if someone were to see them, it might make them curious enough to want to investigate further. At that point, he was getting just a bit paranoid and knew it.

The two sat down for lunch with their backs to the rock and looked over the scene panning out in front of them. The water which was some distance away and below them glistened in the sunlight, now that the clouds had departed. A warm breeze blew off the water and up the slope.

"This is still nice and warm. I'm sure that a month from now it will be getting quite a bit cooler as fall settles in," Elizabeth relayed idly.

"You're right about that," Matthew agreed. "You know, Barnes was quite the craftsman. He made very intricate furniture and headstones. Thinking back on how he designed the hidden compartments in the dressers and the stone in the cemetery, I bet he made this so it would open a certain way too. Nothing he made required a lot of force to work, and I doubt that this will be any different."

"You're probably on the right track. Do you have any ideas?" she asked.

"I've been going over that in my mind. There aren't any levers or depressions to hook a crowbar or a prod into, at least as far as I can see. So that might mean that the stone isn't supposed to be moved outward. Maybe the small one has to be pushed inwards," he said thoughtfully.

"How would you do that? If you hit it with a hammer you'd break the stone and probably jam it in the hole, wouldn't you?"

"That's what I was thinking. Barnes was pretty smart, and the close fit of the stones must have taken him some time to achieve. If it was meant to open using force, he wouldn't have made it so well. I think that a minimal amount of force will be required," he stated emphatically.

"I can see that it's come to you how to get it to work, hasn't it?"

"Yep, it sure has. I need a piece of wood, something like a short piece of two by four and a good size hammer. They're in the truck, I'll go get them."

Twenty-five minutes later, the two were back in the cave. Matthew had Elizabeth hold the wood so the small end of it was pushed against the center of the smaller stone at right angles to the wall.

"Okay Elizabeth, don't be scared, I won't miss and hit you. I've done this with Dad lots of times," he said to reassure her.

He touched the end of the wood with the hammer and took it away to swing. The impact was fairly solid, but nothing happened. He swung again, only a little harder this time. Again nothing happened. He bent over and ran his fingers along the seam in the rock.

"It has moved inwards ever so slightly. I think it's starting to move. A few more times and a little harder, and we should see some positive results," he informed her.

Five more good solid hits and the small stone had moved in about half an inch. Looking at the wall closely showed that the large stone had been forced outward. The two got back into position, and several more heavy hits forced the big stone out far enough to grab it and wiggle it out of the wall. It fell to the floor of the cave with a thud.

Shining the flashlight into the hole, the two saw an old heavy iron bar with a protrusion on the back side near the middle of the bar. The stone that was being hit had pushed against the end of what looked like a lever. When the one end of the bar was pushed deeper into the hole, the other end pushed the big stone out like a fulcrum. A closer look at the bar revealed that it was made of bronze.

Shining into the back of the hole, the two saw an old metal box. Reaching in, Matthew pulled out the box and, after brushing it off, looked it over.

"It looks like it's made of brass, doesn't it, Matt?"

"I think it might be bronze too, that's why they haven't corroded. I can't open it here. It's locked, and it would be a shame to ruin the box. We'll take it home and open it there with the picks I made."

"Let's put the stones back the way they were and the metal bar too so we can open it again if need be," she mentioned.

"Good idea. You never know."

A bit of grunt work and both were perspiring somewhat, but the stones were back in place again. After smearing a bit of dirt on them, the stones looked like they did before they were disturbed. The tools and everything they brought with them was taken back to the truck, and they drove off. Buddy was happy to be on the road again.

"Wow, this is great, we finally seem to have solved

this mystery too," Elizabeth said with an ear-to-ear grin.

"Boy, oh boy, this has been quite the exciting time we've had since we've first come to Lilac Cottage. Mom and Dad couldn't have picked a better spot."

"Do you really think that the box has the collection of jewelry in it? It couldn't be something else or just a big joke meant to mislead the authorities if Barnes was caught, could it?" Elizabeth asked.

"Anything is possible, but I doubt it. The whole thing was far too elaborate to just be some kind of prank. Besides, why worry about it? We'll find out soon enough," he assured her.

An hour later, the pair was home and in the garage. Buddy had been given a drink of water, and they'd had a small snack to tide them over till supper. Matthew got his picks ready and the box—which was just over sixteen inches long, twelve inches wide, and six inches high—sat on the workbench. The air compressor had been used to blow out any dirt from inside the lock. Matthew oiled the interior of it too and then blew the excess out, taking any dirt out of the mechanism at the same time, just to make sure everything could move easily.

"All right, are you ready for this," he said to his sister.

"What do you want, a drum roll?" she asked laughingly.

He set to work on the lock for a few minutes. Pulling out the pick, he took a tiny hammer and gently rapped the outside of the lock a few times. The air gun was used to blow out the inside of the lock again before he picked up the tool. "I think that the lock mechanism was a little seized after being unused for so long. Let's see if the tapping helped or not," he said.

Inserting the pick, he worked at the lock and, after a few minutes of fiddling with it, was rewarded with movement and a click. The box was opened and the two stood there with their mouths hanging open. Wrapped up inside was the collection of jewelry that had been missing for over a century. The two stood there stunned by what they saw. It took almost a minute for them to get over the shock of actually seeing the jewelry that was, at their present time, worth many times what it cost to buy the cottage.

"Now what, what do we do with them? We can't very well keep them, can we?" Elizabeth asked.

"To tell you the truth, I really never gave it a lot of thought. I didn't really think that we'd ever find the collection. Now that we have, I almost wish we could, but I don't think it would be fair to the original owners. Four men died, several police officers were wounded, and the people who owned the collection were almost ruined over the theft, including the museum."

"How do we get them back to the owners? It's not like we can just walk up to them and say, here, I think you lost these," Elizabeth mentioned.

"I think that I may just have an idea to take care of it. We can go back and talk to John and Alice, then show him where the jewelry is hidden, just after the men are shot. This way, with Barnes and his friends dead, they won't be able to pull off any more robberies, and the owners will have the collection returned to them."

"What if there is a reward given, what will be done with that?" Elizabeth brought up.

"Let's cross that bridge when we come to it. For now, we should work out the return part first."

The two decided that they still had time to see John and Alice. Their parents would be back the following day and who knew how long they would have to wait before they had the opportunity to travel again? The collection was placed in the back of the clock room, and Buddy fed. Elizabeth checked her records to see when the men were killed and picked a date a month later. After the one hour trip to make arrangements was done, the clock was then set for seventy-two hours. That way they could sleep over in John's home and get all the tasks completed that needed to be done in his time. The clock room clouded over, and the two were gone.

Chapter 62

John, as it turned out, was home and pleasantly surprised to see his friends. The group caught up and made the plans for when the time was available for the extended layover. When the time travelers returned, Matthew explained why they were there and how the two of them had solved the riddles that Barnes had created. Alice was brought up to speed, and the four made plans as to how the stolen property should be returned to the rightful owners.

It was late Saturday afternoon, and the group had a nice supper and an evening socializing together. The future had been changed for John and Alice with the lawyer being killed. There was much information to be given to the two people who actually belonged in that time period. Finally, it was bedtime, and everyone retired.

The next morning the four friends took a trip to the cave, and after a short time the lost treasure was recovered and taken back with them. John and Alice contacted the museum and informed them of the discovery, being careful to leave Matthew and Elizabeth out of the story.

It was a good thing that the four spent part of the evening before coming up with a credible story as to how the cave and the hidden storage place were found. In the end, John and Alice were presented with a reward by the owners and the museum. They had their photos taken, and a story of how these two upstanding members of the community had stumbled upon the hiding place of a treasure thought to be lost forever.

"I feel like a charlatan," John said as Alice nodded in agreement. "We didn't find anything at all. It was the two of you who found it."

"Somebody had to take the credit for finding the jewelry," Matthew said to his friends. "We certainly couldn't, so take the credit and the money. Why don't you open an account in the bank with it? This way we have some extra finances if we come back on another mission to help someone. If necessary, we can always have our names added to the account. That way, we'll have access to the funds if we're back in the past and need a little money in a hurry."

"Yes, you do that, and, if by chance the two of you need some of it, then, by all means, use it," Elizabeth added, thinking of the things the future held for their friends. "Let us know what bank you decide to make the deposit in, too. Because we live in the future, we will know where and when it should be moved in order to keep it safe."

"The two of you have already helped us so much. We don't know how we can ever repay you," Alice said, and John nodded his head that time.

"We're friends living in different times, but we're friends nevertheless. It's almost time for us to leave. Be happy, who knows when we'll see each other again? If you do need us, just leave a note in the clock. We'll keep an eye on it and be back to lend a hand," Matthew said as they hugged each other for possibly the last time—or maybe not.

A short time later, Matthew and Elizabeth were standing in front of the clock in their own time. There was a feeling of loneliness as they looked at the screen on their digital camera. The camera showed a group photo of them and their friends in old time clothes. The picture would be a fine memento for their scrapbook. Looking online, the pair viewed the newspaper photo of their friends being presented with the reward by the museum. Off to one side were two youngsters standing behind the group in the photo.

"I don't think we should ever let Mom and Dad see this picture. They might notice us in the background," he said with a smile.

Chapter 63

Leonard and Kate were back home again and told their young adult children all about the wonderful time they had visiting their old friends. Life soon got back to normal as schoolwork and jobs kept the family busy. The weather had been cooling off as the sun sank lower in the sky.

Almost a month went by and, as Matthew walked down the beach with Buddy, he ran into the little old lady, Mrs. Johnston. Immediately he remembered his promise to look into her brother's disappearance.

"Hello, Mrs. Johnston, I haven't been able to do a lot of research yet, but Elizabeth and I are going to start shortly. Like I said, we may not find anything, but then again we just might. I'm sorry for the delay, I truly hope something comes up. We really would like to help you."

"I really don't expect anything to come of this, but thank you so much for trying. It's nice to have a young man such as yourself for a neighbor. Bring your sister along next time you come this way."

The little lady took his hand in hers and gave it a gentle squeeze before she walked away. Matthew headed for home, and, when he had the chance, he told Elizabeth about his talk with their new little friend. "Let's start reading the diary again and do a thorough search in it for clues. The computer will help us in our investigation, and who knows? Maybe we'll be able to help solve this old mystery. I'm sure you feel the same way I do because I'm ready for another adventure."

She grinned. "Yes, you're right. I am ready for a new mystery."

If they only knew what was in store for them, they might not have felt that way.

THE END ~ QUITE POSSIBLY

About the Author

Leonardus G. Rougoor was born in the Netherlands. His parents and most of his family moved to Canada to start a better life years ago. He was raised on a dairy farm, which made for an abundance of work. Educated in southern Ontario, he tried a number of different jobs before he ended up in a major tool and die shop, starting a lifelong career.

Having a heart for the underdog, although causing many sleepless nights, has been the driving force in a writing career. He now writes in three genres: crime, young adult mystery adventure and the supernatural.

"If you like rejection, become a writer."